A GENTLEMAN'S CURSE

AVENGING LORDS - BOOK 4

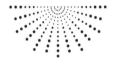

ADELE CLEE

A Gentleman's Curse
Copyright © 2019 Adele Clee
All rights reserved.
ISBN-13: 978-1-9164336–2-5

Cover by **Jay Aheer**

Books by Adele Clee

To Save a Sinner

A Curse of the Heart

What Every Lord Wants

The Secret To Your Surrender

A Simple Case of Seduction

Anything for Love Series

What You Desire

What You Propose

What You Deserve

What You Promised

Lost Ladies of London

The Mysterious Miss Flint

The Deceptive Lady Darby

The Scandalous Lady Sandford

The Daring Miss Darcy

Avenging Lords

At Last the Rogue Returns

A Wicked Wager

Valentine's Vow

A Gentleman's Curse

CHAPTER ONE

"What do you mean the actress is unsuitable?" Hudson Lockhart lounged back in his fireside chair and studied his friend seated opposite. While he wanted to spring to his feet in a state of panic, years of good breeding forced him to arch a brow, nothing more.

"It is as I suspected," Dariell began, the soft burr of his French accent doing little to settle the turmoil whirling in Lockhart's chest. "The woman's greed will be your downfall. While she has the skill necessary to play the role of your wife, she will betray you the moment someone presents a more lucrative offer."

Lockhart gritted his teeth. His pulse rose more than a notch. To combat his growing anxiety, he stared into the fire's flames. On this cold November night, a man daren't drag his horse from the stables and ride as if wolves were nipping at his heels. A distraction might clear his head, but it would not solve his problem.

"And you are certain of this?"

Dariell nodded. "Would I have cautioned you otherwise?"

An oppressive silence descended.

Lockhart closed his eyes briefly. The walls of the small gatekeeper's cottage seemed to close in around him—crushing his spirit. Were his efforts for naught? Years of waiting, months of planning, long hours spent dreaming of the moment he discovered the truth.

The truth?

A contemptuous snigger filled his head. Only two men knew what had happened on that fateful midsummer's eve five years ago. One was dead. A corpse long since buried beneath the ground. The other had no conscience. The other slithered in the shadows—a snake in the grass.

"I understand your urgency, my friend," Dariell continued. "The need for vengeance, it infects the body like a pus-filled wound that will not heal. But there is much at stake. The woman you choose must be a convincing liar, but she must be honest, steadfast in her loyalty, reliable."

Lockhart sighed. Dariell often spoke in riddles, and tonight was no exception.

"I doubt there is a lady in the land whose character boasts of such a contradiction."

A knowing smile played at the corners of Dariell's mouth. Clearly, the Frenchman had a plan but enjoyed making a man wait for the grand revelation. "Perhaps there is one."

Hope sprung to life in Lockhart's chest. "You have someone in mind? Another actress?"

Dariell peered at the window as if watching, waiting for the answer to present itself. "Not an actress, no."

"Who, then?"

The woman needed enough grace and poise to pass as the wife of a nobleman. She needed eyes brimming with passion, and a magnetic sensuality if people were to believe Lockhart had succumbed to marriage. She needed to embrace the role, feel comfortable with a level of intimacy expected when two people were in love.

In short, she needed skill in the art of deception.

Dariell rose to his feet. "Miss Darling strikes me as someone eager to fight for justice. A woman who tends to the needs of her family with such devotion is a woman worthy of your consideration. Do you not agree?"

Miss Darling?

A vision of the blonde-haired lady of the manor who provided food and lodgings entered Lockhart's head. Amongst the *ton*, her plain features would mark her as a wallflower, and yet there was nothing fragile about her countenance. Her heart-shaped face and large blue eyes spoke of timidity, yet she was not afraid to express her opinion.

"The lady cannot look me in the eye," Lockhart said, recalling the numerous times she had blushed in his presence. "She will probably have a fit of the vapours when I draw her into an embrace."

Miss Darling was hardly a beguiling temptress. In bed, she was probably one of those frigid sorts who turned her back and hugged the edge of the mattress.

Dariell ambled over to the window and glanced out into the night. "Passion, it brims beneath her composed facade. It would take the right man to bring such powerful emotions to the fore."

"And you think I possess the skill?"

Dariell glanced back over his shoulder. "You have a charm most women find irresistible. Miss Darling is no different."

Suspicion flared. Dariell's plan stretched to more than a desire to clear Lockhart's name.

Lockhart narrowed his gaze. "I am looking for a temporary wife, not someone to fill the role permanently. So you can stop meddling. Miss Darling is unsuitable."

"She is honest," Dariell persisted.

"Yes, and too pure to play the wife of a scandalous rogue."

Dariell stepped away from the window but hovered near the wooden door that let in too many draughts. "You have no other choice."

The weight of the comment hung heavily in Lockhart's chest. He could not hide away in a ramshackle cottage forever. Soon, his family would learn of his return to England. Soon, they would come to know that he had not perished from a tropical fever but was very much alive and well and out for retribution.

"Surely you can persuade the *ton* you're in love with her," Dariell said, hanging on to the prospect of Miss Darling becoming Lockhart's wife like a dog did a juicy bone.

"Danger lurks in the darkness." The villain thought nothing of committing murder and blaming an innocent man. "I could not ask the lady to risk her life for me, regardless of how much I am willing to pay."

Lockhart's gaze swept to the metal bucket sitting ready to catch raindrops from the leaking roof. The Darlings lacked funds. Judging by the simple meals prepared each evening, things were bleak. Why else would an unmarried woman rent a cottage to a stranger?

"Would you rather see two ladies struggle than offer a solution?" Dariell mocked.

"It is unlike you to play the guilt card."

Why would Dariell not leave it alone? Playing Lockhart's wife might bring Miss Darling financial reward, but the experience would forever taint the lady's spirit. She would have knowledge of a world run by the greedy, the corrupt, the lords and ladies who would do anything to advance their positions. She would know what it meant to be the subject of malicious gossip.

"Regardless," Lockhart continued, "your efforts to persuade me are in vain. Miss Darling would never leave her sister."

Dariell's hand settled on the doorknob. "Not unless someone else took on the role of caring for Miss Emily."

Before Lockhart could form a response, Dariell opened the cottage door. From the feminine shriek outside, it was clear supper had arrived.

4

"Ah, Miss Darling," the Frenchman said, gesturing for the lady to enter. "Forgive me. I did not mean to startle you."

"Startle me? I almost dropped the pot on my toes." As always, the lady's tone carried a hint of humour that lessened the blow. "Would you mind offering Emily your arm, monsieur?"

"Mind? It would be a pleasure."

Dariell stepped back as Claudia Darling entered the room. As had been the case for most nights this last month, Lockhart stood and moved to offer assistance.

"It is easier if I place the pot on the table," Miss Darling said. Her gaze flicked in his direction but did not remain there for long. Soon she would give a rushed recital of the night's menu followed by an apology for the lack of variety.

Lockhart found the iron stand and placed it on the crude round table near the far wall. "And what delights await us tonight?" he said in the rich drawl that always left the lady flustered.

"Pheasant casserole with parsnips and carrots." She placed the heavy pot on the stand, breathed a relieved sigh and flexed her fingers. Miss Darling insisted on bringing supper each evening though she had numerous servants capable of seeing to the task. "I know it is the third time this week that you've—"

"Pheasant is a particular favourite of mine," Lockhart interrupted. He lifted the lid and inhaled the woody aroma of game and thyme. "And I am grateful for a hot meal."

A blush touched her cheeks, and she shrank back towards the door. Somehow, she found the courage to look at him directly. "There is no need to be polite."

The depth of her sapphire-blue gaze held him in thrall though he maintained an indifferent expression. Miss Darling could not act the part of his wife. Not because her innocence made her unsuitable, but because he was in danger of devouring her naive little mouth, of ravishing every inch of purity from her sumptuous body.

Such was the way of wicked men.

"And I have brought a baked apple tart." Miss Emily Darling approached the table whilst clinging on to Dariell's arm. Every evening, she accompanied her sister on the short walk from the manor house named Falaura Glen.

Dariell placed the dessert on the table. "And it smells delicious."

Miss Emily smiled as if the compliment were the pinnacle of her life's achievements. "You are most kind, monsieur." She turned and looked at Dariell, though having lost her sight as a child, gazed somewhere beyond his shoulder.

Silence ensued.

"Would you care to dine with us, Miss Darling?" Every evening, Lockhart invited them to stay for supper, but they invariably declined. Tonight, he felt compelled to be more persuasive than usual. "My friend is weary of my less than enthralling conversation."

Miss Darling gave a nervous smile as she scanned the breadth of his chest. "We thank you for the offer, sir, but we ate two hours ago and should get back to the house."

Two hours ago? Lockhart could never get used to dining at six.

"It is cold out. Won't you at least warm yourselves by the fire before venturing home?"

A shiver shook the lady's shoulders, and she drew her drab shawl across her chest. "A brisk walk is a perfect remedy for cold bones."

If the woman could not remain in a room with him for five minutes, how on earth was she to share his bed? No. Miss Darling was a most unsuitable candidate, indeed.

"Still, I would not want you to catch a chill on my account."

Miss Darling raised her chin. "I have a hardy constitution."

"Then humour me," Lockhart countered, desperate to prove Dariell wrong, desperate to prove this lady lacked the wherewithal to tackle the vipers in the pit called the *ton*. Yes, wiping the smug grin off his friend's face was the reason for his persistence.

"May we stay?" Miss Emily asked. "Just this once. It won't hurt to have a small bite to eat, and I am keen to hear Monsieur Dariell's opinion on Plato's ancient theories of the soul."

Dariell's eyes brightened. "And I would be delighted to hear your views on the subject."

Lockhart suppressed a smirk. He turned to Miss Darling and arched a brow. "Well? Will you disappoint two people who clearly have a shared interest in philosophy?"

A faint huff of annoyance left the lady's lips. "What loving sister would deny her sibling a moment of pleasure?"

What loving wife would deny her husband the same?

Lockhart gestured to the table. "Then allow me to escort you to your seat."

He offered his arm though judging by the flash of horror in Miss Darling's eyes she did not relish the prospect of touching him. Being a man used to taking charge, he captured her dainty hand, ignored how soft and warm it felt, and placed it in the crook of his arm.

"It has been some time since I escorted a woman to dinner." More than five years to be precise. "Permit me this one indulgence."

She cast him a sidelong glance but continued to hold his arm. "You strike me as a man who's used the same line many times, Mr Lockhart."

"On the contrary, Miss Darling, I never grovel for a lady's attention. But I should like to play escort to you all the same."

Her bottom lip quivered, but she held her composure and inclined her head by way of acceptance. Lockhart almost gave a triumphant cheer for having advanced a few paces in this battle of wills.

The next hour passed quickly, the conversation interspersed

with awkward moments of silence. Perhaps neither lady felt comfortable dining in the company of men.

After consuming a glass of wine—a particularly fine claret Dariell had brought back from London—Miss Darling's shoulders relaxed. Aided by the soft glow of candlelight and the intimate seating arrangement around the small table, the lady grew a little more comfortable in his presence.

"Have you visited London recently, Miss Darling?" Lockhart doubted she had the funds to travel to the nearest coaching inn but a desire to prove Dariell wrong forced him to pry.

The lady dabbed her mouth with her napkin though she had long since finished her meal. "My duties keep me at Falaura Glen, sir, and I am not one for the hustle and bustle of city life."

Lockhart glanced at Dariell and raised a brow.

As he suspected, this lady was ill-suited to play his wife.

"And what keeps you amused in the country?" Lockhart asked. No doubt she spent her days reading poetry or squinting over a needlework frame. "I'm told there's a monthly assembly in Flamstead." Not that he had an interest in attending.

Miss Darling glanced at her sister, a look of pity passing over her features. "I'm afraid I make a rather clumsy dancer, sir."

It was a lie. A perfectly constructed lie used to spare her sister's feelings. A moral lie if such a thing existed.

Dariell looked at Lockhart. His satisfied smile conveyed his belief that Miss Darling would be a perfect wife.

"Do you dance, Miss Emily?" Dariell asked much to the shock of her sibling whose eyes grew as wide as saucers.

Miss Darling glared across the table. She looked ready to leap from her seat and throttle Dariell for his foolish comment. "I took you for an intelligent man, monsieur."

The need to protect her sister radiated like a flaming beacon. She was not afraid to speak her mind when it mattered.

Damnation!

Yet another reason why this lady was the ideal candidate.

"My affliction makes dancing impossible, monsieur," Miss Emily said without a hint of embarrassment.

Dariell inhaled deeply. "One needs only to hear the music and move their feet to dance. With the help of a supportive partner, there is no reason why you cannot waltz about the floor."

"Waltz, monsieur?" Miss Emily's illuminating smile lit up the room. It was as if someone had just offered her a chance to experience heaven here on earth. One could not fail to share in the lady's apparent joy.

Lockhart sensed Miss Darling's sudden panic.

Miss Emily clutched her hands to her chest. "You believe such a thing is possible? Possible for someone like me?"

"I am certain. With your permission, I am happy to be your tutor."

Lockhart shifted his gaze to Miss Darling.

Water swam in her eyes. Nerves, excitement and fear were all etched on her dainty face. He wished they were on such intimate terms that she might confide in him, allow him to experience the wild flurry of emotions that made her want to cry.

Dariell was right.

Miss Darling concealed a fiercely passionate nature beneath her prim facade.

Dare he say, he was intrigued. He had an overwhelming urge to be the one to unlock the lady's darkest secrets.

"You would not mind me stepping on your toes, monsieur?" Miss Emily said before glancing in her sister's direction. "What do you say? Might Monsieur Dariell teach me to dance?" Every word brimmed with hope. "We can use the library if we move the chairs."

"Of course he may." Miss Darling bit down on her bottom lip and dabbed her finger to the corner of her eye. "Though we cannot pay you for your time, monsieur."

"The pleasure of seeing your sister glide about the floor would be payment enough."

Silence descended.

Miss Darling came to her feet. "Well, thank you for supper, but we must return to the house before the servants send out a search party."

Lockhart stood and moved around the table. "May I walk with you?"

The lady shook her head. "That won't be necessary."

"Will you not permit me this one indulgence?" he said, offering a wicked grin.

A faint smile touched her lips. "I think I have indulged you enough this evening, Mr Lockhart."

He captured her hand and bowed low. It crossed his mind to inform her that he was a man with an insatiable appetite, but he simply said, "Then I bid you good night, Miss Darling. I look forward to seeing what delights you have to offer tomorrow evening."

"Delights?" She snatched her hand back.

"Will it be pheasant or might I hope for goose?"

Her cheeks coloured. "If you hope for goose, you will be sorely disappointed."

An odd feeling settled in his chest upon noting her mild embarrassment. The urge to drop a purse full of coins into her palm proved overwhelming. A woman so humble might struggle to convey the bearing of an affluent aristocrat. How would she fare living in the luxury afforded a man of his wealth?

Dariell assisted Emily Darling to the door. He promised to call at the house the next day and discuss the arrangements for her first lesson. After returning the lady to the care of her sister, he bid them both a good evening, watched them walk away and then closed the door.

Neither man spoke as they cleared away the plates, ready for the footman who came to collect them every evening. It was not until Dariell had stoked the fire and they settled into their chairs that Lockhart broached the subject of Emily Darling.

"That's the first time I've seen you take a genuine interest in a woman," Lockhart said.

Dariell saw no merit in meaningless liaisons. So what was it about Emily Darling he found intriguing?

"I am interested in anyone with a pure heart and kind soul."

Lockhart snorted. "Then why the hell are you friends with me?"

Amusement flashed in Dariell's dark eyes. "For the reasons I have just mentioned. You are an honest man still trying to find the right path."

"Your interests in Miss Emily run deeper than appreciating her character," Lockhart said, eager to steer the conversation away from his own failings.

"Perhaps."

"It does not bother you that the lady is blind?"

"Why would it when she can see better than those with the gift of sight?"

Dariell had a point. Some people spent a lifetime unable to see the beauty of their surroundings, unable to appreciate the love radiating from their children's innocent faces. Some parents failed to see their child's strengths and only focused on their weaknesses.

Lockhart stared at the fire's amber flames.

The empty feeling returned—a crippling hopelessness a man ought not dwell on. Except for his friends, Lockhart was alone in the world. He doubted his family would welcome him with open arms like the prodigal son.

"You are thinking of your return home," Dariell said. It was a statement, not a question.

"Is it home anymore? I am not so sure."

"Home, it is anywhere love resides. You have friends who care for you there."

His friends—Greystone, Drake and Valentine—were like

brothers. Now they were all married, and he would embrace their wives as his sisters.

"You have always been a good friend, Dariell." Damn. Thoughts of home brought various emotions to the fore.

"Then as your good friend, I ask that you accept my counsel regarding the matter of your wife." Dariell sat forward. "With Miss Darling at your side, success shall be yours."

During the years Lockhart had known the Frenchman, he'd had a gift for predicting the outcome of events, a gift for seeing each man's destined path. If Dariell believed in Miss Darling, who was he to argue?

"You have not been wrong yet."

"Trust me. Miss Darling, she is a perfect choice."

Lockhart sighed.

The actress would have indulged in after-dark activities. A romp beneath the bedsheets might have made the whole process less tiresome. That said, perhaps it was easier to sleep next to a virgin. With no hope of settling between Miss Darling's soft thighs, he could focus on the grim task ahead.

"Well?" Dariell persisted. "Will you approach Miss Darling with a proposition?"

"What choice do I have?"

"None." Dariell chuckled.

"Then tonight, I shall visit the manor and make Miss Darling a scandalous offer."

No doubt one the lady would refuse.

CHAPTER TWO

"Must you walk so quickly?" Emily panted as they marched back to the house. "No matter how hard you try, you'll not escape the biting wind."

"It's not the wind I am trying to escape." Claudia slowed her pace before her sister tripped and stumbled. It was the dark, brooding gentleman staying in the cottage that caused a fluttering panic in her chest.

"Each night, we creep to the cottage as if a wolf lives there." Emily's breathing settled to a steadier pace. "Each night, we leave as if the creature might pounce from behind a tree and tear our flesh from our bones."

Claudia could not dispute Emily's claim. In her defence, Mr Lockhart looked eager to sink his teeth into someone's pulsing vein. "Is it not right to be nervous when visiting an unmarried gentleman?"

One could not deny Mr Lockhart had a hypnotic charm. Claudia had made the mistake of staring into those chestnut-brown eyes, had made the mistake of noting the gold flecks that glowed whenever his voice turned smooth and suggestive. As a woman with no hope or opportunity of ever dabbling in affairs of the heart, she might easily fall under his seductive spell.

"And yet tonight your fear stems from more than the man's marital status." Having lost her sight at the age of ten due to an illness, Emily had learnt to hone her other senses. Consequently, it was as if she could read Claudia's mind.

"I am not afraid of Mr Lockhart."

"You're afraid to like him," Emily countered. "I can hear the hesitance in your voice when you're in his company."

"We know nothing about the gentleman"—and she used the term loosely for there was an air of sinful wickedness about his countenance—"other than he has spent the last five years living abroad."

Mr Lockhart might be a master criminal. A thief! A murderer!

Why else was he hiding in a cottage in the Hertfordshire countryside?

It was easier to think the worst. Only in fairy tales did a handsome knight arrive to rescue a damsel in distress. *Distressed* and *desperate* certainly described her current predicament. Beneath Mr Thorncroft's polite facade lay a savage brute. Of that she was certain. The mild threats would soon escalate when she failed to settle the debt. And while Mr Lockhart paid handsomely to rent a run-down cottage, it was not enough to keep the real wolf from their door.

"Anyone who has such a kind and considerate friend as Monsieur Dariell must have a good and honest heart," Emily said in the dreamy tone of one suffering from a mild infatuation.

"Perhaps."

Monsieur Dariell was the most pleasant man Claudia had ever met. He seemed wise beyond his years. Not once had he looked upon Emily with pity but treated her as a woman without a debilitating affliction.

"Describe him again," Emily said as they approached the

small portico supported by two Doric columns, the entrance to their modest-sized manor house.

"Well, he has soft full lips and wavy black hair that falls rakishly over his brow." A chuckle burst from Claudia's mouth in a stream of white mist. "He has a strong physique and a mischievous twinkle in his eyes whilst still looking scholarly."

Emily squeezed Claudia's arm and laughed, too. "I am not talking about Mr Lockhart."

"I know you're not, but one cannot help but admire such a virile male specimen." And the man had a smile that turned her insides to blancmange.

"Are Monsieur Dariell's eyes as kind as his voice?" Emily persisted. "I imagine they are."

"They are indeed. Every mannerism conveys depth of character. And yet despite being slight of frame, he possesses a physical strength beyond that which I have seen before."

On one of her daily walks with Emily, Claudia had witnessed Monsieur Dariell and Mr Lockhart out in the field practising some strange form of combat.

"What's his most striking feature, do you think?"

That was an easy question, one Emily has asked before, but Claudia humoured her all the same. "I would say his hair. It's as black as ebony and tied back in a queue."

A satisfied smile illuminated Emily's face.

They entered the house and made their way to the drawing room. A healthy fire blazed in the grate, candles flickered in the lamps. The welcoming sight was enough to chase the chill from their bones. Mrs Bitton had placed two small glasses of sherry on the side table ready for their return, and so they sank into their usual seats to reflect on the night's event.

"How do you truly feel about Monsieur Dariell teaching me to dance?" Emily clutched her glass between her palms and took a sip of sherry. "Do you think it's foolish?"

Claudia could not lie, but she did not wish to ruin a moment of happiness. "I think it is a wonderful idea, but it will take time and perseverance. No doubt Monsieur Dariell is a patient teacher."

Emily sighed as she gazed at the fire. "To glide once around the floor in the arms of a gentleman would be a dream come true."

"It would," Claudia said, sharing in her sister's fantasy.

They sat in silence for a brief time. Doubtless, Emily imagined a magical moment on the dance floor, while Claudia's thoughts turned frosty as she anticipated Mr Thorncroft's arrival the next morning. The man wanted money or her hand in marriage. She could give him neither.

"Would you mind if I went to bed?" Emily said, stifling a yawn.

"Of course not." Claudia rose to her feet. Perhaps Emily wanted to dream of Monsieur Dariell without disruption. "Let me help you. Let me escort you to the first-floor landing."

Emily stood, too. Gripping her glass with one hand, she batted the air with the other while searching for the side table. Claudia longed to offer assistance, but Emily craved independence.

After placing her glass down, Emily held out her arms and drew Claudia into their usual nightly embrace. "Very well. But then you must let me find my own way."

"Agreed."

Emily held Claudia's arm as they left the drawing room and mounted the dimly lit staircase. Once safely clear of the top step, Emily tugged her arm free and whispered, "Pleasant dreams."

Claudia lingered in the gloom and watched her sister edge her way along the wall as she navigated the corridor.

When Emily entered her bedchamber, and the house plunged into silence once more, Claudia returned to the drawing room and quickly downed another two glasses of sherry. Liquor was said to help people forget their problems. She slipped off her boots and stockings and stretched out on the sofa before the fire. In the morning she had the farrier's bill to pay. Mrs Bitton had requested the funds to settle their account with the tea dealer, she had to approve the grocery order, and the footmen needed new shirts.

But the stress of household business was not the reason nausea roiled in her stomach. No, while Emily lay in a snug bed and pondered the prospect of dancing the waltz, Claudia closed her eyes and contemplated her fate. The thought of meeting Mr Thorncroft tomorrow filled her with dread. The man was a vile letch looking for any excuse to trap her into marriage. She could only keep him at bay for so long.

Who knew when he would tire of her excuses?

Who knew when the blackguard would strike?

Mr Lockhart had entered the drawing room. Claudia could not see him through the misty veil of her dream, but that did not mean he wasn't there. The smell of his cologne filled her head—oriental rose infused with incense and the warm woody notes that gave the scent its masculine depth.

She felt the soft touch of his fingers trace the line of her jaw. Heat warmed her chest, the exciting sensation moving in a southerly direction as she imagined him climbing on top of her on the worn sofa in front of the fire.

The first thread of consciousness came when she heard her own soft hum of pleasure. The faint whiff of brandy and wine reached her then, dragging her out of her trance. A large hand took hold of her bare foot, forcing her to open her eyes and sit bolt upright.

A shriek caught in her throat as she noted the handsome gentleman staring at her from a kneeling position on the Persian rug.

"Mr Lockhart!"

Claudia rubbed her eyes with the heels of her palms, convinced she was still dreaming.

"Do not call out," he whispered. "I come merely to discuss a matter of some importance. A private matter spoken only in the strictest confidence."

Claudia's head spun—probably because she had drunk far too much sherry in an effort to banish thoughts of Mr Thorncroft's visit.

"How did you get in here?" She snatched her bare foot from his grasp and scrambled to tuck her legs beneath her skirts. But not before Mr Lockhart had taken an admiring peek at her ankles.

"The front door was open. I simply turned the knob and walked in. After noting the light spilling out beneath the door, I thought to try in here first."

Claudia gulped. She tried to look him in the eye but failed. "And if there had been no light, what would you have done then?" Would he have crept upstairs and into her bedchamber?

Mr Lockhart brushed a hand through the tantalising lock of hair falling over his brow. "I would have stolen up to your room," he said in the soothing voice that made the hairs on her nape prickle, "slipped inside and spoken to you there."

It seems she had the measure of this man though she had to admire his honesty. During his time at Falaura Glen, he'd had many opportunities to take liberties. The fact he had always been above reproach meant she had to trust his word now.

Claudia gathered her courage and shuffled to sit straight, though he remained in a submissive position.

"What is so important, sir, that you would enter my home uninvited?"

A sudden panic rushed through her chest. Had he come to withdraw Monsieur Dariell's offer to tutor Emily? Oh, she would have to drop to her knees, too, and beg him to reconsider.

A dark, solemn look swept over his features as his arrogant

facade faltered. For a moment, she saw pain and torment in his eyes. "I come to you on a matter of life and death."

The words carried a menacing undertone. Good Lord, surely he was teasing.

"That is a rather dramatic statement, sir."

"Nonetheless, it is the truth. My life is in danger, Miss Darling."

"In danger?" Claudia clutched her hands to her breast. She glanced at the window with some trepidation. Was that why a man with his intelligence and aesthetic appeal had locked himself away in a cottage?

Mr Lockhart inclined his head, his expression grave. "I come tonight to beg for your assistance."

Beg? She doubted a man with his charm had ever begged for anything in his life.

Intrigued, she asked, "You wish to remain in the cottage for an indefinite period?" Heavens above, perhaps this gentleman was the answer to her prayers. With a regular income, she could meet Mr Thorncroft's demands.

The deep furrow between his brows dashed her hopes. "I must return to London within the week."

Return to London?

Disappointment sank to the pit of her stomach like a brick in a water barrel. "You agreed to a two-month tenancy."

Would Monsieur Dariell be leaving, too?

"And I shall more than compensate you for my need to vacate the premises."

Claudia could not hide her despair.

"Do not look so downhearted, Miss Darling," he continued in the flirtatious voice she found unnerving. "I have a proposition that may be to your benefit. I can see how much you enjoy my company and I would never abandon a friend in need."

They were far from friends, barely even acquaintances, and

yet the thought of him leaving Falaura Glen created an unexpected anxiety that stemmed from more than her need for money.

Keen to dismiss the feeling as foolish, she forced herself to meet his gaze. "You have certainly piqued my curiosity."

"I possess a certain skill for rousing a lady's interest."

Good Lord! Was this an attempt at seduction?

Did he think to bed the mistress of the manor before taking his leave?

"You will find I am unlike other women, Mr Lockhart." It was a small lie, but he was not to know. "Feigned words of affection are unlikely to provoke a reaction. Speak plainly. Tell me what you're doing here. Tell me what you want."

The rogue smiled. His tongue swept over his kissable lips, and she resisted the urge to moisten her own mouth. "To be blunt, Miss Darling, I want you."

"Me!"

Saints preserve her!

What on earth did he mean?

Claudia struggled to catch her breath as her pulse pounded in the base of her throat. The smell of Mr Lockhart's cologne swirled in her head, making her dizzy. The mischievous glint in his eye made her hands tremble with excitement, not fear.

The man was far too close for comfort. Claudia flicked her fingers towards the fireside chair. "Sit down, Mr Lockhart. How can I concentrate when you're crawling about on bended knees like a grateful peasant?"

The gentleman inclined his head. When he stood, he seemed so tall, so broad and large. His thighs were eye level, and she could not help but steal a furtive glance at the solid muscles filling his breeches.

He dropped into the chair with the languid grace born of an aristocrat. The smug grin playing on his lips spoke of arrogance, of the satisfaction gleaned from knowing he had unsettled her composure.

As difficult as it was to remain indifferent, she refused to fall under his spell.

"There seems to be a miscommunication, sir. Regardless of your intentions, I am not any man's possession." And she would say the same to Mr Thorncroft first thing in the morning.

Mr Lockhart steepled his fingers as he watched her with an intensity that almost made her drop her gaze. She didn't. For some reason, she felt empowered. He needed something from her, and she couldn't help but feel flattered.

"I will not lie. The thought of possessing your mind and body, Miss Darling, has a strange appeal."

So the wolf had decided to make an appearance.

Not wishing to flounder under the heat of his stare, she said, "Of course it does. What else would one expect from a scoundrel?"

He laughed. "Scoundrels lie and deceive. Scoundrels use and abuse. I come to you with honesty, with the truth that I would not be a warm-blooded male if I did not fantasise about taking you to bed."

Claudia's cheeks flamed. No doubt they were a bright shade of crimson. Try as she might to hide her naivety, something always gave her away.

"Finding a bed partner is not considered a life and death situation. And I am no man's mistress, sir, so you can be on your way."

Her sharp tone failed to wipe the smirk from his face. "No, I never once thought that you were." He sat forward. "What I want is for you to come with me to London. What I want is for you to live with me. Sleep with me. Pretend to be my wife."

Stunned did not even begin to describe her reaction to his shocking declaration. Had she been standing, her knees would have buckled and she would have ended up a crumpled heap on the floor.

"I beg your pardon," she managed to say because clearly she had misheard.

He exhaled deeply, held his tongue while he scanned her with a scrutiny that sent a shiver from her neck to her navel. "My family believes I murdered a man," he eventually said, though she wished he'd remained silent. "Someone wanted rid of me and so framed me for a murder I did not commit. I must go home and confront the demons of my past, Miss Darling. Proving my innocence is my priority."

"I—I see."

What else could one say when hit with such a terrifying revelation?

An awkward silence descended, the sound broken only by the crackle of the fire's flames.

"I am innocent of any crime," Mr Lockhart persisted. "You have no need to fear me."

She hardly knew him. And while he looked strong enough to beat the life from a man, she doubted he had the heart to do so unprovoked. But what did proving his innocence have to do with needing a wife?

"No," she whispered. "I am not afraid of you, Mr Lockhart." He did make her nervous but not for the reason he might think.

You're afraid to like him.

A relieved sigh left his lips and his gaze softened. "Then you give me hope, Miss Darling. Hope that I have never dared dream of before."

The fact she wasn't afraid did not mean he wasn't dangerous. Mr Lockhart knew what to say to elicit the desired response. A man with his charm might easily convince a woman she was in love.

Live with me. Sleep with me. Pretend to be my wife.

The words echoed in her mind like a siren's song luring her with the prospect of excitement and pleasure. Every reader of

22

mythology knew that to follow such a bewitching call brought nothing but disaster.

"None of what you have said explains the reason you're here, sir. Why do you want someone to pretend to be your wife? And what makes you think I would be remotely interested in the role?"

Mr Lockhart lounged back in the chair, his rakish smile returning. "Do you not crave adventure? We would reside in a townhouse in Mayfair, attend balls, soirees, the theatre."

"The lavish pursuits of the aristocracy do not interest me."

"I will pay handsomely for your assistance. A thousand pounds for one week out of your busy schedule."

A thousand pounds!

She almost slid off the sofa.

The gentleman had more money than sense.

A vision of her slapping the banknotes into Mr Thorncroft's outstretched palm flashed into her mind. She would not bandy words when she told him never to darken her door again.

"You have not answered my question, sir." Claudia sensed his reluctance to offer a more detailed explanation. His answer might make the notion of earning a thousand pounds less tempting. "Why do you need a wife?"

"Who else can a man trust if not his own wife?"

"Stop being evasive. And you're not asking me to be your wife. You're asking me to take part in a deception."

He stretched out his legs and crossed them at the ankles. "As always, Miss Darling, your directness leaves me no option but to answer, though I fear I do so at the detriment of my persuasive argument."

"Then as a man who believes he has been duped, sir, I am sure you understand the need for honesty."

"Indeed." He inclined his head respectfully, though the rakish lock fell over his brow, distracting her momentarily. "I am afraid I suffer from a gentleman's curse, Miss Darling."

"A gentleman's curse?" Was there such a thing?

"I suspect the traitor—the man responsible for my situation— is a member of my own family. Money, land and enriching one's bloodline are but a few reasons why someone might want to see me hang from the gallows. Envy, greed and pride flourish amongst the ranks of the landed gentry."

Such vices were apparent in those who wished to advance their position—Mr Thorncroft being a prime example.

"Allow me to offer my condolences," she said. Family were supposed to be the ones a person turned to in times of need. "It saddens me to think you speak the truth."

There was a sudden change in his bearing. He straightened, gritted his teeth and said, "I cannot forgive them, any of them." Bitterness dripped from every word. "I cannot forgive the one who stabbed me in the back, nor those who stood by idly, those who failed to come to my aid."

No, that much was evident.

"But why do you want your family to think you're married?" As soon as she'd spoken, a plausible reason entered her head. "Ah, I see. A gentleman's curse passes to his male offspring. What is yours would one day belong to your son. Should the motive be money, getting rid of you would not serve the villain's evil end."

Mr Lockhart arched a brow but did not confirm or deny her theory. "I mean to lure the devil out. But to do so, I must lay a trap."

"And you intend to use me as bait?"

Regardless of whether the money would bring an end to her troubles or not, Claudia could not accept such a ridiculous proposition. Even if—in a moment of fancy—she might like a change of scenery, might like to sit in a plush box at the theatre and watch a play, she could not leave Emily.

Mr Lockhart rose to his feet. "A decision made now would be a decision made in haste. Take a little time to contemplate my offer. Let me have your answer tomorrow."

Claudia did not need time to think. There could be but one answer to such a shocking proposal and that was no.

"Very well," she said, paying him the courtesy of agreeing to his request. "I shall call on you at the cottage tomorrow."

He lingered. Stared. Not once did he divert his gaze. "Until tomorrow, Miss Darling," he eventually said before turning on his heels and striding towards the door.

"Wait!" The command burst from her lips. The nagging question in her mind would have an answer it seemed. "What makes you think I am up to the task of aiding you in your quest for justice?"

The corners of his mouth twitched as he glanced back over his shoulder. "Honesty is a rare trait. You have it in abundance."

Was that it?

She could not help but be a little disappointed. Could he not have said he liked her, that she possessed a refined grace, a radiant beauty that made her an ideal candidate? Could he not have said that her strength of heart and courage appealed to him, too?

"Will your family not wonder why you did not write to them and inform them of your marriage?"

"Why would they?" He shrugged. "My family think I'm dead."

CHAPTER THREE

The mantel clock struck ten. No sooner had the last chime rung through the drawing room than the clip of Mr Thorncroft's boots echoed in the hall. The man was prompt. No doubt he had been up at dawn planning how his day of wickedness might end.

Claudia sat in the chair, her eyes fixed on the door, repeating her refusal over and over until confident she had the wherewithal to recite it aloud.

The door creaked open, and Dickinson appeared. "Mr Thorncroft to see you, ma'am."

"Show him in, Dickinson."

A hard lump formed in Claudia's throat as she anticipated locking gazes with the arrogant braggart. The man had the beady eyes of a bird of prey—cold, sharp, eagerly calculating the moment to strike.

Mr Thorncroft marched into the room, the end of his walking cane hitting the floor as if it were a third foot. He did not smile when he bowed. His small mouth and thin lips formed the usual grim expression.

"Miss Darling, I'm thankful you could receive me."

26

"I am not a lady who goes back on her word." Besides, he had left her with no choice. "As this is not a social call, sir, perhaps you should sit so we may discuss our business."

Mr Thorncroft stared down his long, pointed nose. Perhaps he wanted her to pander to his whims, to fall at his feet, grateful he had offered another means to repay the debt.

"Business is better discussed while taking refreshment."

Refreshment? She wanted to make her point quickly not partake in idle chatter.

"Then Dickinson will bring tea, though I shall not be joining you."

Whilst lying awake in bed during the early hours, trying to banish all thoughts of Mr Lockhart's exciting proposal, Claudia decided it was time Mr Thorncroft heard the truth. She would not continue to feed his delusions of grandeur.

"Please sit, sir." She gestured to the chair opposite.

After a moment's pause, he thrust his cane at Dickinson, flicked out his coattails and dropped into the seat.

Claudia wasted no time. The sooner this man was out of her house, the better.

"Well, Mr Thorncroft, I trust you have taken the time to consider the offer you made at our last meeting. Marriage is a serious affair, a union not to be taken lightly."

Unless a man wanted to prove himself innocent of murder.

"Borrowing money with no intention of repaying the debt is a serious affair, Miss Darling." His hollow cheeks conveyed his disapproval. "I cannot imagine what your father was thinking."

Neither could she.

Richard Darling was too proud to take a loan. He cared too much for his daughters to leave them in such a precarious predicament, especially when his passing meant their finances were significantly reduced. The entailed property in Berkshire had passed to a distant relative, so too had the modest yearly income. He had purchased Falaura Glen in its current state a year before her mother died, and they had remained there ever since.

"If only there were receipts to show what my father did with the money," she said.

How odd that no one knew anything of his lavish expenditure and yet Mr Thorncroft had the papers to prove his claim.

Mr Thorncroft's head fell slowly forward as he sharpened his gaze. "I might offer an explanation, but it is not for the ears of a gently bred lady, my dear."

Insulted, for how dare he imply that her father was anything other than an honest and moral gentleman, she said, "I do not care for your sordid implications, sir." Her hands trembled as every fibre in her body wanted to kick this scoundrel down the length of the drive. "And it is wrong to cast aspersions on the character of a man who is no longer here to defend his position."

Rather than appear affronted by her sudden outburst, Mr Thorncroft managed a faint smile.

"Your loyalty to your kin does you credit, Miss Darling. Any man would be grateful to have such a faithful and honest wife at his side."

"So I am told."

Mr Lockhart had said a similar thing, too. Not that she wanted to appear shallow, but she would like to think she had other attributes besides a desire to speak her mind.

A mild look of panic passed briefly over Mr Thorncroft's features. "You have had an offer from another gentleman in the parish?"

Perhaps she would give this toad a reason for concern. "Yes, as a matter of fact, I have." Remembering Mr Lockhart's need for secrecy, she added, "Though, as I told the gentleman in question, I have no intention of marrying."

A timely knock on the door brought Mrs Bitton with the tea tray. The fact she had not sent a footman said more about the housekeeper's protective nature than their current staff shortage.

Silence descended as Mrs Bitton placed the tray on the stand beside Claudia's chair and poured for the gentleman. Numerous times she cast a scowl at Mr Thorncroft whenever he diverted his attention. When she left the room, she wedged the door open.

"Who is he?" Mr Thorncroft said as soon as they were alone. He did not give her a chance to answer—not that she would have broken a confidence—before saying, "Your only hope of being rid of the debt is to marry me. I thought I had made that clear."

"Tea?" Claudia gripped the saucer and offered Mr Thorncroft the beverage.

He took hold of it, but the rattle of the china cup showed his annoyance. After gulping the hot drink down until he'd drained every drop, he stood and returned the china to the tea tray.

"Just in case there should be any doubt as to my claim," he said, delving into the inside pocket of his coat and removing a folded note, "the magistrate has assessed my case and agrees you must pay the debt forthwith."

He thrust the note at her, and she took it in the hope he would return to his seat. It was difficult enough sitting opposite the man without him hovering over her like the crow of death ready to peck her eyes from their sockets.

When he failed to move, Claudia gestured to the chair opposite until he obliged.

She peeled back the crisp folds, observed the signature of the man acting for the Crown but who took bribes when his wife overindulged on her frequent trips to town.

"And Mr Hollingsworth based his decision solely on a piece of paper that bears my father's signature?"

"It is a legally binding document." Mr Thorncroft stared in the menacing way that made every hair on her body stand to attention. "The magistrate agrees and will assign the case to the assizes should you fail to repay the debt. It clearly says that should death occur I may recover the sum from the deceased's estate."

Claudia scanned the document written in Mr Thorncroft's

hand. There were no signs of tampering. The writing was fluid and even. At the bottom, her father's signature acted as the damning mark.

Perhaps it was the need to get rid of this devil that brought Mr Lockhart's proposal to the forefront of her mind. Perhaps it was the thrill of a challenge that caused excitement to flutter whenever she thought about the role he wanted her to play. One thing was certain. She would rather spend a week with Mr Lockhart than a lifetime with Mr Thorncroft.

A thousand pounds for one week out of your busy schedule.

The debt was fifteen hundred pounds.

Mr Lockhart seemed desperate enough to pay more.

But Claudia couldn't leave her sister. How would Emily cope in her absence? Then another idea took root. Would Mr Lockhart consider taking Emily with them?

The options bounded back and forth in her head until Mr Thorncroft cast an arrogant grin and said, "It is time you accepted your fate, Miss Darling. Agree to be my wife, and I shall wipe the debt."

Nothing in the world would make her believe she was destined to marry this conceited fool. Had the man a conscience, one might think he had been awake half the night consumed with guilt for his misdeeds. But the dark shadows beneath his eyes were a permanent feature.

"I shall make a pact with you, Mr Thorncroft," she said, desperate to get rid of him for she could not bear the sight of his vanity a moment longer. "Permit me one week. One week to pay the debt. Should I fail in the task, I will agree to be your wife. Together we will visit Mr Hollingsworth where he will witness our agreement. However, I require my own signed copy of the document."

She would be damned before she'd trust either of the fools. Something strange was afoot. She just couldn't prove it.

Mr Thorncroft sat in silence.

30

"Well? Are you in agreement, sir?"

"Where do you propose to find fifteen hundred pounds in a week," he eventually said, "when you have failed to pay the debt these last twelve months?"

"That is my affair."

The final word sent a tingle down the length of her spine. Mr Lockhart had mentioned sharing his bed. Surely that was only for appearance's sake. Surely he did not expect to take liberties for his thousand pounds.

Mr Thorncroft narrowed his gaze in suspicion. "And if I refuse?"

It would mean selling the house, moving to a small cottage, but such things took time. She could sell furniture, paintings, perhaps raise enough to satisfy the gentleman.

"I could never marry a man who lacked an ounce of Christian charity."

Mr Thorncroft's expression remained sombre. He pursed his thin lips. "Very well. I shall give you one week to pay the debt in full. I shall return home and draw up a contract, and we will visit the magistrate today."

"Agreed." Claudia came to her feet. There was nothing more to say, and she needed a nip of sherry to quell her nerves.

As a gentleman, Mr Thorncroft had no option but to stand, too. He bowed, appeared eager to be on his way. One could not pledge their soul to the devil without making their mark, and Mr Thorncroft would want to see her name scrawled in blood.

"I shall return in due course to convey you to Meadowbrook."

Claudia offered a weak smile. "Then you will not object if my sister accompanies us." Emily would act as her chaperone should Mr Thorncroft have dishonest intentions.

That meant she would have to reveal the full extent of their troubles. She would have to tell Emily the truth if Mr Lockhart agreed she could accompany them to London.

"No," he huffed. "I have no objection."

"My sister must be part of the arrangement, as I intend to care for her always. Any man who wishes to be my husband must accept that Emily will live with us."

A muscle in the man's cheek twitched. He gave a half smile though his eyes remained as cold as the morning frost coating the blades of grass. "You want that written into our agreement?"

"I do."

He muttered beneath his breath, inclined his head and promised to return. Without another word, he swung around and marched from the room. She heard him snipe at Dickinson for some petty misdemeanour before the front door opened and closed.

Claudia dropped into the chair, her knees about to buckle under the strain of her predicament. So much for a nip of sherry. She contemplated downing the contents of the decanter.

The day would prove long and taxing. A frank talk with Emily was long overdue, and the thought of a twenty-minute carriage ride to Meadowbrook filled her with dread. Once she'd given her oath—and ensured she had a witness to the fact that payment of the debt brought an end to the matter—she would descend on Mr Lockhart, ready to make a bargain.

"I heard Mr Thorncroft leave." Emily's voice dragged Claudia from her reverie.

"He has an important errand to run," Claudia replied, looking up to find her sister hugging the doorframe. "How long have you been there?"

"Long enough to snoop." Emily straightened and entered the room.

For weeks, ever since Mr Lockhart and Monsieur Dariell arrived at Falaura Glen, Emily had been practising walking unaided. She had memorised the number of steps required to reach the sofa.

"Long enough to hear of the debt that brings the man to our door most weeks," Emily added. She reached out, found the arm of the sofa and edged around before taking a seat. "Why did you not tell me he is trying to force you to marry?"

There was no right way of answering. It had been wrong to keep secrets. Despite wanting to protect Emily from the truth, Claudia had done her sister a disservice.

"I didn't want you to worry."

Emily's life was hard without wicked men like Mr Thorncroft causing mischief.

"Just because I cannot see does not mean I am too weak to share in your troubles."

Guilt wrapped around Claudia's heart like a strangling vine. She had sworn an oath to their father, a promise to take care of Emily. "I do not think you weak at all. You're the strongest, most courageous woman I know."

Emily smiled but the expression soon faded. "Surely you don't believe Father incurred such a huge debt? He was always so frugal. Ever since Mother made him buy this house, he had to be mindful of his expenditure."

Claudia didn't know what to believe. "Mr Thorncroft has the papers to prove his claim. The magistrate agrees that the signature belongs to Father, and I am of the same view." She had studied it in some detail through the lens of her magnifying glass.

Emily gripped the arm of the sofa. "Then all is lost. Despite what Mother wanted, we must sell the house and get rid of Mr Thorncroft for good."

Upon first glance of the quaint manor house during one of their weekend excursions, her mother had insisted her father purchase the property. Anna Darling often acted on impulse. She believed the house held the key to her family's destiny, said she felt the truth of it deep in her bones. And so they had moved from Berkshire to Hertfordshire and leased the entailed property. Twelve months later, her mother perished from a fever.

"You know Mother and her whims," Claudia said.

"I'm not sure they were whims. Monsieur Dariell said that the truth of all things lies in the heart, not the head. She loved it here. We love it here. But needs must."

Claudia fell silent.

She was so lost in the myriad of thoughts filling her head she could no longer hear the whispers of her heart.

"There is another option," Claudia said, knowing Emily would catch the hint of trepidation in her voice.

Emily jumped to her feet but kept her balance. "You are not marrying Mr Thorncroft. I would rather beg on the streets than know you must suffer his company daily."

It was not his daily company but his nightly company that made the thought unbearable.

"Marrying Mr Thorncroft is not an option I am willing to consider. But Mr Lockhart came to visit last night and made me a rather lucrative offer."

Open-mouthed, Emily flopped down into the seat. "Mr Lockhart wants to marry you. Why did you not say so before? I am not surprised. There is something in his voice that is different when he speaks to you."

The bubbling excitement returned to plague Claudia's stomach. Oh, it was ridiculous. "He has not offered marriage but is willing to pay for my assistance."

Claudia told Emily the details of her conversation with the enigmatic Mr Lockhart.

"A thousand pounds?" Emily exhaled. "If we sold Mother's jewellery and a few paintings, we would have enough to pay Mr Thorncroft."

"Precisely." That had to be the priority now.

After a brief silence, Emily said, "But we know nothing about Mr Lockhart. You would be risking everything if you helped in this deception."

True.

But when given limited options, did one choose the fallen angel or the evil devil?

"He has friends in high places—a lord, a viscount. And Monsieur Dariell is a man above reproach."

A smile brightened Emily's face. "Yes, he is."

"Besides, I've never been to London, to a ball or the theatre. With so many engagements the week will pass quickly. You could come, too."

"Me? Oh, no! I couldn't." Emily remained rigid in the seat. "I am just learning to navigate my way around here on my own. It has taken months to pluck up the courage."

Being an overprotective father, Richard Darling had insisted Emily have a chaperone at all times. Under his watchful eye, Emily believed herself inadequate, an invalid incapable of doing anything unaided. Now, she was making progress, and the prospect of learning to dance was a feat Claudia never thought possible.

"I cannot leave you here alone." Claudia winced. She hated being the one to put doubt back into her sister's mind.

"But I won't be alone. Mrs Bitton and Dickinson and the other servants are here. And Monsieur Dariell is not leaving else he would not have made arrangements to teach me to dance."

Emily had such confidence in the Frenchman's integrity it touched Claudia's heart. She didn't want to be the one to dash Emily's hopes and dreams, but it would be better for them both if she came to London, too.

"I shall speak to Mr Lockhart when we take him his supper later this evening."

"He may not wish to speak honestly if I am there. I shall invite Monsieur Dariell to take supper here, and you may dine with Mr Lockhart."

Claudia's nervous gulp reached her sister's sharp ears.

"If you're contemplating spending a week with him in London, you must learn to like him," Emily continued with some amusement.

Learning to like Mr Lockhart wouldn't be a problem.

Learning to forget about him when the week was up would prove infinitely more difficult. But she could not think of that now. Nor could she think about her reputation. Was it not better to spend her days a scandalous spinster than the wife of the most abhorrent man ever to make her acquaintance?

Besides, she would do anything to ensure Emily always had a home at Falaura Glen.

One week was hardly a sacrifice. She could spend one week with a handsome scoundrel if it meant bringing an end to her troubles. What harm could it do?

CHAPTER FOUR

T he night was cold. A biting wind nipped at Claudia's cheeks as she walked down the drive leading to the thatched cottage. The heat from the pot of rabbit stew she carried seeped through the thick blanket protecting her hands.

Emily had sent a note to Monsieur Dariell asking him to dine at the manor. Having accepted the offer, the Frenchman had passed Claudia trudging along the path. Refusing his offer of help, she had merely smiled to hide the sudden rush of trepidation that took hold whenever she thought about being alone with Mr Lockhart.

When she arrived at the cottage, the gentleman in question was standing outside propped against the door, staring up at the inky sky. A scattering of stars drew his gaze in numerous directions. Moonlight illuminated his striking profile. Never had she seen a man with such a strong jaw.

It wasn't his tall, athletic form that forced her to catch her breath, nor his captivating countenance. It was the look of wonder in his eyes as he stared at the heavens. The yearning returned, the tug deep in her core. A lady might live a lifetime and never have a man admire her like that.

When Mr Lockhart noticed her, he straightened. The mask of a sinner fell back into place. With a wicked grin capable of rendering the most experienced courtesan helpless, he sauntered towards her and took hold of the pot.

Nerves threatened to leave her speechless.

How was it she could deal with a rogue like Mr Thorncroft but crumpled beneath the weight of Mr Lockhart's stare?

"You look cold," he said in the smooth way that hinted at amusement. "Come inside. Let me take your cloak, and you can warm yourself by the fire."

How was it he made a kind gesture sound like a rake's seductive repartee?

"Thank you," she managed to say without her teeth chattering. "I can barely feel my toes."

"I am more than happy to massage your feet if it will help to get the blood pumping."

Claudia swallowed. "That won't be necessary." Never had a man spoken to her so intimately.

Mr Lockhart smiled, proof he was teasing her. "Come. Lead the way, Miss Darling. My stomach is growling like an angry bear."

No doubt such a virile gentleman required more than a measly helping of rabbit stew to feed his muscles. And yet, judging by his trim physique, he was not one to overindulge, either.

Claudia opened the cottage door and stepped back for him to enter. Mr Lockhart placed the pot on the stand in the middle of the table. He had laid two place settings, poured two glasses of red wine. Perhaps he thought to numb her senses in the hope she would accept his ludicrous proposal.

"How is it we're dining alone?" Mr Lockhart came to stand behind her, his words breezing past her ear as he lowered his head to speak. "Are you pandering to Dariell's desire for privacy or mine?"

"I said I would call to discuss your proposition." Claudia held her breath as Mr Lockhart's hands swept over her shoulders, his fingers pulling the ends of the silk ribbon securing her cloak.

"Then you have given the matter serious thought?"

He was standing so close she almost closed her eyes and leant back against his broad chest. "I have."

"Good."

He untied the bow and slipped the cloak off her shoulders. When he stepped away, the gnawing ache inside returned. The gentleman always sent her nerves scattering and yet, truth be told, she welcomed his attention.

"Then let us sit and discuss your decision over supper." Mr Lockhart hung her cloak on the coat stand near the door and then played the role of footman by pulling out her chair.

"Do you intend to serve me, too?" she said to lighten the mood, for the atmosphere thrummed with intensity.

"If that is what you want." He paused. "I need you, Miss Darling, and will do whatever it takes to win your favour."

"You will do anything?" Claudia chuckled as she took a seat.

Mr Lockhart shook out her napkin and draped it across her lap. "Anything to ease your fears, anything to ensure your comfort and mental wellbeing."

A foolish woman might be flattered, might relish the prospect of having Mr Lockhart at her beck and call. But this was about deception, Claudia reminded herself, and this man knew how to make a woman feel desirable.

"Then sit down, sir, for I cannot concentrate when you loiter."

When Mr Lockhart dropped into the seat opposite, Claudia wondered if she had been hasty in her instruction. The man had a devilish glint in his eyes that sent her heart fluttering like a host of bewildered butterflies.

Heaven help her.

How could she sleep in his bed when she couldn't even look him in the eye?

Claudia remained silent in a desperate attempt to gather her wits while Mr Lockhart proved a master with a ladle and filled both their plates without spilling a drop.

"So," he began after tasting a mouthful of stew and giving a nod of approval, "am I to wait until the end of the evening to hear your answer?"

Claudia placed her cutlery down and dabbed her lips with her napkin.

Look at him, damn it, else he'll think you weak.

She raised her chin. "I have a few stipulations if I am to accept your proposal."

"Only a few?" He smiled. "I could think of ten questions a gently bred virgin might ask."

"Heavens, you're keen to make assumptions, sir."

Mr Lockhart arched a brow. "Please. It is a compliment to your character, not a criticism."

Still, he should not presume to know her. "Perhaps I eloped with a lover, and my father caught up with us before we reached Gretna Green. Perhaps, as mistress of the manor, I have a penchant for stable boys."

Amusement replaced his initial look of surprise. "Then for once, I wish I was born to the lower ranks and destined to care for horses. There is nothing like a rampant roll in the hay."

Heat rose to her cheeks.

Oh, she hated how he had the means to unsettle her so easily.

"As long as one has a thick enough blanket," she replied with affected confidence.

"Indeed." He raised his glass in salute. "To frolicking in forbidden places."

Being forced to raise her glass, too, it appeared she agreed. They both sipped their wine, their gazes remaining locked for all of a few seconds.

"Would you care to hear them?" he said as he lowered his glass and ran his tongue over his bottom lip.

"Hear them?"

"The questions you should ask."

Claudia managed a weak smile. "Certainly."

He lounged back in the wooden chair. "You should ask how we plan to make others believe we're in love. You should ask what I wear to bed. If I plan to make love to other women whilst partaking in our little game of deception."

"Do you?" she suddenly said as jealousy slithered through her veins for his imagined infidelity.

"What? Sleep naked? Of course."

She quickly dismissed the vision filling her head. "Do you plan to bed other women while playing the doting husband?"

Mr Lockhart straightened, his gaze growing intense as he stared at her across the table. "When in a committed relationship, you shall never meet a more faithful gentleman."

"You class me assisting you in deception as being in a committed relationship?"

"I'm saying that you will have my undivided attention, Miss Darling. As your husband, legally or not, I shall remain devoted, dutiful in my care and consideration."

The heat from her cheeks moved in a southerly direction.

How wonderful it must be to hear those words and know a man meant them.

"And you think people will believe ours is a love match?" she asked, addressing his first point. "It is impossible to feign love."

An arrogant smirk made him appear devilish. "The look of love and the look of lust are similar."

"I disagree," she said, noting the way his gaze dropped to the swell of her breasts. "Love is conveyed through eye contact." And so she had no hope of being convincing. "Lust involves detailed scrutiny of the whole body."

Without warning, Mr Lockhart pushed out of the chair.

"Show me." He snatched his glass and swallowed a mouthful of wine before skirting around the table. "Give me your hand, Miss Darling."

She should insist he sit down for he was intent on embarrassing her. And yet the defiant woman inside, the one who had found the courage to deal with Mr Thorncroft, wanted to show this man that she could be bold, too.

"I am more than happy to demonstrate my meaning," she said, placing her hand in his.

With the absence of gloves, the touch of his skin sent her pulse racing. He drew her to her feet and led her to the centre of the room.

"Let us pretend we are at Lady Cotterill's ball. We have escaped to the terrace, desperate for a minute alone." He kept a firm hold of her hand. "Music drifts out from the ballroom. Stars twinkle in a clear sky."

"It sounds beautiful."

"It is." The arrogance faded for a moment as he stared at her. "Now show me. Teach me the difference between the look of love and that of lust."

He spoke as if she were an expert. In truth, she was just a naive girl experienced in fanciful dreams. Still, she closed her eyes briefly and attempted to step into the role. After all, this might be his way of testing her ability to act.

"Which emotion shall I demonstrate first?" she whispered.

"Lust. Show me what lust looks like to you, Miss Darling."

Pushing aside her embarrassment, and with her eyes still closed, Claudia focused on the warmth of his skin radiating through her palm. She pictured his tongue sweeping over his lips, the muscular thighs bulging against material of his breeches, recalled the tickle of his hot breath at her nape.

When she opened her eyes, she looked at him as if ravenous to taste him, to touch him, to devour every inch of his body. She scanned the breadth of his chest, the broad shoulders, his mouth, his hair. A hum left her lips.

It was easy when she wasn't looking into his eyes.

"Strange," he said softly. "I feel the heat of your desire."

42

"Then perhaps I am a good actress."

"Yes, perhaps you are."

Still, she did not look at him.

"Show me love, Miss Darling. In your mind, how is it different?"

Love was felt on a deeper level. Great poets spoke of a soul connection, told of the eyes being the gateway to a higher plane. With lust, images fed the body's cravings. With love, the opposite was true. The emotion rose from the chest and was conveyed through the eyes.

As if she knew a sorcerer's trick, Claudia imagined that love enveloped her heart. It did not take long for heat to radiate from the organ and flood her body. Slowly she raised her lids and looked directly into Mr Lockhart's brown eyes.

The sight stole her breath.

Not because he was the most handsome man ever to make her acquaintance, but because she sensed a connection there. The longer she stared at the gold flecks around his pupils—and the longer she imagined loving this man—the more the connection grew.

Mr Lockhart remained rooted to the spot. His breathing grew shallow. While Claudia fought the urge to cup his cheek, she noticed his head moving towards hers. His glance at her lips told her all she needed to know.

"Kissing was not part of the bargain," she said, pressing her fingers to his lips when he came too close. She dropped her hand and stepped back. "Did you not sense the difference? Did love and lust appear the same to you?"

"Oh, I sensed the difference. But it so happens that both times I thought only of devouring your pretty mouth."

Claudia sighed. Mr Lockhart reminded her of a naughty boy in the schoolroom.

"And if you accept my proposal," he continued, "you will have to kiss me at some point. Why not now?"

Lockhart took pleasure in the look of shock and then annoyance that marred Miss Darling's delicate features. He had wanted to kiss her the moment she blushed when he offered to massage her toes. No doubt she tasted of everything that was right with the world—of honesty, integrity, of clean and wholesome living.

"Why would I need to kiss you when I have not accepted your proposal?" Her argument drew him from his amorous musings.

She had a point. Even so, a man couldn't help but try. Well, if he couldn't kiss her, he might as well tease her. "But you will accept."

"How do you know I will?"

"Because you have a kind heart, Miss Darling, and because you need the money."

She appeared both flattered and insulted by his direct reply. "What makes you think I need your money?"

Did she think he was blind and stupid?

He gestured to the tin bucket, to the simple meal still gracing their plates. "You're struggling to make repairs to the property. You make excuses for the lack of variety when serving supper. And your wardrobe is rather limited, to say the least." He challenged her to argue with his accurate observations.

"What is wrong with this dress?" She tugged at the striped brown skirt that did little to enhance her figure.

"It's ugly."

"It is warm and extremely comfortable."

"It is too drab for my wife."

"I am not your wife."

"Not yet. Admit you need the money. Admit I am the answer to your prayers." If they were going to tackle his family together, he had to get past her defences. "If we have any hope of helping each other, then there must be honesty between us."

Miss Darling fell silent.

Her gaze turned meditative.

From the deep frown marring her brow, her troubles were far greater than he first suspected. Or was it the thought of spending a week in his company that caused her distress?

"If you want directness, sir, you shall have it," she eventually said, her tone determined. "Yes, I need the money, but a thousand pounds is not enough to encourage me to sleep in your bed."

He jerked his head back. "I am not paying you to make love to me. And a thousand pounds is ample considering you'll have a new wardrobe at your disposal."

She blinked rapidly. "You want me to lie next to you each night when you have already admitted to sleeping naked. And there's every chance someone might recognise me in the future. For such a blight to my reputation, I require two thousand pounds."

Lockhart rubbed his chin as he studied her. One had to admire anyone willing to fight for their position. "Fifteen hundred. And that is my final offer."

"Seventeen."

"Done."

Her eyes grew wide with shock, and she struggled to keep the satisfied smile at bay. "And you must wear a nightshirt to bed."

"A nightshirt?" he scoffed. Did the lady not know that he could seduce her with one toe? One toe drawn slowly up the lower leg sent tingles of pleasure directly to the sensitive spot between a lady's thighs. "Agreed."

"And my sister must accompany us."

"That is out of the question," he replied in a tone that said the request was not up for negotiation. "She will remain here. Dariell will ensure her safety."

"Monsieur Dariell cannot take residency in the house." Panic infused each word.

"For appearance's sake, you will hire him as her dance tutor. He will remain in this cottage and visit her daily."

"No, that will not do." Miss Darling shook her head five times or more. "Should someone learn of my absence and see them together, she will be the subject of gossip."

Better that than for Lockhart's enemies to use her as a pawn. While he hated focusing on the lady's weakness, being blind only made her an easy target.

Lockhart inhaled deeply. "Let me remind you of the reason behind my proposal, Miss Darling." Talking of that fateful night brought the memories flooding back—the blood, the cold, lifeless eyes staring back at him. "An innocent man was murdered. Murdered," he repeated, in case she had not understood the severity of his situation. "The culprit will look for ways to hurt me, of that I am convinced. I can protect you, but I cannot protect your sister, too."

Fear filled her eyes. "You think this person might try to hurt me?"

"I don't know what he will do, but—" Guilt made it impossible to finish the sentence. "Perhaps I am asking too much. Perhaps you should forget my proposal, forget you ever met me."

A brief look of panic marred her dainty features. The lady turned away from him. She dropped into her seat at the table, captured the wine glass and gulped the contents.

Long seconds passed.

"I led you to believe I would help you," she said in a melancholic tone, though she did not tear her gaze away from the single drop of claret swimming in the bottom of the glass. "And I agreed to accept an extortionate sum in payment."

"I'm strong enough to deal with rejection, Miss Darling." And yet the weight of disappointment in his chest was like nothing he had felt before. "I shall have to find another way to achieve my goal."

"Life can be cruel and unfair," she said, though still would not look at him.

He moved to kneel beside her, took hold of her chin between

his fingers and drew her around to face him. "Life can be beautiful, too, of that I am assured."

Her sombre gaze searched his face. "Perhaps there is a compromise."

"I am all ears," he said, hope springing to life in his heart once again.

Miss Darling pursed her lips while deep in thought.

"Dariell is trustworthy," Lockhart added. "I would not suggest he remain here were he not above reproach."

"I know. The man's character is as easy to read as a page in an open book."

"It is a book of great depth and wisdom."

"That is what Emily admires about him." Miss Darling sighed. "London is but thirty miles away. I do not have to be seen at Falaura Glen every day. What if you brought me home twice during the week? I could go into Flamstead, attend church. The locals would be none the wiser. Mrs Bitton can say I'm ill should anyone call."

Lockhart watched her intently as she continued with her garbled excuses.

"You're not worried about the gossips," he said, sensing the real cause of her anxiety. "You're worried about how your sister will cope in your absence."

She looked at him from beneath half-closed lids. "Is it so obvious? Emily craves independence, but I'm frightened to let her go."

Lockhart couldn't help but smile. "That is the most honest thing you've said all evening." There was hope yet, hope that they could form a union strong enough to bring down every devious scoundrel ever to darken his door. "What if I escort you home three times during the week? Between Dariell and your housekeeper, I am confident we can come up with a plan that will work to our mutual benefit."

A genuine smile brightened her countenance. "You would do that?"

"It is the least I can do under the circumstances. Besides, I sense your sister is desperate for a challenge."

Miss Darling's striking blue gaze dropped to his lips. "I imagine it will be a challenge for us all."

CHAPTER FIVE

For an hour, Lockhart had sat opposite Miss Darling, as his newly purchased carriage rattled along the narrow lanes and bobbed up and down in rain-filled ruts, and neither had spoken.

Tension sucked all air from the confined space. The draught blowing in from the small gap in the open window did little to relieve her anxiety.

The lady had sobbed upon leaving her sister. Tears welled in her eyes whenever she noticed a milestone marking the distance to London. Perhaps he should have drawn the blinds. But plunging them into darkness would only send her nerves scattering.

Doubtless, he had made a mistake.

Despite Miss Darling's protestations to the contrary, he feared she would collapse under the weight of his burden. The week would bring many trials. Danger lurked in the shadows. Evil lingered behind warm smiles and kind gestures. The *ton* behaved like the devil's brood come to wreak mischief and mayhem.

"Are you cold?" he suddenly asked when the silence became deafening. For all his confidence and courage, he needed some reassurance that she would keep her end of the bargain. "I can close the window."

"No. I hardly slept a wink last night, and the cool breeze is keeping me awake."

"The bustling streets of London are but an hour away. Take a nap. It might help to liven your spirits."

For the first time since setting out on their journey, she looked at him directly. "I couldn't possibly sleep knowing you're watching me."

Lockhart snorted. "What do you think I'll be doing tonight when we climb into bed? I like to read for an hour and suspect the late nights will leave you exhausted."

The lady was used to country hours. Supper at six, not midnight. Snoozing by the fire, not dancing and making merry.

"You mean you're serious about that?"

Lockhart frowned. "Balls and routs go on until the early hours."

"No, I mean you're serious about us sharing a bed. It's not as though your family will storm into your bedchamber and demand evidence of our betrothal."

"We *will* sleep together, Miss Darling." The serious edge to his tone should leave her in no doubt. "It is for the servants' sake that I insist."

"The servants?" She drew her brows tightly together. "Why would they care?"

Clearly the lady knew nothing of life in town. "My friend Lord Greystone hired all the staff from the Registry. Consequently, they have no loyalty and may accept bribes for information."

Her shoulders sagged. "So home will be a potential battle-ground, too?"

Home? There was no such place. Not anymore.

"I am the only person you should trust, Miss Darling."

She contemplated the comment before saying, "Claudia, you

must call me Claudia else there's every chance you'll inadvertently make a mistake."

"As I said, we must learn to share a certain intimacy if we are to convince others ours is a love match. Most people call me Lockhart, but you may call me Hudson, if you so wish."

"Hudson," she repeated as if the word held special meaning. "Perhaps we should use this time to become better acquainted with our story."

"Our story?"

"Where did we meet? When did we marry?" She glanced at her gloved hand. "Do I not have a ring? A token of your love and abiding affection?"

Lockhart had made a rough sketch of events in his mind. "Your father served as an officer in the 8th dragoons in Meerut. We met at a dance held by the regiment who invited a few British gentlemen living in the area. I attended as a guest of Lord Valentine."

"And I suppose my name is not Darling."

"You were Miss Adams—a relatively common name should anyone wish to pry. But you will avoid questions regarding your family's background."

"But I know nothing about India other than it's hot," she gabbled in a panic.

"Then when in bed this evening, I shall paint a vivid picture. One you're unlikely to forget."

A blush crept up her neck to colour her cheeks. "And you must tell me about your friends, although I feel as if I have known Monsieur Dariell for a lifetime."

"He has that effect on people."

Claudia gave a sad sigh. "I hope Emily will manage at home in my absence."

Without asking permission, he reached over and took hold of her hand resting in her lap. She should get used to his sudden touch if they wished to make their relationship appear convincing. "Your sister is stronger than you think."

She did not snatch her hand away. "I'm sure you're right. Besides, a week will pass in no time."

A week might not be long enough to trap the villain. Once settled into her new position, Lockhart hoped Miss Darling might be flexible if he needed her assistance a little longer. There was no point mentioning it now.

"I do have a ring," he said to distract her from thoughts of Falaura Glen. "Would you like me to place it on your finger or shall I simply give you the box?"

Perhaps she didn't mean to grip his hand, nor for her eyes to widen with excitement. After all, this was all part of the deception.

"You put it on. Then if someone asks about the moment I first glimpsed the ring, I can tell a half truth."

"Then you should remove your glove." Lockhart released her hand and delved into the inside pocket of his coat. He removed the black box, raised the lid and presented the ring for her inspection.

Miss Darling's eyes almost bulged from their sockets as she gawped at the amethyst and diamond halo ring. He had spared no expense. The traitor would know Lockhart had amassed great wealth while working abroad these last five years.

"You can touch it," Lockhart said, trying to sit still as the carriage rocked back and forth. "It is yours now."

Miss Darling swallowed audibly as she traced the circular cluster of diamonds with her fingertip. "You mean it is mine for the next week."

"Indeed."

For some obscure reason, his fingers shook as he pulled the ring from its velvet cushion. Miss Darling's fingers trembled, too, as he pushed the gold band slowly down over her knuckle. How strange that it was a perfect fit.

"Is it a family heirloom?" she asked, still gaping in awe.

Lockhart scoffed at the question. Fake or not, his wife deserved better than a ring given by a host of hypocrites.

"No. It is a ring of my own choosing, not one handed down through generations."

"Oh." She examined the sparkling gems gracing her finger. "One purchased purely for the deception? I doubt you would want to honour the future Mrs Lockhart with a ring worn by another woman. Ladies tend to be rather pedantic about such things."

How fortunate he had no intention of ever marrying. "Some men are born for bachelorhood. Some men prefer the freedom that comes with remaining unattached."

Miss Darling's gaze turned inquisitive. "And you place yourself in this category of gentlemen?"

"I do." And he was not ashamed to admit it.

"Naturally, circumstances lead you to distrust people's motives. If one cannot trust their kin what hope have they of trusting a wife?"

"Precisely." Evidently, Miss Darling was one of the few women who could accurately hear the unspoken.

Lockhart doubted he would ever trust another living soul. His friends were like brothers, and he hated that a small part of him reserved doubt over their loyalty. He did not trust the lady seated opposite, either, which was why he hoped to see the matter of vengeance concluded quickly.

"So you have no desire to produce an heir?" Miss Darling scanned the carriage's plush interior—the blue velvet seats, the silk blind with a gold tassel. "Are men of means not eager to secure their wealth for future generations?"

"For the living, money is a necessary evil. My friends will enjoy my fortune when I'm dead."

"Money is the cause of most people's problems." Tiny furrows appeared between her brows.

"Including yours." Had she not been desperate for funds, she would not be sitting opposite him now.

"My father was a little lapse in his accounting."

"You could marry. There must be a wealthy squire in the district keen to find a wife."

"And have him send my sister to an institute when he grows weary and considers her a burden?"

"So you're just as distrusting." It was a small comfort to know he wasn't the only person suspicious of other people's motives.

"I, too, know that snakes hide in the grass waiting for the right moment to strike."

"Then we have something in common, Miss Darling." Though he doubted she had a relative who wanted to frame her for murder. Doubted her betrothed had deserted her and married her sibling.

"Claudia," she corrected. "You must become accustomed to using my given name, Hudson. And while both of us lack faith in the integrity of others, there must be an element of trust between us for your plan to succeed."

His plan? His plan amounted to walking into the ballroom and hoping his brother died from the shock. His plan amounted to his sister-in-law dropping to her knees, poor and destitute, while he refused every request for help.

Both were unlikely.

Should he tell Miss Darling that they had little hope of success? Should he tell her that this elaborate deception might only serve to open old wounds? He might never discover his family's motive for wanting him dead. He might swing from the gallows—an innocent man—and the gentleman's curse would claim yet another victim.

"How long have we been married?" Miss Darling asked.

"Twelve months."

"I need a specific date. Ladies often ask such things."

He shrugged.

"What about the second of November?" she suggested.

"The second it is. We were married by the Reverend Fischer in a small makeshift chapel in Meerut because St John's church is in the process of being built."

Miss Darling nodded. "The information will prove useful, but when two people are in love, the place hardly matters."

"No, I don't suppose it does." The mere mention of marriage reminded him of why he needed a wife to help him deceive his family. "You are currently with child."

"With child?" Miss Darling placed her hand on her stomach. "Oh, I see. Your family must think I am carrying your heir."

"Indeed." Lockhart needed to prove a point. "I want them to think I am deliriously happy." He wanted Selina Lockhart to wallow in guilt and regret. "I want them to see that my life is unhindered by the evil wrought upon me."

Miss Darling stared down her nose in silent disapproval. She rubbed the mist from the window and looked out, feigned interest in the trees whipping by.

"What?" he pressed. "You disagree with my motive?"

Did the prospect of his wife bearing a child not give him a reason to return to clear his name?

Her gaze flicked in his direction. "Vengeance is an illusion."

"Did Dariell tell you that?" Lockhart snorted.

Had his friend been preaching about man's eagerness to corrupt his soul?

Had he insisted Miss Darling was a good choice because he knew she would continue to taunt Lockhart, to question his reasoning?

"You think the truth will make you happy," Miss Darling said. "It won't."

Lockhart folded his arms across his chest. "Then what would make me happy, pray tell?"

She raised her chin. "Acceptance."

"Acceptance?" he mocked.

This guileless maiden was even more naive than he suspected. She knew nothing of life's trials and tribulations. She might want for money, but no one had ever stripped away her character and trampled it into the dirt. No one had ever manipulated the truth to hold her to ransom.

"Accept what happened to you. Find the truth and move on. Ruining lives will not bring you the peace you crave. Hurting others will not lessen the pain."

The need to fight, the need to punish those responsible, burned inside him like a constant flame. Acceptance left no room for justice. And who wanted to live in a world without justice?

"Thankfully, I am not paying you for your opinion, Miss Darling." His blunt response forced her to inhale sharply.

The lady's gaze shot back to the window, misted once again from the heat of their breath. This time she did not bother to wipe away the droplets but watched them trickle slowly down the pane.

Tension returned to crush the air from the confined space.

They had made some progress on their journey. She had spoken without blushing, without the surreptitious glances she stole whenever she struggled to look him in the eye. Having more or less told her she was as good as the hired help, it was up to him to fill the silence.

"The first disagreement is always the hardest," he said in a lighthearted tone to show he was not annoyed. "I'm told reconciliation is often rewarding."

Kissing after a heated argument was said to cause an explosion of passion.

"We are allowed to disagree," she said without looking at him.

Had Miss Darling been his lover, he would have taken her chin, drew her mouth to his and delved so deep inside she would forget the reason for her petulance.

"We are," he agreed. He was used to the company of men. Men shouted and swore. Fists flew. They made their point, the argument soon forgotten. "Disagreements are healthy. Through differing opinions, we will come to know each other better."

"Yes, I suspect we will disagree on many things, Mr Lockhart."

"What happened to using our given names?"

She looked at him for longer than a few seconds. "A lady often addresses her husband formally when slightly annoyed."

He could not tell if she spoke in earnest or in jest.

"What would I have to do for you to call me Hudson?" He had never been one to pander to a lady's capricious moods. For his wife, he might make an exception. For his wife, he might consider seducing her into submission.

"Do not speak to me as if this arrangement is one-sided," she snapped. When making a point, she lost all trace of nerves. "We are assisting each other. Remember that, and we will find the wherewithal to muddle through."

To say her contradicting character traits fascinated him was an understatement. Devil take him, Dariell was right. This lady had enough humility to be the *darling* of the *ton*. She had enough self-worth to put every disreputable rogue in his place.

"You're right. I often speak without thought." He could be magnanimous. He could be an arrogant arse, too, but this lady roused the gentleman in him. "You may find it hard to bear my company."

Miss Darling's mouth curled into a weak smile. "It's surprising what a lady will put up with when faced with the prospect of earning seventeen hundred pounds."

CHAPTER SIX

L ondon was not the vibrant metropolis Claudia had
envisioned. Well, not at five in the evening when smothered
by a grey blanket of fog. While aware of the plight of the impov-
erished, she had expected to see ladies in fine gowns prome-
nading down streets lined with carriages. But it was as if a
malevolent presence filled the air, chasing people into their
homes, choking those who'd found the courage to step outdoors.

"Is it always so dismal?" Claudia asked as the sight threatened
to suck her spirits down into its murky depths.

"Not in the summer."

Mr Lockhart's mood matched the depressing scene outside.
He had fallen into a tense silence since passing through the turnpike, since the noise of the bustling city reached their ears. While
Claudia had watched the hazy figures of men carrying torches to
prevent accidents on the road, he had shrunk back into the shadows. Subdued. Solemn.

Not knowing what to say or how to soothe him—for they
were strangers after all—she had stared into the gloom while
worrying about how Emily was coping at home.

The week would be long and tiresome if they continued like this.

Brooding only created barricades.

"Are you thinking about the past?" she said, keeping her gaze fixed on the window.

He did not reply.

"You're replaying the events that led to you leaving." Most people did a similar thing when struggling with a problem. "You're letting bitterness consume your rational thoughts."

Whether her assessment proved accurate was immaterial. Her only motive was to tempt him to converse.

"Are you sure Dariell has not enrolled you in his school of insight?" Mr Lockhart eventually said, though his voice held a hint of mockery. "You appear to have an innate ability to read my thoughts."

Claudia smiled inwardly and gave herself an imaginary pat on the back for a job well done. "Is it not part of the human condition to analyse the past?"

"Is that what you think I am doing, Miss Darling?"

"Most definitely."

He straightened. "Then what else would you have me do? What would Dariell suggest?"

Oh, what was it the Frenchman said about the heart? Emily would know. She listened intently whenever Monsieur Dariell spoke.

"We should be busy constructing a plan, not dwelling on something beyond our control."

"We?" Even in the dark confines of the carriage, she saw the suspicious glint that played in his eyes whenever someone challenged him.

Claudia retaliated with a smile. "I am your wife and have a vested interest in the outcome."

"A vested interest? Ah, you mean money. Have no fear, Miss

Darling. I shall ensure you're paid even if I'm hauled to the gallows and left to dangle from the neck until dead."

"Don't say that." A sharp pain stabbed her chest when she pictured him meeting his demise. "From what you've said, your brother is the only one who knows about your supposed involvement in the murder. I doubt he will call a constable and bring shame upon the Lockhart name."

"My brother's silence came at a price," he said, a menacing aura radiating from him once again.

"Do you speak of the five years you spent abroad?"

"Of the five long, laborious years."

"We've reverted to speaking about the past again," she said. "Let us focus on the present."

The sudden jerk of the carriage proved a timely intervention. The vehicle slowed and rumbled to a halt. Through the haze, Claudia noted a white townhouse with an excessive number of windows.

"Where are we?" she asked.

"Home. Well, for the next week, at least."

"I mean where in London."

"Russell Square. Lord Greystone leased the property on my behalf. It comes with a modest staff, and Dariell hired a lady's maid to assist you. She's French. He also made arrangements for your wardrobe. Madame Armand is a talented modiste who exceeded his expectations."

Her wardrobe?

Claudia suppressed the chuckle bubbling in her throat. The last time she'd worn a new dress fashion dictated straighter skirts and shorter sleeves. The rush of excitement had nothing to do with vanity. For once, she could indulge her desires without worrying about paying the bill.

"You will need to pick a dress for the masquerade ball this evening. Your maid has skill in making alterations but will—"

"You expect me to attend a ball this evening?" Panic ensued.

She needed more time to prepare, more time to settle into her new role.

Mr Lockhart nodded. "We leave at ten."

Ten? She lay curled up in bed at nine most nights.

Ten! That gave her less than five hours to prepare.

A footman appeared at the carriage window, the shiny buttons on his mustard coat attracting her attention. He opened the door, dropped the steps and assisted Claudia to the pavement.

Mr Lockhart exited the carriage. He placed his hand at the small of Claudia's back and guided her towards the front door. It took a tremendous effort not to gasp in shock at the intimate gesture. Heavens, she would have to get used to a certain level of familiarity, and quickly.

They spent the next thirty minutes meeting the servants who would attend them during their stay in Russell Square. It became apparent that Mr Lockhart had leased the house for six months. What would he tell them when Claudia packed her valise and fled in the middle of the night? How would he explain her sudden departure? Not that it mattered. Whatever happened once the week was out was not her concern.

The housekeeper, Mrs Brewster—a woman whose serious countenance conveyed pride in her position—gave them a tour of the house.

"You understand that my wife and I wish to share the same bedchamber," Mr Lockhart said when the housekeeper escorted them to the master suite.

Claudia stared at the four-poster bed. She blinked numerous times to banish the image of a muscular male body sprawled across the mattress. Perhaps she might negotiate the terms of their agreement once they returned from the masquerade.

"Yes, sir. Lord Greystone expressed your preferences."

What? Had Mr Lockhart told his friend of his desire to sleep with his wife?

"I have moved Mrs Lockhart's clothes into the dressing room

as instructed." Mrs Brewster gestured to the open door on their left which led into a side room dominated by two large armoires.

Nerves fluttered in Claudia's stomach. Surely Mr Lockhart didn't expect her to undress while he watched.

"Excellent." Mr Lockhart's arm slid around Claudia's waist, and his hand settled on her hip. "Having spent months on a ship bound for England, we're used to living in close quarters."

As master of the house he had no need to explain, but the comment added a certain credibility to their story.

"Please send Lissette up in five minutes," Claudia said, forcing a smile. She had to find something to distract her thoughts from the warm fingers caressing her hip. "I must choose a dress for the masquerade ball."

"I trust Lord Greystone informed you we're dining out tonight," Mr Lockhart said, "though I shall still require a light repast at seven."

"He did, and yes, sir." Mrs Brewster turned to Claudia. "On the matter of dinner, ma'am, I shall have next week's menus sent up for your approval."

"Thank you, Mrs Brewster." Claudia was keen to get rid of the housekeeper so her husband might stop with the pretence. "That will be all for now."

As soon as the housekeeper exited the room and closed the door, Claudia swung around. "Must you be so open in your affections, sir?" she whispered.

A sinful grin played on the gentleman's lips. She decided she preferred this look to the glum mood he had succumbed to earlier.

"My darling, we have to set the scene for our play." He captured her chin between his fingers and planted a kiss on her forehead. "Tonight, we will have to jump on the mattress until the bed squeaks. I suggest you start practising pleasurable moans."

Oh, he was incorrigible. He seemed to be enjoying his new role far too much.

"There is no need to call me *darling*," she countered. "And I am certain married couples do not rut like wild animals."

Mr Lockhart laughed. He stepped back and released her chin. "I shall call you darling in case I make a *faux pas* and use your real name. And the right gentleman will most definitely rouse a howl from your luscious lips. Let's hope it is your husband."

His gaze dropped to her mouth as hunger flashed in his eyes.

"That is a look of lust, Mr Lockhart, when we are supposed to be in love."

"Ah, you want love, Miss Darling?" Slowly, and with an intensity that stole her breath, Hudson Lockhart met her gaze. "Then I shall give you love."

The energy in the air sparked to life as he stared deeply into her eyes. The gold striped wallpaper and gilt-framed pictures all blurred into the background as he became her focus. Mr Lockhart looked at her as if she were a priceless jewel, unlike anything he had seen before. He looked at her as if she were the air he needed to breathe.

Heat swirled in Claudia's stomach. A desperate ache filled her heart. The sensitive place between her legs pulsed. Her fingers itched to touch him, all of him. The difference between love and lust became blurred as she imagined being drawn to his chest, being kissed by his expert mouth, caressed by his expert hands.

A light rap on the door shattered the spell.

"Who is it?" Claudia called in a strained voice while she continued to stare at her husband.

"It is I, Lissette, madame."

"You should let her in." Mr Lockhart's smooth tones continued to soothe and caress.

"Should I?"

"A man might take liberties if given a chance."

"You sent for me, madame," Lissette called from beyond the door.

"She has but a few hours to make any adjustments to your gown," Mr Lockhart added.

Claudia blinked to bring herself back to reality. "Give me a moment, Lissette," she said, glancing over her shoulder before turning back to the gentleman who could grace the stage with such a convincing performance. "With such fine acting skills, I imagine no one will doubt our story."

He smiled. "The same might be said for you. Not once did you look away."

"If ever we find ourselves destitute, we can always work in the theatre."

His smile faded. "Tonight, you will need to give your best performance. You must not drop your guard until we are alone once again in this room."

"I understand." Nerves threatened to consume her, but she kept them at bay.

Mr Lockhart lingered for a moment before inclining his head and striding to the door.

He stopped as his hand settled on the knob, though he did not turn to face her when he spoke. "I ask a great deal, I know. But I would not have brought you here were I not confident you had the strength to deal with the task." He did not wait for a response but opened the door and gestured for Lissette to enter. "I shall be in the study should you need me."

The words tugged at a place deep in her core. The day she *needed* him would be the day she packed her valise and took the mail coach back to Falaura Glen.

Claudia might have sunk into a melancholic mood if left to contemplate the great task that lay ahead, but Lissette was a lively woman whose vivacious personality lifted one's spirits.

"Oh, wait until you see Madame Armand's creations," Lissette said as she closed the bedchamber door and hurried to the dressing room. "The modiste, she has worked miracles. Miracles."

Excitement fluttered to life in Claudia's chest, banishing all prospect of her sinking into the doldrums.

"Come," Lissette beckoned, holding out her hand. "Come see."

The lofty matrons would consider Lissette too familiar for a lady's maid, but she put Claudia at ease, and that was all that mattered.

Claudia followed Lissette into the dressing room. The maid flung back the door of the armoire to reveal a host of silk gowns in an array of colours. Monsieur Dariell had spared no expense when instructing the modiste in matters of her wardrobe.

"You are to attend the masquerade tonight, no?" Lissette beamed.

"Yes." Feeling somewhat overwhelmed, Claudia added, "Though having never ventured to town, I don't have the first clue what to wear."

"Let me see." Lissette pursed her lips and narrowed her gaze. "Perhaps you should look at the masks." The maid did not wait for an answer but pulled a hatbox from the top shelf. She placed it on the floor, lifted the lid and removed two sparkling creations. "We have the proud peacock or the red devil."

Claudia admired the masks in Lissette's hands. The blood-red mask was rimmed in black silk, boasted red and black feathers and a large onyx stone between the brows. Tiny teal jewels decorated the bronze arabesque swirls on the other mask. A teal feather served as a backdrop for a fan of small peacock feathers. The mask looked exotic and far more mysterious than the bold red one.

"Peacocks are proud creatures," Claudia agreed. "Is there a gown that might suit it, do you think?"

Lissette's eyes widened. "Is there a gown? Madame, there is a gown that will make every man in the room stop and stare." The maid returned the masks to the box before drawing a cerulean blue dress from the armoire.

A soft sigh left Claudia's lips.

The blue silk taffeta was trimmed in gold brocade. The sleeves were designed to bare the shoulders, the bodice cut scandalously low. Heavens, how would she wear such an elegant gown without looking like an imposter? One would need a natural sensuality, the confidence of royalty. Yet she was a mere country girl.

Panic surfaced.

And she thought feigning love proved challenging.

"Isn't it marvellous, madame?" Lissette hung the dress back on the hook. She bent down, opened a drawer and withdrew a length of blue velvet ribbon. "Monsieur Dariell, he chose this choker. He said a lady has no need for jewels when she sparkles like the stars in the night sky."

Claudia snorted. Perhaps Monsieur Dariell had another lady in mind when he chose the wardrobe.

"Well, I must try on the dress and hope it needs minimal alterations. I'm told you're skilled with a needle and thread."

"*Oui*, madame. I learnt my trade in Paris."

"Paris? You served as a lady's maid there before coming to England?"

A chuckle escaped Lissette's lips. "This is my first position in a grand house. I came to England to work for Madame Armand five years ago. Monsieur Dariell, he asked me to serve you, and I owe him a debt of gratitude that I long to repay."

Claudia drew her brows together in confusion. She wasn't sure which question to ask first. "You're a seamstress?"

Lissette nodded. "Monsieur Dariell said you are a lady without prejudice."

Claudia pondered the maid's comment. The Frenchman had been staying at Falaura Glen when Claudia accepted Mr Lockhart's proposal.

"When did Monsieur Dariell tell you that?"

"A week ago, madame, during his last visit to the modiste."

A week ago?

Then he was definitely speaking about someone else. Mr Lockhart must have approached another woman with the same proposition. Ridiculous as it was, Claudia couldn't help but feel disappointed. She was the second choice—the inferior model.

"And what is the debt you owe Monsieur Dariell?"

Lissette hung her head and cast her gaze to the floor. "It is a shameful subject, madame. Please, do not make me speak of it."

Claudia was not one to judge, nor was she one to pry. Besides, the notion that Mr Lockhart had not been completely honest left a sour taste in her mouth. Pain throbbed in the base of her throat as she held on to the feeling that she had been naive, naive to imagine he saw something in her other than a usefulness to serve his own ends.

"Then I shall try on the dress so you may make the alterations." Claudia raised her chin and kept her voice even. She would approach the task of playing Mr Lockhart's wife as she would any other chore—with a determination to do her best whilst remaining indifferent.

"I doubt we will need to make any adjustments, madame." Lissette removed the gown from the armoire, shook out the material and held it against Claudia's body. "Monsieur Dariell, he was most precise in his measurements."

Of course he was! Mr Lockhart had chosen her because she resembled the previous candidate.

Heat crept up Claudia's neck to burn her cheeks, punishment for believing Mr Lockhart's lofty praise of her character. If she hadn't already made a pact with one devil—in promising to marry Mr Thorncroft—she would have gathered her valise and taken the next mail coach home.

But there was more at stake than her fragile pride.

Claudia needed the seventeen hundred pounds he had promised. Emily needed a sister with the strength and courage to see this task through, not one whose vanity had led her to believe the gentleman held her in high regard.

"Nevertheless," Claudia began, resigned to take her role seriously, "we won't know if the dress fits if I do not try it on."

If Mr Lockhart wanted a devoted wife, that's what he would get. Claudia would give a performance worthy of royal patronage, a performance to show him she was far from second best.

CHAPTER SEVEN

"What the hell's keeping her?" Lockhart muttered to himself as he paced the hall, stopping every few steps to examine his pocket watch should the long-case clock need winding.

Perhaps the dress she'd chosen for the masquerade needed extensive alterations.

Perhaps Miss Darling's courage had abandoned her at this crucial stage.

He was about to mount the stairs, hunt her down and berate her for her tardiness when the sound of feminine laughter reached his ears. The hushed mutterings of a conversation—*thank you* being the only audible words—preceded the rustle of material.

Lissette appeared. She descended the stairs wearing a mischievous grin—the look of a woman who had a secret she was desperate to tell. The maid curtsied when she reached the hall before disappearing through the door leading down to the kitchen.

Somewhat confused by Lissette's excited expression, Lockhart's attention swept back to the stairs.

The seconds ticked.

He watched and waited.

His heart pounded hard in anticipation.

With the slow, graceful steps of a duchess, Miss Darling approached the stairs in a breathtaking gown of cerulean blue. Her golden hair was swept up in an elegant coiffure. One long curl snaked around her neck to dangle seductively over her shoulder. The minx kept her mask high to hide her face. Lockhart didn't know if her eyes swam with excitement or fear, not until she descended the stairs with a sensual sway, trailing her fingers down the length of the bannister like a skilled temptress might tease a man's throbbing shaft.

Lockhart held his breath.

For one so innocent, Miss Darling certainly knew how to seduce her husband.

She stopped on the bottom stair so that they were almost eye level.

"The peacock reveals his fan in a display of courtship," he said, hoping to prompt her to lower her mask. "From your choice this evening, I can only surmise that you intend to woo me, my darling."

Her blue eyes sparked to life, the hue enhanced by the teal gems covering the bronze mask. "I wish for every person in the ballroom to know how much I desire my husband. Is that not what this evening is about?"

The evening was about shocking his brother and wiping the arrogant grin off his face, about proving Selina had a heart of stone. So why did it cross his mind to capture Miss Darling in his arms and remain at home?

"Then before we leave for Comte de Lancey's masquerade, lower your mask and permit me to judge your ability to rouse a reaction."

He was confident she would rise to the challenge.

"Very well." The lady lowered her mask in the teasing way a courtesan might slip out of a silk chemise.

Something had changed during the hours she had spent alone

with Lissette. It had nothing to do with the magnificence of her gown, or the way the sapphire comb sparkled in her blonde hair. It had nothing to do with the scandalously low neckline that offered him an opportunity to admire her ample breasts.

No, the lady had a steely look in her eyes, harder, more determined than before. Her resolute chin looked capable of sustaining more than a few knocks.

Miss Darling had slipped into the role of his wife as easily as any skilled actress, and yet in doing so she had lost something of herself, lost the innocence he found just as fascinating.

As a man who could not recall the last time he'd taken a woman to his bed, he scanned the delightful swell of her breasts once again. "If I'm to spend the evening feigning love, Miss Darling, permit me a moment to bathe in the lust flowing through my veins."

The lady arched a coy brow. Had Lissette been giving her lessons? After all, the maid had dressed the finest whores in France.

"I wonder if I was not mistaken," she said. "Perhaps when a man loves his wife he lusts after her, too."

Lockhart had to agree. He could not envisage living with a woman he did not want to bed. "I imagine if I loved you, my darling, I would want to pleasure you until you clasped my buttocks and cried my name."

Despite sucking in numerous breaths, Miss Darling's cheeks turned a pretty shade of pink. Ah, there she was, the woman in the ugly dress who brought him supper each night and panicked about pheasant. The woman who struggled to look him in the eye.

"Then I am thankful we are only pretending," she said, as the naive maiden shrank back behind the curtain to give the actress centre stage.

Lockhart laughed. If only his task were to bed Claudia Darling. It would make for a far more interesting game than a need for vengeance.

"You may have a different view once the week is out," he said, for he relished a challenge.

"Yes, in a week I may hate you." Thankfully, her voice lacked conviction.

"But for now you love me. Let's not forget that. Let's not forget why we're here."

"I have not forgotten."

Silence ensued.

"You look beautiful," he said, and he meant it.

Rather than accept the compliment and smile as other ladies were wont to do, a sadness passed over her features.

"Are you thinking about Miss Emily, about Falaura Glen?" he asked.

She exhaled. "I am always thinking about Emily."

"No doubt she will enjoy hearing your tales of the ball tonight." Lockhart offered his arm. "We really must be on our way. Come, our carriage awaits."

Miss Darling wrapped her fingers around his biceps rather than place her hand lightly in the crook. "Let us hope we cause a stir tonight."

"Cause a stir? Madam, we will be the talk of the *ton*."

The Comte de Lancey was a man possessed of extravagant tastes coupled with a desire to please. Consequently, a horde of eager revellers had squashed into the elaborate ballroom of his Mayfair mansion. Hermits, magicians and many characters from Greek mythology mingled with those whose desire to dress for the occasion extended to naught but a simple mask.

Buffoonery topped most people's agendas. Fools believed their masks rendered them invisible. The rakes and scoundrels grasped any opportunity to make mischief. As with all masquerades, the air in the room carried a licentious undertone that infected all those in the vicinity.

Greystone had secured Lockhart's invitation. The comte cared more about the quantity of guests than their quality. Assured of Terence's attendance, Lockhart had specifically chosen this event to make his appearance. The black domino and mask gave him anonymity until the grand reveal. While the masquerade made it more difficult to locate Terence in the crowd, Lockhart's friends had gathered to offer support and assistance.

Had Devlin Drake hidden himself beneath a shroud, Lockhart would recognise him in a room packed with people. The giant stood a head taller than most men. As a man unamused by tomfoolery, Drake had forgone a costume.

"Come, let me introduce you to my friends," Lockhart said as he led Miss Darling to the far side of the room. The lady gripped his arm as if they were walking through Whitechapel at midnight draped in diamonds and pearls. "Relax. I shall not leave your side."

"Promise."

"I promise."

They squeezed past a monk telling bawdy tales to anyone willing to stop and listen, past a Roman emperor with knobbly knees intent on flashing them to every passer-by. Numerous men raised their masks. None were interested in the man dressed in the same black domino as a hundred other guests. All focused their hungry gazes on Miss Darling's luscious breasts.

Devil take it. Lockhart would lay odds he'd have a fist fight before the night was out.

"You look ready for your bed, Drake." Lockhart raised his mask as he joined his friends. It had been a little over a month since he had last set eyes on the men who'd dragged him from a pit of despair and given him a reason to live.

Drake's smile enveloped Lockhart like a warm embrace as

their gazes locked. "I am, and if I don't leave soon I shall punch one of these fools making inappropriate gestures to my wife."

Lockhart noted the lady at Drake's side, dressed as a shepherdess and wielding a crook. She was Drake's opposite in every way—petite, dainty, with kind eyes beneath her mask.

Introductions were made.

Valentine and Greystone, both dressed in plain black dominoes, patted Lockhart numerous times on the back, though their curious gazes lingered on the lady at his side. He met the women who had captured his friends' hearts. Juliet was the delicate lady who held the giant, Drake, in thrall. Aveline's intelligent eyes were surely the reason Valentine had fallen in love. And Lydia's lively spirit had captured Greystone's heart. Greystone's playful exterior belied the intelligent, methodical, hardworking man whose business acumen had helped to secure all their fortunes.

"Welcome home," Greystone said, his gaze flicking in Claudia's direction by way of prompting an introduction. "I trust everything in Russell Square meets with your approval."

"It does," Lockhart said, confused at his own reluctance to present Miss Darling. Perhaps it was because these men knew the truth, and he liked playing husband, liked keeping Miss Darling all to himself.

Valentine fixed a stare and bowed low. "As my friend seems somewhat lapse when it comes to manners, Mrs Lockhart, let me welcome you to London."

Miss Darling smiled. "Thank you, my lord, though I must admit to preferring the peace of the country," she said, remembering what Lockhart had said about remaining in character, even with his friends. "And I like devoting my time to my husband without unnecessary distractions."

Valentine's smile expressed approval.

Lockhart turned to look at her. He gazed into her innocent blue eyes—eyes that did not look so innocent tonight—without looking at her breasts. "The next few hours will pass quickly and we will be alone again soon."

The other six people in the group gaped.

Greystone arched an inquiring brow. "May we know your wife's name or is it to remain a closely guarded secret?"

"Of course." Lockhart inclined his head. "Allow me to present Mrs Claudia Lockhart, wife of an infamous rogue."

All three ladies broke into excited chatter, inviting Miss Darling to tea, to a shopping trip at the Burlington Arcade, to a meeting with a group of ladies who studied literature as a means of enlightenment.

Lockhart cast his friends a look that conveyed the depth of his fear, conveyed the dangers Miss Darling faced once Terence Lockhart learnt the truth.

"There is plenty of time to shop for new bonnets," Lord Valentine said. "I doubt Lockhart will leave Claudia's side during —" He broke off abruptly and turned to Miss Darling. "May I call you Claudia?"

"Certainly."

"What Valentine is trying to say," Greystone interrupted, "is that Lockhart is besotted with his wife and will, no doubt, monopolise her attention whilst in town."

"And we must make time to reunite with family," Lockhart added, though keeping his hands from wringing his brother's neck would prove problematic. "Speaking of which, I assume Terence is here this evening."

Drake nodded to a point near the orchestra. "Terence is wearing the burgundy domino and Scaramouch mask. Selina has come as Minerva though some have mistaken her for Athena." Drake snorted. "Roman, Greek, they are pretty much the same."

"I would have to disagree," Aveline countered.

While Aveline and Drake conversed about the Roman goddess taking her influence from the Greeks, Lockhart scanned the crowd, searching for his quarry.

Bitterness formed like bile in his throat when he located Selina Lockhart. The ebony-haired coquette had the gall to look sad, subdued. He had wanted to wipe the arrogance from her face, wanted to knock her off her polished marble pedestal and see her grovel. While Terence spoke to friends, she simply stared at the jugglers and then at those dancing the quadrille.

"De Lancey has spared no expense when it comes to entertainment," Lockhart said. "He's hired every sideshow act except for a performing monkey."

Valentine raised his mask and sharpened his gaze. "Dariell told you, didn't he?"

"Told me what?"

"That I have developed a dislike of the creatures."

"A dislike of sideshow acts?"

Valentine groaned. "Of monkeys."

"Did you not befriend that monkey who stole from the market in Ghaziabad?" Lockhart said, finding the conversation amusing, for Dariell had spoken about the night Raja attacked Valentine at the Westminster Pit.

"That animal did not maul my face and try to scratch out my eyes."

Drake chuckled as he pointed to Valentine's cheek. "If you look closely, you can still see the scar."

Valentine slapped his friend's hand away. "At least I don't get down on all fours and growl at dogs."

"I was trying to train the lazy animal," Drake countered.

Nothing had changed during Lockhart's absence. His friends knew how to lighten his mood, brighten his spirits. But one glimpse at Terence was enough to rouse the devil inside.

"Shall we dance, Claudia?" Lockhart said as the first few strains of the waltz echoed through the room. He would have a moment alone to school his partner in deception before approaching his brother. It was imperative Miss Darling looked happy and vivacious when they made their first move.

"You wish to dance the waltz?" She seemed nervous.

"I told you. I intend to keep you close. Give Juliet your mask and Drake will hold mine." Not everyone waited until the grand reveal.

Miss Darling did as he asked.

When they walked out onto the dance floor, he felt the gossips' piercing stares, heard their curious whispers.

"You love me," he breathed. "Every person in this room must be in no doubt."

"And you love me," she said, allowing him to clasp her hand and draw her into the required embrace. "Do try to keep your gaze eye level."

Lockhart smiled as his hand settled on her back. "I've more chance of calling a constable and admitting to murder," he said, sweeping her into the dance. "Surely you'd not begrudge your husband one small indulgence."

"Indulging you is becoming a habit." Miss Darling returned his smile. She seemed genuinely amused, but then she was a good actress.

"Habit? Rather a pleasurable pastime I hope, not a chore."

They moved about the floor in perfect time to the music. For a country maiden, Miss Darling possessed the elegance one needed for such a graceful dance. Yes, she might have stumbled once or twice had he not been strong enough to support her but that stemmed from a lack of experience as opposed to a lack of skill.

As they travelled and swayed through the steps, his focus shifted. He had meant to use the opportunity to gain his brother's attention and yet gazing into Miss Darling's eyes and feigning love proved distracting.

"There is a reason we are dancing," she said. Her level of perception was as sharp as his own. "You want your brother to notice you. You want to witness his reaction."

Lockhart had wanted to burst into the ballroom like a violent storm set to whip the room into a frenzy. He wanted to charge at

Terence and drive his fist down his brother's throat, for the simple fact that he'd lacked the strength to help clear Lockhart's name.

But this was a complicated game.

One that took patience and perseverance.

"And how might I do that when I cannot stop looking at you?" Lockhart took the opportunity to admire Miss Darling more closely. Her golden hair shimmered like silk in the candlelight. The sapphires decorating the comb added an ethereal appeal. The rise and fall of their movements on the floor matched the undulation of her milky-white breasts as her breath came quicker.

"Your need to prove a point must not distract you from your plan," she said.

"Prove a point?" Did Miss Darling know of his history with Selina? Did she know he wanted the vixen to rue the day she married his brother? Surely not.

"To prove to the villain that his actions did not ruin your life." Pity flashed briefly in her eyes. "We have a limited time to achieve success. We must make every moment count."

Selina's duplicity had helped stoke the fire of vengeance—had given him a reason to live. And while he fantasised about seducing the woman pretending to be his wife, that was not why he was here.

"Then let us move nearer to the orchestra," Lockhart said.

Terence was still deep in conversation, his Scaramouch mask pulled high on his forehead, the long, pointed nose resembling a devil's horn. Did his brother not know that in the *commedia dell'arte* it was the mask of vanity and the mask of a coward?

"I know of a way to gain his attention," she said as they were but a few feet away. "Pull me closer and whisper into my ear."

Unable to refuse an opportunity to feel Miss Darling's body pressed against his, Lockhart did as she asked. "Aren't you even a little intrigued to see me naked in bed?" he whispered in a soft teasing breath.

He felt a shiver run through her body, but the actress tilted her head back and laughed loud enough to draw attention. The incessant hum of laughter filling the room diminished. He heard his name carried on a breeze of whispers. From the corner of his eye, Lockhart noted those in the vicinity turn towards the floor and stare. Deciding not to meet his brother's gaze, not yet at least, he captured Miss Darling's hand and drew her from the floor.

"Where are we going?" she said, hurrying to keep his pace.

"To the terrace." Terence would follow. And the garden would afford some privacy should either of them fly into a rage, should they end up needing to release five years of pent-up frustration.

"But it's so cold out, and I don't have my wrapper."

"I shall keep you warm."

The terrace doors were closed to keep the freezing fog at bay. Lockhart opened the door, slipped outside with Miss Darling and closed it again. The frigid air smelt sterile until one inhaled deeply and almost choked on the coal smoke. Cold nipped at his cheeks and his breath came in puffs of mist. A white blanket of frost covered the lawn. Through the haze, ice sparkled like crystals as it clung to foliage and branches.

"How long must we stay out here?" Miss Darling shivered as she scanned the deserted terrace.

"Not long." He unfastened his black silk cloak—part of his ridiculous domino costume—and draped it around Miss Darling's shoulders. "This should keep you warm."

She inhaled deeply. "It smells of you."

"In a good way, I hope."

"In an extremely good way."

They looked into each other's eyes. His fingers stroked the delicate skin below her collarbone as he drew the edges of the cloak across her chest. This time, he did not need to feign emotion. He did not pretend to feel anything other than a rush of apprehension and the carnal lust that always thrummed in his veins when he stood so close to Claudia Darling.

"I have a suggestion," he said, shuffling back a few steps to lean against the wall, "though I am not sure you will approve."

"Tell me you don't plan to stay out here all night." She shuddered as the words left her trembling lips.

"No." He smiled. "Come here." He captured the ends of the cloak and pulled her to his chest. "Let me wrap my arms around you. It will add credence to our story as well as keep the cold from settling into your bones."

They were so close their breath mingled in the frigid air. Despite being dressed like a duchess—one who oozed with the confidence of her station—the furrows across her brow conveyed the true nature of the woman he was about to embrace, perhaps even kiss.

"We are merely actors playing roles," he reminded her.

He had convinced himself of that, too.

"Even actors must have some reservations when forcing intimacy with a stranger."

"A stranger?" Lockhart arched a brow. "Besides my friends, you know more about me than anyone else in that room."

She raised her chin a fraction. It was enough to draw his attention to the pouting lips eager to make a point. "I know only what you tell me. How do I know what is real? How can I tell the difference between words spoken from the heart and the lines you have spent months rehearsing?"

Without thought, he cupped her cold cheek. "Can you not feel the tenderness in my touch? There is a naivety about you that rouses the gentleman in me. There is a purity to your character that makes me want to devour your mouth in the hope I might feel goodness in my heart, too." He paused briefly and wondered what it must be like to feel something other than hatred for his kin. "That is real. That is true. It draws me to you like a moth to a flame." And yet part of him wanted to run, wanted to put a vast ocean between them.

Raised voices on the other side of the terrace doors captured their attention.

"There is no time to discuss this further," he whispered with some urgency. "But I am going to kiss you now, Miss Darling."

With wild eyes, she glanced quickly at the glass doors. "You should know I have never kissed a man."

"Never?"

"Never."

Knowing he would be the first gentleman to taste her proved highly arousing. "Then think of this as your opening night. And you know what actors say."

"No. What do they say?"

"One's performance improves with practice."

CHAPTER EIGHT

The sight of Mr Lockhart moistening his lips was enough to rob Claudia of all rational thought. She forgot about the cold nipping her cheeks, forgot that her fingers were numb, forgot she was his second choice and should tell him to go to the devil.

Lord, he was about to kiss her and pay seventeen hundred pounds for the privilege.

Did that not make her the most expensive courtesan to grace the ballroom this evening?

The thought should have made her gather up her skirts and race back to Falaura Glen. But she would rather kiss Mr Lockhart once than have Mr Thorncroft's lips smother hers night after night.

Mr Lockhart lowered his head and stared at her with a smouldering heat that made him look positively sinful. Nerves pushed to the fore as he came closer, close enough that she breathed in the woody tones of his cologne.

Oh, why was he taking his time?

Why did he not hurry?

Her heart hammered so hard in her chest she had no choice

but to take control. Grabbing the lapels of Mr Lockhart's black waistcoat, she squeezed her eyes shut and pressed her lips to his so fiercely it hurt.

The gentleman tore his mouth away. "Good God, woman. You may suffer from stage fright, but there's no need to assault the cast."

"Forgive me … I …" Heat flooded her cheeks. "Oh, just kiss me, sir, and have done with it."

"That is what I am attempting to do."

"You were lingering for too long."

"Lingering? It's called seduction."

"I think you forget why we—"

Mr Lockhart's lips came crashing down on hers—wild and wicked—bursting with passion, not panic. His mouth slid over hers with surprising skill, so warm, so wet, so thoroughly commanding. Every nerve in her body sparked to life to bask in the sweet sensation.

With a hunger that stole her breath, he coaxed her lips apart. Her legs almost buckled when he moaned into her mouth and the first touch of his tongue teased her to respond. He continued to stroke, to taste, to explore with a need that went beyond the duties of a fake husband. Every slick movement fed her desire. Every caress tugged deep in her core.

Hudson Lockhart knew how to please a woman.

Hudson Lockhart knew how to take what he wanted.

A pleasurable hum resonated in the back of his throat, the sound like a siren's song tempting her to move closer to this idyllic shore, to dive into these forbidden waters.

Oh, she'd imagined kissing him many times this last month— but never like this.

Random lines from Coleridge's poem entered her mind.

Alone … Alone on a wide sea! My soul in agony.

Her soul craved a companion.

Looking for something to ease the yearning inside, she touched her tongue to his. The erotic sensation seemed to draw the strength from her muscles. She sagged against his chest, permitting him to plunder, to take whatever he needed.

Hudson Lockhart wasted no time.

Merciful heaven.

Hot hands slipped from her back to cup and caress her buttocks. Each tangle of their tongues fed her craving. With every masterful thrust into her mouth, he rocked against her in an erotic dance that made her head spin. Heat pooled low and heavy in her loins until she could think of nothing other than touching his bare skin, of bringing relief to the desperate ache between her thighs.

The lustful urges gripping him showed no signs of abating. Had they been somewhere private, she would have surrendered to these waves of wanton pleasure.

Nothing had ever felt so divine.

The sweet music of passion that carried her in its undulating rhythm was suddenly drowned out by the lively notes of a Scottish reel spilling out into the night. The hum of conversation and laughter became more discernible. A discreet cough drew her out of the sensual world where she indulged her fantasies with a man she could no longer consider a stranger.

"Hudson?" In that one word, the masculine voice conveyed shock and confusion.

Mr Lockhart seemed oblivious to the interruption—or was that part of his plan? Indeed, he did not tear his lips away but continued to trail fiery kisses across her cheek to the sensitive spot below her ear.

"Remember you love me," he whispered.

This man was so skilled in the art of giving pleasure how could she forget?

The gentleman hovering at their side coughed again. "Hudson?"

Lockhart raised his head and stared at the two people who had invaded their moment of intimacy and brought Claudia crashing back to reality with a bump.

"Hudson?" the man with hair as black as Mr Lockhart's—but whose countenance lacked his brother's magnetic appeal—repeated for the third time. It was hard to take him seriously with the pointed nose of the Scaramouch mask perched on top of his head. "Good God! It *is* you. You're alive?"

"It appears so," Lockhart replied with an air of indifference. His hands slipped to his sides as he straightened. "Tropical fevers can make a man seem as though he's knocking on death's door. I'm afraid Lord Greystone was somewhat premature in his correspondence."

Claudia studied Terence Lockhart's face. Confusion did not turn to elation as he absorbed the news. "What the hell possessed you to come home?" The cold look of fear filled his eyes.

"One can only stand the heat for so long, and my wife longed to return to England."

"Your wife?" The lady with equally dark hair, shivering in the flimsy fabric of her Minerva costume, gasped. "You did not think to write and tell us you survived? You did not think to tell us you're married?"

Selina Lockhart's distress seemed justified under the circumstances. The watery evidence of pain and disappointment swam in her eyes.

Lockhart's hand came to rest on Claudia's back. His other hand settled on her stomach. It took every ounce of restraint she possessed not to gasp at the intimate gesture.

"I feared you might try to prevent our return," Lockhart said, "and we wish for our child to be born in England."

The lady's face turned ashen as she gaped at the large masculine hand cradling their imagined babe. Imagined or not, Hudson's caring caress played havoc with Claudia's mind.

What woman wouldn't want such a strong and powerful man as her protector?

What woman wouldn't want to have a piece of Hudson Lockhart to love and cherish?

Terence Lockhart wrapped his arm around his wife and rubbed her shoulder affectionately.

Selina shrugged out of his embrace. "You're with child?" Rapid breaths and wet sniffs spoke of an inner torment.

"Indeed," Claudia replied, feigning happiness at the prospect. "With the Lord's blessing, our child will be born in May."

Selina covered her eyes with her hands.

"You must forgive our odd reaction," Terence said, embarrassment staining his cheeks. "We have spent five years hoping for the same, but to no avail."

Selina was barren?

Did Mr Lockhart know? Was his sister-in-law's inability to conceive part of the reason he wanted a wife and heir, to prove he was a better man than the brother who'd abandoned him five years ago?

"I can only imagine how distressing that might be," Lockhart said, his voice laced with sympathy. In reality, he probably found the news satisfying.

Indeed, Mr Lockhart had every right to be both angry and suspicious. Had Claudia spent five years separated from Emily, she would hug her sister so tightly she'd struggle to catch her breath. These aloof exchanges failed to convey an ounce of love or compassion for Hudson Lockhart's plight.

"And you think it wise to return to London?" Terence cast a covert glance in Claudia's direction. "After the incident at the inn, did we not agree you would remain abroad indefinitely?"

Lockhart straightened and tugged at the cuffs of his coat. Claudia felt the loss of his warm hands instantly. Still, the anger she sensed raging inside her husband burned hot enough to thaw the freezing fog.

"You can speak openly in front of my wife. We have no secrets."

That was not entirely true. He had failed to mention she was his second choice.

Terence arched a brow in surprise. "Then she knows you risk your neck coming here."

Lockhart shrugged. "Other than you, who knows of the crime? Has anyone ever found the body?" Lockhart's heavy sigh sent a puff of white mist into the air. "Has anyone ever come forward to incriminate me?"

"Not that I am aware," Terence replied, still looking less than pleased about his brother's return.

"Then I do not see the problem."

"God damn it, Hudson," Terence suddenly snapped through gritted teeth. He dragged the mask off his head and jabbed it at Lockhart. "Seeing you might prompt someone's memory. Do you not care if you're hauled to the gallows? You endanger us all by being here. We all face ruination if the truth comes to light, including your wife and your unborn child."

Said in a more earnest tone, one might have believed Terence Lockhart cared for his brother. But the words showed concern for his own interests first and foremost.

"Claudia supports my decision to discover the truth about what happened that night," Mr Lockhart said. "Regardless of the outcome."

"The truth?" Selina blurted. "We all know what happened, Hudson. Although we were the ones who remained at home, we have all suffered."

"Suffered?" Lockhart's disdainful snort suggested he despised this woman.

Selina drew back her shoulders. "Your mother has not smiled since the night you left. Your father is on his deathbed. Because of you, he's lost the will to live. Justin visits him daily hoping to persuade him to change his will, and there is not a night that goes by when I don't wake in a cold sweat, when I don't blame myself for what happened." Selina inhaled deeply after finishing her lecture, and then her shoulders sagged.

Claudia turned to Mr Lockhart and whispered, "Justin?"

"Justin Perigrew. My cousin and my father's godson." Lockhart turned to his brother. "No doubt Justin is keen to inherit my share of the family fortune. Father wrote a few months after I arrived in India, informing me he'd struck me from his will."

"What did you expect?" Terence waved the ridiculous mask again. "He thinks you ran away from your responsibilities. He thinks you deserted your family to run amok with your friends."

"And now he thinks you're dead," Selina added.

In all honesty, it was hard to absorb the amount of information being batted back and forth. So Mr Lockhart had been disinherited. Was that the villain's plan all along? Was money the motive? If so, they should attempt to discover what other amendments his father had made to his will.

It would also help if Mr Lockhart explained precisely what had happened on that fateful night. Claudia was somewhat surprised at herself for not enquiring before. Then again, she was being paid for her services. Should it matter what caused him to flee to India all those years ago?

"I intend to call on them tomorrow, though doubt I'll receive a warm welcome." There was a sadness in Mr Lockhart's voice that for all his bravado he could not disguise. For no reason other than to soothe him, Claudia reached for his hand and gripped his fingers.

"You should leave them be," Selina said, throwing deadly daggers their way. "Your parents have been through enough, we all have. You should take your wife far away from here and never return."

Since her initial outburst, Selina Lockhart's nerves appeared unhinged. Guilt and an element of remorse flashed in her dark eyes. Anger lingered there, too. Everyone had suffered greatly it seemed.

"The longer you stay here, the more you put your life at risk," Terence added. His tone lacked compassion, and he shuffled on the spot as if Mr Lockhart was an irritation, an annoying scratch he couldn't quite reach.

"Perhaps you developed a hearing impediment during my absence," Mr Lockhart said coldly. "I am not the young man you chased away with morbid tales of the hangman's noose." Mr Lockhart laced his fingers with Claudia's. He brought her hand to his lips and placed a chaste kiss on her knuckles. "My wife wishes to remain in London, and so London is where we shall stay."

"Then she is as foolish as you are," Terence spat.

A growl resonated in the back of Mr Lockhart's throat. "Say what you like about me, but do not dare speak ill of my wife."

Claudia's heart fluttered. Heat filled her chest. While she embraced her role as a spinster and mistress of the manor, there was something comforting about knowing a man would fight to protect her. Even when he was merely acting the part.

"How times change." Selina scowled. "You used to be a man who cared only for himself."

Lockhart stared down his nose. "That is a lie."

A look passed between them—unspoken words that hinted at dark secrets. If Emily were here, she would note the animosity in the air, a mutual disrespect that neither Mr Lockhart nor Selina could hide.

"You're too blind to see your own hypocrisy." Selina's mirthless chuckle conveyed her contempt. "You say you care about your wife and yet you're willing to risk her ending up poor and destitute and living in the workhouse."

A figure hovering on the other side of the glass doors captured Claudia's attention. Mr Drake guarded the exit, his large frame filling the space, preventing anyone from escaping out onto the terrace. Mr Lockhart's other friends were there, ready to jump to his defence at a moment's notice.

Despite being paid to be his wife, Claudia felt a shred of loyalty to Mr Lockhart, too. Indeed, his sibling was not interested in asking her name. Neither Terence nor Selina cared that their brother had not perished from a fever. Neither cared that he had come home, nor that they might expect another addition to the family.

"My husband is not a fool." The words burst from Claudia's lips to mark her annoyance. "Do you honestly think he would put his wife and child at risk? Surely you know him well enough to know he would fight to the death to protect those he loves?" Claudia sucked in a breath. "Clearly, you know nothing of the man you abandoned five years ago."

Mr Lockhart squeezed her fingers.

"And my name is Claudia, in case you should be remotely interested in congratulating us on our marriage. But wait. You're too self-absorbed to consider our thoughts and feelings."

Once she had started, she couldn't stop.

Much like the moment she'd locked lips with Hudson Lockhart. She cast the gentleman a sidelong glance, noted the smug grin playing on those full lips, lips capable of rendering an innocent lady helpless.

Mr Lockhart cleared his throat. "My wife has said all that's needed. I shall visit our parents tomorrow, if only that they might learn their son is alive before hearing the news from malicious gossips."

Keeping a firm grip of Claudia's hand, Mr Lockhart moved to walk past them.

"Hudson, wait!" Terence called. Evidently, he still had much to say.

Mr Lockhart did not reply. As they stepped up to the terrace door, Mr Drake pushed it open and threw a menacing glare Terence Lockhart's way.

"Hudson!" Terence cried. "For the love of God, you cannot stay here."

Mr Lockhart glanced back at his brother. "I listened to you once but never again." His brown eyes turned dark and predatory. For a second, he looked capable of ripping a man's heart from his chest. "Now that I'm older and wiser, I shall do as I damn well please."

CHAPTER NINE

Hatred, he could deal with. The emotion had been Lockhart's permanent companion these last five years. It lived in his chest like a parasite, thrived on any opportunity to rear its ugly head and feed on anyone who dared offer a challenge.

But now another emotion fought to rid him of his disease. This one had no name or label. It was like a forgotten word on the tip of his tongue. No matter how hard he tried, he could not claim it.

Lockhart traipsed behind Miss Darling as she climbed the stairs, heading for their bedchamber. The cerulean gown clung to her hips to accentuate the sensual sway. Lust simmered in his blood. Kissing her had only intensified his craving. But that was not the nameless sensation that sent anger at his brother fading into the background.

Was it pride he felt?

Miss Darling shone amongst the ladies of the *ton*. Gentlemen leered, taken by her vivacious countenance. Had he not kept her firmly at his side, every rake and rogue would have sought her company on the dance floor.

Was it gratitude?

Despite knowing it was all an act, a surge of warmth had flooded his chest when she'd berated Terence and Selina for their lack of thought and care. Hearing her good opinion of him had played havoc with his mind. It roused a determination to be the best version of himself, the best version just for her.

It was all rather odd—all rather baffling.

Consequently, he'd remained silent during the carriage ride home. Numerous times, she had praised his loyal friends in an attempt to restore his flagging equilibrium. He admired that about her, too. Unlike Selina Lockhart, there wasn't a selfish bone in Miss Darling's body.

When she opened the door to their bedchamber, a flurry of excitement dragged him from his musings. She glanced back over her shoulder as if unsure if he would follow. This charming game they played would distract him long enough to keep all anger and frustration at bay.

"Thank heavens someone had the foresight to light the fire." Miss Darling raced to warm her hands in front of the amber flames. "My fingers and toes are still numb."

After fifteen minutes spent conversing with his friends, they had left the comte's masquerade before supper. It was not an entirely selfish decision. A woman with so pure a heart as Miss Darling did not deserve to be stripped and whipped by the gossips. Lord knows what lies Selina had spouted in his absence. No doubt Lockhart was the dissipated rogue who sought entertainment in warmer climates. The vixen had to make some excuse for marrying his brother.

"I instructed Mrs Brewster to keep the fire going all night." Else a man might be tempted to snuggle next to a warm body when slipping into a cold bed.

"How extravagant."

Lockhart watched her rub her fingers together to get the blood flowing again. She was dressed like a duchess, yet her actions reminded him of those huddled around a brazier in a dingy alley. He rather liked that she could be herself in his company. There were times during this game that he wasn't sure what was real and what was done for the benefit of deception.

"Lissette will be up in a moment," she said, failing to look at him. "Sharing a room makes undressing awkward."

"Why?" He relished the prospect of having another opportunity to tease her. "You're my wife. I shall lounge back on the bed and watch you attend to your ablutions." An erotic vision of her standing naked in a hip bath flashed into his mind.

Her head shot round, her eyes wide with alarm. "You cannot stay while I undress." She lowered her voice to a whisper. "Oh, can I not say I have my … my monthly …"

"Courses?"

"Yes, and so must sleep in another room."

Lockhart chuckled to himself. Never had a woman made excuses to avoid sharing his bed. No woman had ever discussed a subject considered taboo.

"How can you use that excuse when you're supposed to be carrying my child?"

Miss Darling huffed and puffed. "Considerate husbands leave the room when their wives undress."

"And scandalous rogues take every opportunity to see their wives naked."

"You're not a scandalous rogue. You're just a little misguided."

"Misguided?" he almost said but thought better of it. Now that the conversation had turned to his failings, he decided to grant his wife's request. "I shall go and pour us both a brandy. A nip will prevent a chill and settle your nerves. Send Lissette down to the study once you're ready to receive me."

Ready to receive me?

He had never spoken those words to a woman, although with

his rampant imagination he could turn a respectable phrase into something licentious.

An anxious smile played on her lips. "I trust you have a night-shirt." Her gaze journeyed over his chest. "If not, now would be the time to find a suitable alternative."

He was hoping she might make allowances, that after sharing a heated kiss on the terrace she might be eager for more. "I can always wear a shirt." Then again, she had asked him to wear one to bed not keep it on for the whole night.

A rap on the door brought Lissette.

Lockhart left them alone.

Time spent sitting behind the desk in the study afforded him an opportunity to contemplate the night's events. He had hardly received the welcome home one might expect. Did guilt form the basis of Terence's frustrations? No doubt he'd replayed the events of that fateful night many times over the years. Had Terence always loved Selina? He'd wasted no time in marrying the woman. Is that why he encouraged Lockhart to flee?

Lockhart gathered his glass from the silver tray on the desk and swallowed a mouthful of brandy. The amber liquid did little to settle the restlessness within. The game had begun. He had moved into position. Tomorrow, he would make his next move, and then he would wait for a counterattack.

It would come.

He was certain.

He spent the next thirty minutes contemplating all the possible scenarios before a knock on the door drew him from his reverie.

"Enter."

Lissette came into the room, her eyes sparkling with mischief. "Mrs Lockhart, she says you may attend her now, sir."

Attend her?

Oh, the lady would get his undivided attention for the next hour at least.

"Thank you, Lissette."

Lissette curtsied and left the room.

Lockhart poured two glasses of brandy and mounted the stairs. The anticipation of what awaited him beyond the bedchamber door raised a satisfied smile. Indeed, he almost chuckled aloud when plotting the ways he might tease the woman currently waiting in bed.

Gripping both glasses in one hand, he turned the doorknob and entered the room.

Miss Darling's faint gasp reached his ears. The lady sat propped up against a mound of pillows. Like a virgin on her wedding night, unease flickered in her eyes. With the fire still burning in the grate, she had no reason to be cold. Yet she'd thrust her hands beneath the gold coverlet and pulled it up to her chin.

"Your brandy," he said, placing the glass on the side table next to the bed.

She offered him a weak smile, but his attention shifted to the silky blonde tresses spilling over her shoulders. During the month he'd stayed at the cottage, he had never seen her hair down. She looked virtuous, angelic, so beautiful it only made him want her all the more.

"You look more relaxed with your hair loose," he said to justify why he happened to be staring for so long. His rampant imagination formed images of what lay beneath the blankets. She had trim ankles—he knew that much—perhaps shapely calves, too, and soft thighs that flared into curved hips and—

Damnation!

If he didn't dampen his ardour, she'd get a shock once he'd stripped to his shirt.

Deciding conversation was the best way to proceed if he hoped to think of anything other than Miss Darling's naked body, he said, "What were your initial impressions of Terence and Selina?"

Miss Darling straightened a little upon hearing the question. "A small part of me pitied them. Though I doubt they have suffered as you have. The sight of you caused them both great pain."

"And the large part?"

"Despised them for not welcoming you home, for not throwing their arms around you, for not giving you the comfort you deserve."

He sipped his brandy while studying her over the rim of the glass. Her honesty hit a nerve. It took an effort to dismiss the heavy cloud of sadness forming. "I despise them, too, for the reasons you so eloquently explained."

Silence descended.

"Were they always so cold and unfeeling?" she asked.

Lockhart wasn't sure where to take this conversation. He suspected this was the first question of many, and so he placed his glass on the mantel and set about slowly undressing.

"No, not always."

Memories came flooding back.

Being the younger brother, Terence had once respected Lockhart's opinion. For a time they were inseparable. They went riding together, hunting, played piquet. They often vied for the same girl's attention—all part of the game—all part of brotherly camaraderie.

"You don't have to tell me anything," Miss Darling said. "We can blow out the candles and go to sleep. But if you need to talk, know that what is spoken between us is said in the strictest confidence. Know I would never betray a trust."

"I know," he said as his chest grew warm and the strange feeling of nerves and excitement surfaced again. Perhaps he was standing too close to the fire. Perhaps, despite believing he could never trust anyone fully, this odd connection he shared with Miss Darling meant she was different.

"We used to be close," he said, shrugging out of his black coat and throwing it over the chair flanking the fire. "It changed in those last few months before I fled to India. It changed when I grew closer to Selina."

"Selina?" Miss Darling seemed puzzled. "Was that before or after she married your brother?"

"Before." He tugged at the ends of his cravat and loosened the knot. "While we'd failed to make any formal announcement, our parents expected we would marry. The night I left for Portsmouth, I asked her to join me, to elope, but she declined."

"Oh, I see." Miss Darling fell silent as she stared, trance-like, at the swirling pattern on the coverlet.

"One might say that being rivals in love is a good motive to commit murder," he said, his thoughts returning to Terence as he pulled the cravat from around his neck. The motion made him think of what it might be like to feel the rough strands of the hangman's rope chafing his skin.

"That explains why the lady had conflicting emotions upon seeing you." Miss Darling sighed. "Nothing about this situation is simple." She paused and did not look at him directly when she said, "Do you still love her?"

Love? He knew nothing of the emotion.

He'd been a young man, blinded by beauty, believing in loyalty, believing that any sentiment expressed came from the heart. *Lies* and *deceit* were foreign words, murder something one read about in the broadsheets.

"No." In truth, he wasn't sure if he had loved her at all. "She married my brother three weeks after I left these shores." Surely that told Miss Darling all she needed to know.

After a moment of reflection, she said, "People do inconceivable things when frightened and under pressure. I understand what it is like to act out of a sense of hopelessness."

The comment drew his thoughts back to the problems at Falaura Glen.

"Your situation must be desperate for a woman of your good character to accept my proposal, for you to leave your sister alone." The more time he spent with Miss Darling, the more he admired her strength and tenacity. A pang of guilt stabbed his chest. He should not have made the financial reward too tempting to resist.

Her shoulders sagged. "Yes, *desperate* is one way of describing my predicament, and Emily is always in my thoughts. I must trust that Monsieur Dariell is a man of his word."

"I can assure you he is."

Silence descended once more.

Lockhart turned to face the fire. He watched the flames dance and flicker as he unbuttoned his waistcoat and tossed it to join the other garments on the chair. When he tugged his shirt out of his breeches, he heard Miss Darling's faint gasp.

A surge of respect for the lady surfaced. "Would you prefer if I undressed elsewhere?" He did not turn around though part of him longed to see anxiety flash in her eyes. It was the only time he could be certain he was witnessing the truth.

Lockhart could almost hear the internal cogs turning as she pondered his question.

"I told you I would never betray a trust," she said with a sudden determination. "This is a partnership for our mutual bene-fit. No matter how difficult it might be, I promised to act as your wife, and so that is what I will do."

Claudia Darling was unlike any woman he had met. A steely resolve flowed through her veins. At times, she appeared shy, timid, and yet he had witnessed her wrath, tasted the raw passion buried beneath the prim exterior. If she loved a man, she would cross the ends of the earth to be at his side. She was too good for him, too kind, too loving.

Lockhart turned to face her, surprised by his urge to worship her as she deserved. "I trust that means you're happy for me to undress here," he said in the teasing tone he used to disguise any genuine feelings.

She forced a smile. "I can always close my eyes."

"With your inquisitive mind, I imagine there would be lots of peeking."

A chuckle escaped her. "You know me so well, husband."

He laughed, despite feeling an odd sense of comfort at her use of the endearment. To distract his mind, he perched on the edge of the bed, removed his shoes and the rest of his clothes until his shirt was the only garment covering his modesty.

"You promised to tell me about India," she said nervously. "You said you would paint a vivid picture. One I am unlikely to forget."

He *had* said that, but merely to tease her about joining him in bed. No doubt she sought a distraction, a means to draw her mind away from a fear of sleeping next to a half-naked man.

"Then we will talk for an hour instead of reading."

Lockhart moved to the washstand. He fought the urge to drag his shirt over his head and use a cold cloth to douse the flames of lust licking his skin. After drying his hands and face on a towel, he blew out the candles and moved towards the bed.

"Wait!" she said, panic rising when he grabbed the edge of the coverlet, ready to yank it back. "I am losing faith in Monsieur Dariell's character."

"In Dariell's character?" He couldn't hide his shock at her odd outburst. "Why?"

Miss Darling clutched the coverlet to her chest as if she may lose her head should she let go. "Perhaps it is because he is French."

"You dislike the French?"

"No. Perhaps his nationality accounts for his taste in clothes."

"Forgive me, but I'm struggling to follow your train of thought." Nerves had affected her logic.

She dropped her gaze to her chest. "Monsieur Dariell instructed the modiste to design bedroom attire, too."

"And?"

"My nightdress—if one can call it that—is silk."

Lockhart pursed his lips. He didn't know whether to chuckle, salute his friend's foresight or grab a pillow and blanket and retreat to the dressing room.

"I could hardly tell Lissette it was unsuitable and that I'd wear the one I brought with me," Miss Darling continued. "From the look she gave I doubt she thinks it will be on for long."

The heat warming his chest journeyed southwards as visions of her naked form danced in his mind. "May I see the nightgown?"

"Of course not. And *nightgown* is a term I would use loosely."

It was worth a try.

"Look, I shall close my eyes as I slip into bed." Had the lady forgotten he'd delved deep into her mouth and roused a sigh of pleasure? Hell, now was not the time to think of that, either. "If you hold the coverlet tightly to your chest, there's no reason I should see your body or the gown."

Looking somewhat appeased, and after a moment's contemplation, she nodded.

Slipping beneath the sheets played havoc with his body. Knowing she wore a scandalous nightgown while lying a mere foot away sent blood surging to his cock. There was only one thing for it—other than taking himself in hand, and he wasn't about to do that in front of a lady—and so he turned on his side to face her and propped himself up on his elbow.

"You want me to tell you about India."

Miss Darling shuffled onto her side whilst remaining huddled in her cocoon. "Oh, yes. I've heard tell it's so hot you cannot sleep at night."

Hot, but nowhere near as hot as he felt now.

"Not all year." Lockhart smiled as she stared at him all wide-eyed and innocent. "In the summer the heat is stifling. Sweat trickles down your back. Humidity is low, making it difficult to breathe. When the Loo comes—"

"The Loo?" Miss Darling wrinkled her nose.

"It's a strong, dusty wind that blows from the west during the summer."

"Surely that helps to keep cool."

The scorching wind devastated the landscape, ruined vegetation. "The gusts are so hot people call them the evil winds. Just before the onset of the monsoon season, the *Kali Andhi* comes—a violent, squalling dust storm that reduces visibility."

Miss Darling's sweet mouth dropped open.

God, how he wanted to kiss her again.

"And what's it like during the monsoons?" She clasped her hands together in prayer and placed them between her cheek and the pillow as she edged a little closer.

There was not much to say about the torrential rain, rain that sometimes fell for days and days, but he would say anything as long as he had Miss Darling's undivided attention.

"Storms roll in so quickly you've little time to prepare," he said, relishing the look of wonder and excitement in her eyes. "The clouds are dark and heavy and filled with moisture. The rains can last for months. Droplets drench the skin in seconds." He reached out and smoothed a strand of hair from her brow. She did not flinch or protest. "I've always found the rain cleansing. I've stood outside until my clothes are sodden and rain runs off the tip of my nose like water from a tap."

Miss Darling chuckled.

She should laugh more often. Her eyes shone, bright and vibrant. A vitality for life radiated from every fibre of her being.

"When caught in a sudden shower I do tend to dawdle," she said.

"Perhaps we might look for an opportunity to share the experience." They were talking about being out in the rain and yet the intimacy of the moment roused his desire on a level deeper than he had ever known.

"Yes, we must."

Silence slipped over them like a silk veil.

Miss Darling held his gaze, which was a feat in itself as he knew lust lingered there.

"Did you meet many English ladies whilst abroad?"

Lockhart wondered what prompted the question. "Some. The British over in India try to recreate the life they had at home. Ladies call on their friends and take tea. They gossip and complain about the weather." He found them rather tedious.

"And the gentlemen?"

"Hunt cheetahs rather than foxes."

"I wouldn't want to flush a cheetah out of a hole."

"No, Miss Darling." Lockhart laughed. "Neither would I."

When their amusement faded, he waited for her to ask another question. She didn't. She glanced at the fire burning low in the grate. Despite numerous attempts to stifle a yawn, she failed miserably.

But he did not want to go to sleep. He wanted to look at her, to hear her voice, to talk until sunrise.

"Now that we're considered fully fledged actors," he said, "it is time to test our skill. Let us play a game."

"A game? What would you have us do?"

Was she eager to prolong this moment, too, or did embarrassment about sleeping next to him play a part?

"You understand that married couples who are madly in love have intimate relations on a regular basis."

"No, but I shall take you at your word," she said with some apprehension.

"And you understand that we must make our marriage look convincing."

She hesitated before saying, "Yes, but I am not jumping on the bed whilst wearing this nightgown."

"No, of course not." That would be a step too far when in the company of a man with lascivious intentions. "But we should practise our sighs of pleasure."

"Sighs of pleasure?" Miss Darling jerked her head back. "I couldn't possibly do that."

"Then you admit I am the better actor?"

Would she take the bait?

She arched a brow. "Your argument is weak, sir, as you have had to do little to embrace the role of husband."

"Little? Madam, do you not recall one scandalous kiss on the terrace?"

As she shrugged, the coverlet slipped to reveal an inch of bare shoulder. He had seen naked women many times before but nothing as erotic as a forbidden glimpse of her milky-white skin.

Regrettably, she rectified the problem.

"I'm sure you've kissed many women, and so it was no great hardship. It was different for me as you're the only man I've kissed."

Lockhart gave a boyish wink. "We could practise kissing if you'd like to work on your performance."

She snorted. "It is you who needs practice."

"Me?" He frowned, affronted at the suggestion he lacked skill with his tongue.

"You kiss like a man consumed with lust when you're supposed to kiss like a man in love."

"Is there a difference?" Honestly, he did not know.

"Of course there's a difference."

Ah, the lady had fallen nicely into his trap. "Show me." Before she could protest, he added, "A man needs a tutor if he hopes to learn a new skill."

Miss Darling's gaze dropped to his lips.

"I will need to kiss you again at some point," he pressed. "It is up to you whether it is a kiss full of lust or one that conveys love."

She remained silent for a time. Eventually, she said, "Very well. But you're not to kiss me back."

That was like asking a parched man not to drink from a

stream. Still, he'd not pass up an opportunity to feel her lips on his.

Lockhart squeezed his eyes shut. "Do with me what you will. I shall not open my eyes until you've finished."

"It will be short," she said. "Lust is like a fire in constant need of poking."

Did she know that was an accurate analogy?

"Love," she continued, "is conveyed through a simple but tender touch."

Disappointment flared. He was hoping for an opportunity to tempt her, to devour her mouth as he'd done before.

"Do not move." She shuffled closer, so close her hot breath breezed across his face.

His imagination ran amok. Was she still gripping the coverlet or had she let it slip?

The waiting, the anticipation proved highly arousing.

The first touch of her fingers gliding up to cup his cheek sent a bolt of heat to his loins. He felt her breath again like a mystical breeze whispering ancient secrets. Such was the power this lady had over him. The feel of her lips pressing softly against his was almost his undoing. They were moist and slightly parted, conveyed tenderness while hinting at the possibility of so much more. Yet strangely one kiss was enough to ignite a fire within.

She broke contact, whispered, "If I loved you, I would tell you now."

Then tell me.

A part of him ached to hear the words.

But this was a game, he reminded himself, a game of his own construction.

When she moved away, he opened his eyes to find her shrouded in the coverlet with her head on the pillow. Something lingered in the air between them—a feeling, an emotion he could not identify, more unspoken words and confounding thoughts.

"Good night, Hudson." Her eyes fluttered closed, shutting him out.

Lockhart turned onto his back and stared at the ceiling. "Good night, Claudia," he said, knowing sleep would elude him for hours, knowing that until he drew his last breath, he would never forget that one sweet, gentle kiss.

CHAPTER TEN

Light danced on Claudia's closed eyelids, teasing her gently out of the sweet realms of sleep. Remnants of a dream flickered in her mind, of her running through the wheat fields bordering Falaura Glen, laughing as the midday sun cast a golden hue over the scene. She hiked up her skirts and glanced back over her shoulder, bursting into an excited giggle as she bolted from the gentleman chasing in hot pursuit.

Claudia couldn't see his face clearly, but she was not afraid. She wanted him to catch her. Desperate to keep the dream alive in her conscious memory, she imagined throwing her arms wide in surrender, imagined him scooping her up and swinging her around and around until dizzy.

A pleasurable sigh left her lips.

"Is this a game of illicit moans or is it that you slept well?" The smooth, masculine voice caressed her senses. It took her a moment to realise that it was not the man in her dream who spoke but the man lying next to her in bed.

Hudson Lockhart.

Instead of her heart melting, it hammered hard in her chest. Too scared to open her eyes fully, she peered through half-closed lids. There was a body, a large male body, a bronzed naked male body a mere foot away.

Where the devil was his nightshirt?

Claudia stole a fluttered glance at his face. An arrogant grin played at the corners of his mouth as he watched her intently.

"Since you failed to reply," he continued, moistening his lips as his dark eyes devoured her, "I assume it's my turn." A deep, guttural groan resonated in the back of his throat. "God damn, Claudia, you drive me wild." He winked and said in a less amorous tone, "There, how was that?"

Embarrassment forced a rush of blood to her cheeks. Desire sent it flooding in another direction, too. Her whole body burned. But then she was huddled beneath a heap of blankets.

Except she wasn't beneath the blankets.

Claudia wiggled her toes, the cool air proving her worst fear accurate.

Oh, Mother Mary!

She forced her eyelids apart, forced herself to look at the shirtless rogue propped up on one elbow.

"You've been watching me sleeping?" Claudia winced as she dared to examine her current state of dishabille. She was sprawled like a starfish, a starfish whose silk nightgown happened to be riding halfway up her thighs, clinging to her breasts and erect nipples.

If her cheeks were red before, they must be a dark shade of crimson now.

"I don't know why you're embarrassed," Mr Lockhart said as his hungry gaze slid up and down the entire length of her body. "You look angelic while sleeping, though I doubt an angel would hike up her nightdress while moaning with pleasure."

Mortification threatened to consume her.

"What happened to you wearing a shirt to bed?" she snapped, grabbing the end of the coverlet and pulling it up to her neck. "You made a promise. It was part of our bargain."

"I promised to wear it to bed. I did not promise to keep it on all night."

Claudia couldn't help but take another furtive glance at Mr Lockhart's muscular physique.

Lord have mercy!

Every fibre of her being itched to run her hands over the bulging contours, longed to twirl her fingers in the dusting of dark hair on his chest. Thankfully, the bedsheets hugged his waist and hips and—

Hell's bells!

Hudson Lockhart was naked beneath the sheets.

"Wh-what time is it?" Panic held her rigid.

"Nine."

"Nine? But I never sleep late."

"We *were* talking until the early hours." He inhaled deeply, and his chest expanded to torment her all the more. "But you're right. I'm to visit my parents at noon and haven't time to lounge around."

Without offering a word of warning, he threw back the bedsheets and jumped out of bed. Leaving her with a perfect view of his pert buttocks, he reached high, every muscle in his back rippling as he stretched his limbs.

Oh, this man was as cunning as the devil.

No doubt he was about to grab hold of his manhood and piddle into the chamber pot. He took pleasure in unsettling her composure. Naivety made her a prime candidate for teasing. He knew exactly what to do to draw attention to her lack of experience.

Well, not anymore.

Timidity had become rather tiresome.

Lord knows how long he had stared at her breasts while she relaxed in peaceful slumber. At some point in her life, she would see a man naked. It might as well be now. Having shared a bed with him, should she not be a little bolder? Besides, something had changed during the early hours when she'd listened to him speak of the Indian weather. A deeper connection had formed—an intimacy she had never known.

"Then surely I'm to come with you when you visit your parents." Claudia slipped out of bed and padded over to the washstand. Heavens, it was cold. "We should ring for Lissette to bring fresh water and have a maid light the fire."

Claudia did not have to look at Hudson Lockhart to know she had captured his attention. The heat from his gaze journeyed over her back, scorching her skin in its wake.

"Haven't you forgotten something?" he said, his tone low and husky.

Claudia gathered every ounce of courage she possessed and swung around to face him. Satisfaction raced through her when she noted his initial look of surprise. But Mr Lockhart was a man comfortable in his own skin. Mr Lockhart had the confidence of Adonis.

"Have I?" Claudia arched a coy brow.

"You're without your coverlet?"

"So I am." She cast an admiring glance at his manhood, and yet she wanted to gasp in shock. He was so large … so … so utterly masculine. "And you are without your clothes."

"Oddly, it does not seem to bother you now." He stood strong and proud as if wearing a fine garment, expertly tailored, pleasing to the eye.

"I'm a good actress." Claudia shrugged, though realised that was a mistake when the action drew his attention to her breasts. "And it suddenly occurred to me that I have seen statues in books and museums, that I have seen many versions of the male form."

Though none so impressive. If one were judging purely on proportions, Mr Lockhart would attract a crowd.

"Then call Lissette and have her draw you a bath." A playful twinkle sparkled in his eyes. "I have seen the female form many times, too, once more won't make a difference."

Heavens, she was drowning beneath the depths of her inadequacy. She'd have to fight against the current if she hoped to unsettle this gentleman.

"Very well." The words left her lips without conscious thought. It was too late to retract them. Hudson Lockhart had offered a challenge, and she had accepted.

Pushing nerves aside, Claudia rang for the maid.

Mr Lockhart slipped back into bed. He remained propped upright on a mound of pillows as he watched the sudden flurry of activity.

The maid lit the fire. Two footmen carried the tub and made numerous trips upstairs with steaming buckets. Lissette added drops of rosewater to the bath and tied Claudia's hair in a simple chignon.

"Shall I fetch the screen, madame?" Lissette asked.

Claudia stole a glance at Mr Lockhart. Oh, the devil looked thoroughly pleased with the turn of events. He arched an arrogant brow, lounged back and placed his hands behind his head. "Do you need a screen when bathing in front of your husband?"

Claudia's knees trembled at the thought of Hudson Lockhart seeing her naked. Part of her wanted to insist upon a means to protect her modesty. The larger part longed to see the same flash of vulnerability in his eyes she'd seen thirty minutes before.

"I don't need a screen, Lissette." This cat-and-mouse game they played had nothing to do with him hiring her to play his wife. It felt like a courtship, a wild, illicit courtship that broke all of society's rigid rules. "You may leave me now. I shall ring should I need your assistance."

How strange that she did not feel vulnerable. For the first time in her life, the power that came with knowing a man desired her gave her strength beyond her height and slender frame. And her foolish pride insisted on proving she was more than capable of dealing with any test he threw her way.

Lissette left the room and closed the door.

Claudia remained rooted to the spot next to the bathtub.

Hudson Lockhart's sinful grin taunted and seduced both at the same time.

"Your bath will be cold if you linger." His velvet voice reached across the room. "If you're quick, I may have time to *slip* into your water."

Her pulse quickened.

Do it.

Do it now.

Do it before you change your mind and prove you were the second choice.

"Then I'll be quick." She lacked the skill to undress in the titillating way he might like. And so she gathered the hem of the silk nightgown and raised it to her thighs.

Hudson Lockhart's breath hissed between his teeth. "You're not going paddling, my darling. Take it off."

"No, I'm not going paddling." Before nerves consumed her, she drew the garment over her head, tossed it onto the chair and slipped into the warm water without looking at him once.

"Dariell was right," he said when she found the courage to look at him. His satisfied smile had turned dark and positively wicked.

Claudia swallowed deeply as she bent her knees and swished water over her shoulders. "Right about what?" That she would make an excellent second choice?

"You're perfect, perfect for me."

Her heart leapt and skipped a joyful dance.

Did he mean it? Or was it part of the act?

"Perfect to play the wife of a scandalous rogue," he added.

Claudia pursed her lips. Could he not have stopped when he said the word *me*?

Disappointment came in the form of a hard lump in her throat. Tears welled to prove she was a fraud. She scooped water into her cupped hands and wet her face to wash away any evidence of her sudden distress. Confusion clouded her mind. Oh, she was a jumbled mess of contradictions.

Was this a game? Did it mean more to her than that?

Think of Emily.

Think of paying the debt.

Don't think about him.

"Passion burns just beneath the surface," he continued, though she wished he would stop talking. "And yet the innocent woman from Falaura Glen appeals to me just as much as the determined temptress. Why is that?"

"You're asking me?" She clambered to raise her defences. "Sir, are you not taking your role as husband too seriously?"

"Marriage is a serious affair."

"Indeed, it is." Had she not said a similar thing to Mr Thorncroft? "Can you fetch me the towel?" She wiggled her fingers at the chair.

"I can't. I'm not in any fit state to move from this bed."

"Oh." She wasn't entirely sure what he meant, but she needed to get dressed, needed to leave this room and focus on the job he'd hired her to do.

"I doubt you have ever seen a statue in a state of semi-arousal."

"No."

"Would you like to?"

"No!" She shot out of the tub, reached for the robe and wrapped it around her wet body. "Have you sent a note to your parents informing them you're alive?" she asked, banishing all romantic thoughts of this man.

"There's no need. Terence will have called, eager to play the doting son. One must pander to my parents if they hope to receive their inheritance."

"Then at least they'll have time to deal with the shock." Normal conversation helped to settle her ragged emotions. "Other than to update them on the news, what is the purpose of our visit?"

"The purpose?" He frowned. "Madam, you know how to dampen a man's ardour."

She dismissed all prospect of discussing anything sinful. "I must ask you an unpleasant question." She paused, gave him time to object.

"Then ask what you will." He threw back the bedsheets and strolled over to the bathtub. "We agreed to speak plainly."

Claudia moved to the window and stared at the garden below. She heard the splash as he entered the water.

"Do you believe your parents are innocent of any wrongdoing or do you suspect they played a part in what happened on that fateful night?"

He took a few seconds to answer. "Who wants to believe one's parents want them dead?"

"And what if the motive was simply to get rid of you?" The villain had committed murder and blamed Mr Lockhart. Perhaps threatening him with the gallows was simply a means to keep him abroad. "Do you not think you should tell me what happened that night?"

Silence fell as sharp and as swiftly as the guillotine.

Claudia swung around to find him lounging in the bathtub, knees bent and head back, staring at the ceiling. He looked lost, lonely, a boy in need of a loving smile and a tender embrace.

Against her better judgement, she padded over and knelt beside him. Her body ached to bring him the peace he desired. Her heart ached for the broken man who hid beneath an arrogant facade.

"You must tell me what you remember about that night." She spoke in soothing tones hoping to draw him out of his melancholy. "Fate has brought us together. Perhaps I am here to play more than one role, Hudson. Let me be your friend, let me help you solve this problem so you might put the past behind you."

His body remained rigid but his gaze flicked in her direction. "Your words suggest that being my friend is all part of the act. How can a man trust someone paid to be his wife, paid to be his companion?"

Claudia could not argue with his assessment. Were it not for Emily and her agreement with Mr Thorncroft she would tell Hudson Lockhart she didn't want his money. She would stay because she liked him, cared for him a little and wanted to help.

"You're right. You have no reason to trust me. But if you examine your heart, you know I'll not fail you. Let me be your friend. Heavens, I need a friend more than you do."

His chestnut-brown eyes scanned her face for so long she thought he might never speak. "Destiny has bound us together for a time. We would be foolish not to embrace the opportunity to further our acquaintance."

A faint chuckle escaped her. "Now you sound like Dariell."

"I *have* spent five years with the fellow." His weak smile faded.

"Then something lasting and worthwhile came from your banishment."

"Yes, it did." After a lengthy pause, he said, "Are you sure you want to hear the details of that night?"

Claudia nodded. "Without them, I cannot help you find the person responsible."

"Then I shall try to keep it brief." He pushed a wet hand through his hair and sighed. Thirty seconds passed before he spoke. "I always assumed I'd marry Selina. We began an affair, met a few times at a coaching inn on one of the quieter roads some seven miles south of town."

"By affair you mean you had … physical relations."

He responded with a curt nod. "Someone followed us there that night. Selina was adamant we'd been followed before, had grown fretful at the prospect of her father discovering our affair when there'd been no announcement of a formal engagement."

"Did it not occur to you to propose before you began these illicit interludes?"

Lord, she sounded like a hypocrite. Here she was, an unmarried woman, in a bedchamber with a naked man in a bathtub.

"Selina can be persuasive." He shrugged one shoulder. "I was a virile young man. It's a pathetic excuse, but what can I say?"

Did Selina still love him? She had appeared distraught upon hearing of his marriage. What would she do now that Hudson Lockhart had returned? That thought led to other important questions.

"Then I shall ask you again. Did you love Selina? Do you still love her?" An unexpected stab to her heart forced her to catch her breath.

He hesitated. "Will you despise me if I say no? Will you think ill of me if I say that I liked her enough to marry her, but that love never played a part?"

"Liked her? You don't believe that marriage exists for those in love to make a lifelong commitment?"

"Why would I when I was taught that marriage exists only to enhance one's wealth and status?"

Mr Thorncroft was of a similar mind, too. In agreeing to his contract, Claudia had joined the ranks of the cold-hearted cynics.

"Selina's father has wealth and connections," he continued. "It was good enough for my parents and was doubtless good enough for my brother."

"How sad."

"How sad, indeed."

They were straying from the point. This conversation was not about peeling back the layers of his character and hoping she wouldn't cry.

"So you were at the inn, and someone followed you," she reminded him.

"A hulk of a man with a thick neck and bulging eyes. He saw

me staring out of an upper window and gestured to the small wood behind the inn."

"What did you do?"

"I left Selina in the room and trailed after the fiend. He seemed just as eager to avoid the few guests using the inn. We stopped near an old oak tree, and he demanded I hand over the money, demanded I repay the debt."

Claudia frowned. "A gambling debt?"

"I have no notion. Clearly he had mistaken me for someone else. Every time I pleaded ignorance, the brute punched me in the gut." Hudson clenched his teeth. "I was too weak, too foolish. Now, I'd rip his throat out with my bare hands."

"Is that the man you supposedly murdered?" Claudia swallowed past the lump in her throat. During a violent rage, a person's memory might be foggy. Did people not speak of seeing nothing but darkness, of having no recollection of the atrocities committed by their hand?

Hudson nodded. "Selina appeared, weaving through the trees. Fear choked the breath from my lungs. If the blackguard could beat an innocent man, what would he do to a woman?" Anger darkened Lockhart's voice. "The fiend pulled a blade from his boot, threatened to chase her down and slice her throat unless I brought him the money he was promised."

"And so you knew you must protect her."

A deep frown marred his brow as his head shot in Claudia's direction. "I did not kill him if that's what you're implying."

"Of course not. Tell me what happened."

"I don't know what happened. I lurched at the rogue, tried to kick the blade from his hand, but someone hit me hard on the head from behind. The next time I opened my eyes, I was sprawled on the ground clutching the knife."

"And what of the man who came to claim payment of the debt?"

Hudson closed his eyes. His Adam's apple bobbed in his throat.

"There was so much blood," he said, opening his eyes and staring at the water. "Blood on my hands. Blood smeared on the blade. Blood oozing through his shirt and waistcoat from two wounds in his chest."

Claudia took a moment to gather her wits. Hudson Lockhart was not a killer. The fact a man had crept out of the shadows and bludgeoned him proved her point.

"But it's not the blood that revisits me in my nightmares." Hudson gripped the edge of the tub so tightly his knuckles were white. "It's the cold, glazed eyes. During the fight, I saw the darkness in his soul, the anger. And yet as he lay motionless at my side, it was as if a door had closed and I saw nothing."

Claudia covered his hand with hers and rubbed back and forth until his fingers relaxed. One question sprang to mind.

"Where was Selina? Surely she can identify the man who attacked you from behind."

"When the scuffle broke out, I shouted for her to run. I didn't see her again until I regained consciousness. She'd taken the carriage back to London and returned with my brother."

Selina ran away and left him?

Anger bubbled in Claudia's stomach.

"Why on earth did she waste time riding back to London?" Even at breakneck speed, the round trip must have taken more than an hour. "Why did she not run to the coaching inn and alert the proprietor?" If not the proprietor, she might have returned with the coachman. After all, the trustworthy servant ferried her to her illicit liaisons without alerting her parents.

"She said she heard the rogue's bloodcurdling scream and feared I'd killed him. She couldn't risk her father discovering the truth about our clandestine meetings. Terence was the only person she felt she could turn to for help."

Claudia considered the information. An uneasy feeling settled in her chest. Had Selina cared more about saving her reputation than saving the life of her lover? Or had her actions stemmed from wanting to protect the man she loved from being hauled to the magistrate?

"What did Terence do?"

"He sent Selina to wait in the carriage. The coachman came and carried me to the vehicle. To this day, Terence refuses to tell me what he did with the body. Apparently, the less I know the better, should I ever find myself dragged before a judge and jury."

Or perhaps Terence wanted to use the information as blackmail. Time would tell.

"And what about the man who hit you?"

Hudson shrugged. "Terence searched the woods and found no sign of the other man. He fears I may have been confused and hurt my head during the scuffle."

"I see." Every ounce of sense she possessed—which had diminished since deciding to sleep in a bed with a strange man for money—said that Hudson Lockhart was a victim of the worst kind of betrayal. "And how did you end up on a ship bound for India?"

"Would you mind handing me the towel?" He gestured to the chair.

Claudia did as he asked and then returned to stare out of the window while he climbed out of the bathtub.

"Terence commanded the use of Selina's carriage, and we drove directly to Portsmouth," he said as he dried his naked body. Claudia gaped at his faint reflection in the glass. "You can turn around now."

The same nervous excitement she always felt when gazing upon his masculine form rendered her rigid for a moment. "So you have not seen your parents since that night?"

She turned casually to face him, suppressing the sudden flurry of desire. His bronzed skin was damp, the sheen drawing attention to every bulging muscle. His mussed hair made her want to grasp the ends as she succumbed to another one of his salacious kisses.

"No." The small towel covered his modesty as he sat on the edge of the bed. "Terence brought a change of clothes and a few basic items in a valise. He gave me money and bought the ticket."

"And he warned you never to return home else you might swing from the gallows." Terence was either the most considerate brother in the world, or the most devious.

"Indeed."

Claudia tried to focus while noting the rippling muscles in his abdomen and the tantalising trail of dark hair leading down beyond the edge of the towel.

"How did Selina explain her absence to her parents?"

It was almost eighty miles to Portsmouth. They must have been gone for more than a day.

"I assume she couldn't. No doubt that's why she married Terence." Hudson's mouth curled in disdain. "I invited her to come with me, but she hates the heat and hasn't the stomach for such a dangerous crossing."

For love, Claudia would climb mountains, cross vast oceans. Selina's actions told her all she needed to know.

"And so she chose your brother instead."

"I imagine Terence dropped on bended knee, grovelled to her parents and explained how they were foolish and in love. I imagine he offered for her on their return to London. He never told me, and I certainly didn't ask."

Either Terence planned the whole thing out of jealousy, or he had sacrificed his happiness to save his brother. No wonder Mr Lockhart found it difficult to trust people.

Claudia remained silent for a moment.

Hearing the story of that fateful night had affected her in ways she could not comprehend. The overriding feeling was that she must save Hudson Lockhart. Save him from those wicked members of his family who took pleasure in persecuting an innocent man. Save him from the distrust that forged his character, that informed his thoughts and decisions.

And so as they dressed in preparation for the meeting with his parents, one question remained at the forefront of Claudia's mind. Was Terence the villain or the hero of Hudson Lockhart's sad story?

CHAPTER ELEVEN

Nothing had changed during Lockhart's five-year absence. The grey stone exterior of his parents' townhouse reflected the austere reception one would undoubtedly find inside. And while the cold facade forewarned of the true character of both inhabitants, their love of fashionable furnishings spoke of the fickleness and inconstancy that informed his parents' daily lives.

"Are we waiting for something?" Claudia asked as they sat in the carriage, staring at the house. "The butler has opened and closed the door twice."

"Simmonds will be glad of the fresh air." Living inside a prison was stifling. Everyone, bar the mistress, suffered from some form of inadequacy, and she took pleasure in reminding them daily.

"We don't have to go inside." Compassion infused Claudia's tone. "Equally, I am happy to wait here if you'd rather go alone."

Lockhart considered the lady whose presence settled the unease in his chest.

If I loved you, I would tell you now.

Her words drifted through his mind, bringing the memory of

last night's sweet kiss flooding back. It had affected him more than he cared to admit.

"I need you with me," he said, feeling the truth of it deep in his bones. Perhaps they might be friends when this was all over. Perhaps they might be lovers for a time. Both possibilities appealed to him. "And I need another stellar performance."

Her reply came in the form of a curt nod, and yet he wanted her to say she would do anything for him, that she would support him even if he wasn't paying her a penny.

"You should know a little about my mother before we enter." Hester Lockhart knew how to lure the unsuspecting into her trap. "She will appear distraught, yet she will turn her pain and anger towards me. She has a vicious tongue when the mood takes her."

Claudia smiled. "I am used to dealing with those who seek to intimidate. But I appreciate the warning all the same."

Her reply roused his ire. He imagined many people sought to take advantage of the young mistress in charge of Falaura Glen. "Should you need any assistance at home, you only need ask."

She struggled to maintain her smile. He knew her well enough to know something troubled her. "That is most gracious." She shuffled forward. "Come, let us tackle your parents and see if we can discover anything that might help make sense of the night you fled to India."

Lockhart knew a distraction technique when he heard one, but she was right. They could not linger in the carriage all day, and so he assisted his wife to the pavement and escorted her to the front door.

"Welcome home, sir," Simmonds said. The butler's brown eyes flashed with warning, a signal to alert Lockhart of his mother's precarious mood. He inclined his head to Claudia. "Madam."

"I trust Terence visited this morning."

"He did, sir."

Terence had always been the favourite. "Then my mother is expecting us."

A mournful cry exploded from the room on their left. The prolonged wailing sound expressed his mother's crippling anguish.

Simmonds glanced at the ceiling before saying, "I am sure you know the way, sir."

As Lockhart guided Claudia into the drawing room, it struck him that his mother's latest obsession extended to purchasing anything pale blue. The curtains, the new coverings on the chairs and sofa, and the swirling blue and white pattern on the rug made a man feel as if he were floating above the clouds.

His mother lay stretched on a pale blue chaise with gilt legs. A house cap, tied tightly under her chin with a blue silk bow, covered all but a few grey curls. Her white dress made her look pasty and drew one's gaze to the puffy red rings around her eyes.

She looked up although continued to twist and wring her handkerchief in her hands. "So it is true," his mother blurted. "We received word you were dead. Dead, for pity's sake, dead. And now look at you, standing there as if you haven't a care in the world." She flapped her handkerchief in his direction. "Do you mean to put your mother in her grave?"

Feelings of emptiness returned. "As I have already explained to Terence, Lord Greystone acted prematurely in sending his correspondence."

"Greystone? That son of a whoremaster? Can the foolish boy not tell the difference between the living and the dead?" She broke into another ear-piercing sob just for effect.

Lockhart gritted his teeth. A minute had passed, and he was ready to leave and never return. Had it not been for the dainty hand taking hold of his arm he might have acted on impulse. Miss Darling was there to remind him why he had come—purely for information. And yet a small part of him longed for his mother's embrace, ached to hear words of love and comfort.

"Lord Greystone is an intelligent man whose abilities in business led me to make my fortune."

His mother lowered her handkerchief and narrowed her gaze. "So you left England in pursuit of money. You abandoned those who supported you, turned your back on your family, your responsibilities."

It didn't matter what he said, what excuses he gave, his mother would find every reason to express her disappointment. He could drop on bended knee and explain how he was framed for a murder he did not commit, how he'd been forced to flee, confused and alone. But ultimately she would lay the blame at his door.

"How else was I to survive when Father cut off my funds and struck my name from his will?"

His mother scrunched the handkerchief in her fist. "You forced that poor man to act as he did. Heaven knows why you chose to live with heathens. I'm only grateful our estate is not entailed. When the time comes, I daresay you would lease it out and use the money to buy goats."

Goats?

The matron focused on everyone else's failings rather than accept her own. But the conversation raised one crucial question.

Whose name had his father marked next to the estate in Warwickshire?

Terence Lockhart?

Justin Perigrew? Surely not.

There was only one way to find out.

"Being named the heir, I thought Terence would have moved into Alveston Hall," he said, making the obvious assumption. "Selina favours the countryside I seem to recall."

Hester Lockhart raised her chin. "Like any good son, the boy is not one for gallivanting and refuses to leave his father's side."

"Unlike me."

"You do remember your father? The man abandoned by his eldest son? The man on his deathbed?" She flopped back on the chaise and raised a limp hand to her forehead. "None of us are in good health, Hudson. This is all too much."

Oddly, the welfare of Alfred and Hester Lockhart was not his first consideration. His only thought was for his fake wife, the woman carrying his imagined child. They were still standing because his mother hadn't the decency to offer them a seat.

"My wife is with child," he said, anger rising in his chest at Claudia's mistreatment. "She suffers from bouts of dizziness, and so I must insist she sits and rests for a moment."

The matron lowered her hand and considered Claudia through half-closed lids. Based on her obsession for pale blue, his mother should have found Madame Armand's elegant pelisse with ermine cuffs rather pleasing. But Hester Lockhart rarely expressed approval.

"Poor Selina has had an awful time," his mother said, ignoring the kind smile Claudia cast the matron's way. "It's the stress, you know. The stress of tending to ailing parents makes it impossible to conceive. And she is so attentive to our needs."

Despite surviving in a harsh climate, working in harsh conditions, nothing roused frustration like his mother's insensitive comments. Resentment festered. Disappointment cut to the bone. Bitterness seeped from wounds that had never healed.

"Forgive me, Mrs Lockhart," Claudia suddenly said. "If I do not sit down soon, I'm afraid I must take my leave." She turned to Lockhart and placed her hand on his forearm. "I shall wait for you in the carriage."

Clever minx.

His mother craved attention, craved an audience.

"Then I shall bid my mother good day—"

"Oh, do sit down," his mother snapped. "I've got a crick in my neck from staring up at you."

"Thank you, Mrs Lockhart, you are most kind."

Lockhart waited for Claudia to sit before dropping into the chair next to her.

"As I was saying," his mother continued, "Selina is here most days. Your father adores her. Of course, she should have married you, Hudson. The two of you are far more suited. You broke her heart when you left."

Lockhart clenched his jaw. "Things worked out for the best. I never loved Selina, but I do love my wife." He captured Miss Darling's hand and held it tight. It was not a fake gesture to spite his mother, but he had an overwhelming urge to offer support, to take comfort from her touch, too.

"And our child will be born to doting parents," Claudia said in a sweet voice devoid of malice. "For there is no greater gift in this world than being raised in a loving home."

For a moment, his mother appeared dumbstruck. No doubt her devious mind scrambled to decide if the comment carried a veiled attack.

To annoy his mother, Lockhart drew Claudia's hand to his lips and pressed a kiss to her knuckles. "And you will want for nothing as long as I am your protector."

A tense silence ensued though his mother's penetrating stare was sharp enough to pierce skin, draw blood.

"Words fall easily from the lips," the matron sniped. "When one judges character it is best to consider a person's history, my dear, for therein lies the truth. Once a deserter, always a deserter. Isn't that what they say, Hudson?"

A rage to rival the devil's wrath burned in Lockhart's chest. Pain for the boy who had done nothing to feed her hatred lingered there, too. What the hell did his mother want from him? His complete surrender would not be enough. He was wasting his time here.

Indeed, Lockhart was about to jump to his feet when Claudia cleared her throat.

"Once a cynic, always a cynic. Isn't that what they say, Mrs Lockhart?" Claudia raised her chin, though her cheeks flushed pink. "Thankfully, I know enough about Hudson to know he has a good heart, to know he makes sacrifices for his family, to know nothing he has done in his life stems from selfish intentions."

Hester Lockhart snorted and opened her mouth to speak, but Miss Darling did not give her a chance to utter another word.

"When Hudson Lockhart says he will protect me, I believe him. When Hudson Lockhart promises to be a good husband and father, I know he will love his wife and children unconditionally."

Miss Darling turned to face him. He might have wondered if her powerful monologue was part of the script, but the water welling in her eyes implied the words came from an honest place.

"I cannot control what people say, Hudson, but I can choose not to listen." Claudia rose to her feet and cradled her stomach. The gesture stirred something within him, another unnamed emotion. "And I refuse to sit here and watch such a vicious, unprovoked attack."

Lockhart stood, his heart bursting with pride and respect for the woman whose loyalty to her husband flowed like blood in her veins. "Then I shall accompany you. The welfare of you and our child is what matters now."

He caught himself.

The lines between fantasy and reality were becoming blurred. It occurred to Lockhart that he might grieve for the loss of his wife and child once the week was out.

"What?" His mother gasped. "You've been away for five years, and you intend to leave before seeing your father? The man is on his deathbed." She shook her head and muttered, "Oh, why am I surprised?"

Lockhart had every intention of rushing upstairs to pay his respects to the man who'd sired him. "A wise man once told me that acceptance brings peace. Perhaps you might consider that when Terence and Selina return to stir the hornet's nest. Good day, Mother."

"Peace?" the matron mocked.

Pressing his hand to Miss Darling's back, Lockhart guided her to the drawing room door. He did not take a backwards glance or acknowledge his mother further.

"How can a mother have peace when her son insists ..." His mother's words faded to a garbled mumble as he closed his ears to her constant complaining.

❀

Gesturing for Miss Darling to climb the stairs in search of his father, Lockhart followed behind, his gaze fixed on the gentle sway of her hips in the hope of calming his volatile mood.

He opened the door to the master bedchamber to find the room unoccupied. Hearing the squeak of the floorboards across the landing, he decided to investigate.

As soon as he opened the door, the sour stench of sickness attacked his nostrils. With Miss Darling two steps behind, they entered the dark, dingy room lit by a single candle positioned on the bedside table. The flame flickered in protest at the sudden interruption.

Lockhart's gaze searched through the gloom to locate the figure lying motionless in bed, his head lolling to one side. He stepped closer, shocked that his father's once ruddy complexion was now sallow, that his chubby cheeks were sunken and sagged from protruding bones.

"Father?" Guilt stabbed Lockhart's conscience. Despite his father's illness, he could not rouse the love and respect a son should feel for the man who had raised him. How he wished things were different.

"He cannot hear you for he is heavily sedated." Justin Perigrew's jarring voice pierced the morbid atmosphere. Every word conveyed the man's arrogance, the right of entitlement that informed every aspect of his character.

Lockhart noted the rainbow of glass bottles littering the bedside table. The assortment explained the sickly sweet smell that wafted through the air on occasion.

"Sedated with laudanum?" Lockhart turned to face his pompous cousin whose upturned nose saved him from having to thrust his chin in the air when affronted.

"Yes, with laudanum." The fop slunk from the shadows. He dried his hands on a towel and rolled down the sleeves of his shirt. "I administer a dose every four to six hours depending on the pain."

He administered the dose?

"You sleep here?"

Justin Perigrew would slice off an ear to inherit a healthy portion of his uncle's wealth. How else would he afford his Parisian rouge and gentlemen's corsets?

Justin gathered his green brocade coat from the chair and shrugged into it as if it were chainmail and he was preparing for battle. "Someone had to take care of things in your absence." He brushed his hand through his mop of blonde hair. "Someone had to take responsibility while you were away at your leisure."

"Terence is capable of dealing with all family matters." Lockhart felt Claudia's light touch on his back. The simple gesture banished the sense of isolation he experienced when in the presence of family.

Justin's snort of contempt mocked Lockhart's opinion. "Terence objects to me being here, but his after-dark pursuits keep him busy. We should be grateful he finds the time to collect the medicine." His arrogant gaze swept over Claudia as if she were a street hawker selling inferior wares. "Selina, on the other hand, knows what it means to support one's family during trying times."

Anger rose from the fiery pit of Lockhart's stomach.

He'd spent years dreaming of putting this dandy on his arse. Respect for his fake wife prevented him from acting like a bare-knuckle brawler now. One derogatory word said to Miss Darling, and he would not have the strength to control himself.

"Let us step closer to the bed," Claudia said in a hushed voice, "so we may examine your father's symptoms."

"He's dying," Justin snapped. "What is there to examine?"

Claudia arched a brow. "We will be the judge of that, Mr Perigrew."

Justin sucked in his cheeks as he tugged at the black velvet cuffs on his coat. "Then I would hurry. Selina will be here shortly. It might prove awkward having the woman you love in the same room as your wife."

Lockhart ground his teeth. He was about to curse his cousin to the devil when Miss Darling spoke.

"The woman he once courted, Mr Perigrew," Claudia corrected. "A man cannot presume to know another man's thoughts or feelings. Only an arrogant fool might claim otherwise."

Miss Darling turned on her heel and moved to examine the bottles on the bedside table.

Lockhart glared at his snout-nosed cousin. "Do not dare try to undermine my relationship with my wife," he said in a tone dark enough to frighten the devil. "She has the intelligence to see through your pathetic games. I'll not warn you again." Lockhart sneered. "You should wear padded breeches, cousin. I hear they're all the rage in France and will cushion the blow when I drive my fist down your throat and send you flying."

Justin sucked in a breath. It took him a moment to form a reply. "You won't change his mind," he whispered. "Alfred is a man of principle. A man who rewards those who prove themselves worthy, not those who disregard the laws of the land."

Lockhart froze.

His heart thumped against his ribcage though he held his menacing expression. Had Terence or Selina spoken of that night at the inn? Was that why Terence was so adamant Lockhart should leave town? Did he fear what Justin might do? Or had Justin been there on the night of the murder?

"Going on a jaunt across the ocean is hardly considered criminal," Lockhart countered. "But you can calm your greedy little heart. I'm not here for my father's money. I'm here to right the wrongs of the past. So tread carefully lest you get caught in the crossfire."

Justin's bottom lip quivered. He smiled to mask the obvious sign of his anxiety. "Then I shall heed your advice. I imagine the battle will commence as soon as Selina arrives. Protecting your father has become somewhat of a hobby."

With that, the fop snatched his riding crop from the chair and marched from the room.

Lockhart considered grabbing the crop from his hand and whipping him until he'd drawn blood.

"There are an awful lot of bottles here considering your father is taking laudanum to numb the pain and help him sleep." Claudia's voice reached across the room to pull him out of his murderous mood.

Lockhart dragged himself away from the closed door and came to join the lady who was doing a remarkable job of playing his wife. "Perhaps they don't know what ails him and are trying different remedies."

"Pray, who is his doctor? How long has he been suffering like this, and what is the prognosis?"

Guilt took him in a stranglehold this time as he had been too preoccupied with this own problems to consider anything else. "I doubt they would tell me if I asked."

"Perhaps we should wait and ask Selina." Claudia took hold of his father's wrist, examining his pulse before lifting his lids and peering at his pupils.

"Must we?" The lack of clean air in the room made it hard to breathe. Sickness seeped from the walls. The oppressive tension in the house invaded one's spirits, and he was in danger of being overwhelmed by a sudden sense of despair.

"We need to ask a few questions." Claudia frowned as she studied him. "It must be hard when people attack you from every quarter."

A man did not admit to such weaknesses. Not in front of a woman he wanted to impress. "I have a hardy constitution. It will take more than vicious words and veiled insults to bring me down."

Claudia's smile spoke of compassion. "Still, I feel compelled to offer comfort."

"Then I lied. Their comments cut me to the bone." He put his hand to his heart as if mortally wounded. "I need the love of a good woman, my darling, and you're the only one I know."

She tutted. "While I'm here to indulge you to a point, Hudson, you keep moving the boundaries."

"There are no boundaries between a husband and wife."

Claudia rolled her eyes. No doubt she was about to remind him they were merely playing roles, but the creak of a floorboard drew her attention to the door.

Selina swept into the room. Her dark eyes narrowed in disapproval. "Simmonds said you were here." She moved to the chair, tugged off her gloves and dropped them onto the seat.

She had changed since the night he'd left her at the docks in Portsmouth. It was as if someone had blown out the light inside. The worry lines on her brow were a permanent feature. Was Terence not the doting husband she'd hoped? She had only herself to blame. Had she cast aside her doubts and joined him on his voyage things would be different. But then he would not be here now, with Miss Darling playing his loving wife. And that thought affected him more than he could say.

"We waited to see you," Claudia said as she examined the handwritten label on one blue bottle. "This is a homemade cough suppressant, yet the label reveals nothing of its ingredients."

Selina shrugged out of her burgundy pelisse and draped it over the chair. "Terence purchases any medicine we need from a place in New Bond Street."

"What exactly is wrong with my father?" Lockhart demanded. "Justin was somewhat vague."

Selina tugged at the ribbon on her bonnet and removed the hat with care. "He started vomiting, lost his appetite and struggled to find the energy to move from his bed. At night, he often wakes in pain. Terence thinks it's better to give him laudanum, as does Justin."

"But you don't agree," he said.

"If it were my choice, I would hire every available doctor to determine the cause of these ailments."

"How long has he been suffering?" Claudia asked, picking up an odd-looking green bottle and sniffing the contents.

Selina stared down her nose at Claudia. "He's been confused and forgetful for a few years, but things took a downward turn about a month ago." Selina looked at Lockhart. "Around the time your friend Lord Greystone returned to town."

Lockhart frowned. Should he be suspicious of the coincidence, or more disturbed by the fact Selina had been monitoring Lord Greystone's movements? Did she know of the house he'd leased in Russell Square?

"So you and Justin share the responsibility?" he sought to confirm.

"Yes, and occasionally Terence takes his turn when he's not busy elsewhere." There was a bitterness to her tone whenever she mentioned his brother.

"Why not hire a nurse?" Claudia said.

Selina snorted. "Because it's an unnecessary household expense."

Meaning his mother refused to have a stranger in the house or part with precious funds. Of course, all those people involved had an ulterior motive for wanting time alone with Alfred Lockhart.

Perhaps the next step while waiting for the villain to make his move was to investigate Terence's nightly habits.

Who supplied the medicine?

Why had his brother shunned his responsibilities?

Indeed, they had learnt enough for now, and the need to be away from this house proved overwhelming.

"We should leave you to your duties," he said, placing his hand lightly on Miss Darling's back. "We shall return with a doctor tomorrow."

He observed Selina to judge her reaction. She inclined her head, but her expression remained sombre. "As you wish. Noon is best. Justin has an appointment with his tailor, and I shall be here alone."

Was that a veiled warning about Justin?

Was that her way of offering the proverbial olive branch?

He gave a curt nod and guided Claudia towards the door.

Selina waited until they'd left the room before calling him back. "Hudson?"

Lockhart returned and lingered in the doorway. "Yes?"

A weary sigh left Selina's lips. "I—I made a mistake that night on the docks. I should have gone with you to India."

The words should have brought a sense of satisfaction, but they did not. "It's too late for regrets, Selina."

She took a step towards him, hope flashing in her sad eyes. "Perhaps there's still time to salvage something from this mess." She lowered her voice to a whisper. "Perhaps there's still time for us."

A fool would know what she meant.

Lockhart glanced back over his shoulder to see Miss Darling's sweet smile as she waited patiently on the landing. The muscles deep in his core ached to have her. The muscle that was his heart pumped wildly in her presence, too. Even though this was all a game, he could not hurt her to satisfy his own needs for revenge.

He would not make a fool out of his wife even if he was paying for the privilege.

"Forgive me," he said, "but I'm in love with my wife." A part of him almost believed it was true. "My loyalty will always be with her."

And with that, he retreated and closed the door.

CHAPTER TWELVE

H ouses and shopfronts whipped past the carriage window. Costermongers crowded the pavements, selling their wares. The cries of irate coachmen, the constant clatter of horses' hooves, shouts and jeers filled Claudia's head, and yet Selina Lockhart's parting words echoed through the din. It was rude of her to listen, to eavesdrop. But one could not mistake the desperate longing in the woman's voice.

"Selina still loves you." Claudia swallowed past the lump in her throat. "That much is evident."

As the hired help, what right had she to feel jealous?

What right had she to pester him for his opinion?

Hudson drew his attention away from the window though he looked equally lost in thought. "Selina thinks she loves me, but she's mistaken."

"How do you know?" Oh, she sounded so desperate for an answer, so desperate for confirmation this brazen woman meant nothing to him.

Hudson brushed his hand through his dark hair and sat forward. "May I ask you a question?"

"Of course. You may ask me anything. You know that."

He inclined his head respectfully. "Love or reputation? Given a choice, which one would you choose?"

Which one? She did not need to ponder the question. Love. Love was the greatest gift of all. Reputation was a weak and flimsy label based on nothing more than other people's opinions. Hypocrites who enforced rules and secretly broke them.

"Love," she said earnestly. "I would choose love over anything."

"Over money?"

Pangs of guilt and shame hit her in the chest. The question brought to mind her rash bargain with Mr Thorncroft. The impulsive decision stemmed from fear, fear of what might become of Emily should they have no option but to sell Falaura Glen. How would her sister cope in new surroundings? In that respect had Claudia's actions not stemmed from love?

"I choose love," she reiterated.

Hudson flopped back in the seat. "There you have it. If Selina loved me, she would have boarded the ship to India. I have no doubt you would have seized the opportunity."

Claudia was beginning to believe she might do anything for this man. Such was the nature of this strange connection. Still, as much as she disliked Selina, she had to play devil's advocate.

"Perhaps you're letting your emotions cloud your judgement."

His answer came in the form of a mocking snort.

"What if Selina's only thoughts were of saving you?" she continued. "If she'd boarded that ship, you would have been the talk of the *ton*. What if she married your brother to divert attention away from you leaving?"

A heavy silence descended.

Hudson Lockhart narrowed his gaze as he studied her with an intensity that heated her blood. Whatever he saw caused his eyes to flare with awe and wonder, caused his mouth to curl at the corners in a sensual grin.

"Do you know something?" he eventually said, his attentive stare leaving her breathless.

"What?"

"You, my darling, are a sparkling gem amongst a pile of dull pebbles."

Claudia gulped. Never had anyone paid her such a compliment.

"You, my darling, have such a pure and honest heart you would speak the truth even if it meant backing a potential rival."

"Honesty is the foundation for any lasting relationship." Her father had taught her that. Still, she'd not been honest about her reasons for wanting Mr Lockhart's money. "And we're in a private carriage. You don't need to use the endearment for fear of making a *faux pas*."

"No, I don't." The words slipped slowly from confident lips.

Silence descended once more.

This time the air sizzled with a vibrant energy that brought thoughts of his lustful kiss flooding back. To distract her mind, she glanced out of the window just as they stopped at the turnpike heading out of town.

"Where are we going? Certainly not Russell Square."

Hudson Lockhart smiled in the devilish way that sent her heart fluttering. "I wondered when you would notice."

She had heard him give muffled instructions to his coachman but had paid it no heed.

"Tell me, Miss Darling. If I could grant you one wish, what would it be?"

One wish? One wish was not enough.

Various thoughts and images filled her head.

You could kiss me.

You could kiss me so deeply I might never feel alone again.

"Well?" he continued. "What could I do to show my appreciation for your loyalty and abiding friendship?"

You could beg me to stay with you for more than one week.

He didn't wait for her reply. "I'm taking you home, back to Falaura Glen."

"Home?" To Falaura Glen? Claudia should have been elated —she longed to see Emily. But panic sent her pulse racing. "You don't need me to play your wife anymore?" A sharp pain in her throat made it hard to swallow.

He appeared confused. "Of course I need you. I cannot do this alone, not without you. No, I promised you could visit. I know it's a little earlier than expected but—"

Unable to contain the surge of emotion, she darted across the carriage and flung her arms around his neck. She kissed him once on the lips—a chaste kiss of appreciation, of gratitude that their time together had not come to an end.

"Thank you." Claudia wasn't sure why she was thanking him. Yes, she was desperate to see Emily, just as desperate to remain at his side.

Lord, when had things become so complicated?

Hudson brushed his hand gently across her cheek. "Hell, if I'd known you'd be this appreciative I would have brought you home sooner."

Claudia kissed him again, three quick kisses on the lips. She was tired of battling her addiction. With the fourth kiss, she grew bolder. The need to taste him overruled logic and rationale. Indeed, like a slave to her will, he allowed her to take charge. He simply followed her lead—let her coax his lips apart, let her explore his mouth and drink as deeply as she needed to ease the bone-numbing fear inside.

"I trust you're using me to practise your performance," he said when she broke contact to catch her breath. "That kiss spoke of lust, Miss Darling, not gratitude, and certainly not love. If you're confused, perhaps you might permit me to demonstrate the latter."

Oh, how he loved to tease her.

"One cannot deny you need the practice." Claudia could no

longer stop her need to kiss him than she could stop the changing tides. "Show me. Show me what the kiss of love is like for you, Mr Lockhart."

"Certainly." He shuffled around to face her fully. His gaze softened as he looked admiringly at her hair and nose and mouth before staring deeply into her eyes.

The gold flecks circling his pupils gleamed. With every passing hour, he grew more familiar. She could draw his face from memory, recall every line, every detail.

"Don't be impatient," he said when she moistened her lips and sighed.

He cupped her cheeks as if she were as fragile as a porcelain doll. With the pads of his thumbs, he caressed her cheekbones in gentle strokes. Drawing her towards him, he closed his eyes. His hot breath breezed across her lips as he hovered but a centimetre away.

Her heart hammered against her ribcage as she waited for that first magical touch.

When it came, the power of it hit her deep in her core. The essence of the man she'd grown so fond of seemed to penetrate the fine skin, flooding her body with a vibrant glow. That one long, lingering kiss held her captive.

Hudson broke contact but remained just a few inches away. "If I loved you," he whispered, "I would tell you now."

Claudia struggled to catch her breath. Humour was the only way she might save herself from blushing, from drowning beneath these giddy emotions.

"And if I loved you, I would climb on your lap and ravage you senseless."

His hands slipped from her cheeks as he sat back and laughed. "So you agree that love and lust work well together."

"I admit the lines may become blurred sometimes." She missed the warmth of his tender touch, missed the wicked way his tongue thrust into her mouth. "Equally, I lack the experience to make an informed argument."

His sweeping gaze caressed her body. "Oh, I don't know. When it comes to conveying lust you do a remarkable job."

It was easy to lust after a man like Hudson Lockhart.

It would be easy to love the lost boy, too, easy to love the enigmatic rogue who dazzled her with his witty quips and considerate gestures.

Claudia glanced at the diamond and amethyst ring gracing the finger of her left hand. It felt comfortable having it there. It felt right.

"The style suits you," he said. "You can keep it when this is all over." He gave a mirthless chuckle. "A token to remember one wild week in London."

A sudden bout of nausea almost rendered her speechless. She found the courage to look at him, tried to determine whether it was the actor who spoke, her employer or the man who stared at her as if he might devour her whole.

"It has certainly been an adventure." Claudia smiled as she moved to sit in the seat opposite. Heavens, she could play the lead in any Covent Garden show with such a convincing performance.

"Indeed, it has."

After a minute spent feigning interest in barren autumn fields, she said, "No doubt you'll miss your large bed in Russell Square tonight." In the cottage, he slept in one of two twin beds in the same room as Monsieur Dariell. "I trust you're remaining at Falaura Glen and not returning to town."

He seemed puzzled by the comment. "I'll stay in the cottage if you've no objection."

"Why would I object?" After all, he had paid rent for another month.

Despite shrugging, a mischievous glint flashed in his eyes. "Maybe you've grown accustomed to having a half-naked man in your bed."

"Half-naked?" She snorted. "You had cast off your shirt as soon as I closed my eyes."

A guilty smile played on his lips. "All this talk of beds and nakedness might give a man amorous ideas. Perhaps we should use the next two hours wisely and both take a nap. I hardly slept a wink last night and imagine the same might be true tonight."

"What reason might you have for not sleeping tonight?"

"I can think of a few." Without warning, he stretched out his legs and propped his feet up on the seat beside her, and then he closed his eyes.

Claudia watched him for a time, drawn by his handsome countenance, by the peace and serenity surrounding him when he wasn't preoccupied with plotting revenge and playing the doting husband.

Naturally, her thoughts turned to Emily.

She had every faith in her sister's strength and determination. But what if she'd suffered a terrible accident? What if she'd sustained an injury that kept her in bed, that brought all the old fears and insecurities flooding back?

"Stop fretting, Miss Darling, and close your eyes," Hudson said without moving a muscle.

How was it that he could read her so easily and yet he remained a closed book?

Sleep was the only way to calm the chaotic chatter filling her mind, and so she closed her eyes and silently prayed, prayed all was well at Falaura Glen.

It was dusk by the time Lockhart woke and the carriage rattled through the wrought-iron gates and up the gravel drive towards Falaura Glen. He recalled the first time Dariell had mentioned the manor's name, suggesting it might be a perfect place to hide, to lie low. It had sounded rather whimsical to his ears, a place where fairies congregated to learn magic spells and share centuries-old secrets.

Lockhart stole a glance at Claudia Darling sleeping soundly in the seat opposite.

The manor might not be a home for fairies, but there was something magical about its occupant. The lady had a charm that held him captive. *Fascinated* did not begin to describe his feelings. *Beguiled* and *bewitched*, maybe.

Hell, he hoped Dariell had kept his word and taken care of Emily Darling. One small accident would prevent Claudia from returning to town, would ruin Lockhart's plans. It was selfish. But the thought of facing his family without his enchanting temptress at his side proved too painful to bear.

Deciding not to cloud his mind with problems beyond his control, he sat forward and placed his hand on Claudia's knee. She did not flinch at his touch. Indeed, had he been a true rake and rogue he would have ventured a little higher, high enough to caress her soft thigh, high enough to stroke the sweet spot until she begged for more.

"Miss Darling." He shook her gently lest he succumb to his darkest desires. "Claudia, wake up. We've arrived at Falaura Glen. We're home."

The lady's lids fluttered open. It took her a moment to gather her bearings. "Home? Already? But I've only been asleep for five minutes." She straightened, brushed her skirts and patted the sides of her hair.

Lockhart smiled. "You've slept for two hours."

She nibbled her bottom lip, her eyes filled with apprehension. "Did I moan and mumble?"

"Delightfully so," he lied.

A blush touched her cheeks. With a frustrated sigh, she leant forward and peered at the passing trees. "Are you coming up to the house? I thought you'd be eager to see Monsieur Dariell and inform him what you've learnt so far."

And what would Lockhart tell his friend? That his family cared so little, they wanted rid of him for good? That the mystic's wisdom proved accurate and Miss Darling was everything a man might hope for in a wife? That he struggled to see the line separating fantasy from reality?

"Does your sister not take supper at six? One would assume she'd dine with Dariell in your absence."

"At six? Yes, of course." She shook her head. "For some reason, it feels as though I've been away for years."

Lockhart arched a brow. "Is my company so tedious?"

"On the contrary. You're a pleasant companion."

"Pleasant?" he scoffed. "You make me sound like an elderly aunt, one who comes to read to you and assist with needlework. One capable of recalling the ridiculous Latin names of every plant and shrub."

Claudia chuckled. "You're a charming companion," she corrected.

"Madam, unless you wish to insult my masculinity, you must do better than that."

"Very well." She laughed again but then forced a serious expression. "You're a hot-blooded and wickedly sinful companion who holds me enslaved with your expert mouth and impassioned conversation."

He cast an arrogant grin as the carriage rumbled to a halt. "Now that sounds more like me. Perhaps when we return to town, I might show you how hot-blooded and wickedly sinful I am."

The lady's blue eyes sparkled to life. "You mean to wait until then?" she said in such a seductive lilt he had to fight the urge to bend her over the seat, lift her skirts and drive home.

Desire and pure carnal lust thrummed in the air.

They stared at each other, both challenging the other to make the first move. She wanted him. It had nothing to do with the teasing words of an actress. He had tasted the truth. And by God, if he didn't have her, he might go insane.

The rattle of the handle drew him from his musings. The footman yanked open the carriage door and lowered the steps. The housekeeper came galloping down to greet them, almost tripping in her excitement.

"Oh, ma'am, you've come home."

Claudia's sensual smile turned to one of panic as she tore her gaze from him and focused on the woman clutching her hands to her chest.

"Is anything the matter, Mrs Bitton?" Grasping the footman's fingers, Claudia practically jumped from the carriage. "Is it Emily? Has something dreadful happened?"

Lockhart vaulted to the ground and came to stand at Claudia's side. He moved to place his hand at the small of her back but hesitated. They were not in London now, and she was not his wife.

"Why, nothing's the matter, ma'am." Mrs Bitton smiled. "I'm just pleased to see you home safely, that's all." She glanced at him and curtsied. "Sir."

He expected a scowl of disapproval but received an almost grateful grin. Did Mrs Bitton want him to ravage her mistress? Did she hope an honest proposal might be forthcoming?

Claudia's shoulders sagged as she breathed a relieved sigh. "And Emily is well? Have there have been any *visitors*?" The lady shivered upon asking the last question.

For a moment, Mrs Bitton looked puzzled. Recognition finally dawned, and the housekeeper's eyes grew wide and a little fearful. "No visitors, ma'am." The housekeeper's relieved sigh roused his suspicion. Somewhere he had missed a vital clue when it came to understanding these odd facial exchanges. "And let's hope for all our sakes it stays that way."

"Indeed." Claudia cast Lockhart a nervous smile before returning her attention to Mrs Bitton. "Is Emily taking supper in the dining room?" she said, quickly mounting the steps upon hearing the rumble of thunder.

The black clouds in the distance were thick with the promise of rain. The storm would be upon them within the hour unless the wind changed course.

"Oh, I best warn Miss Emily." Mrs Bitton glanced up at the dark sky. "I doubt she's expecting rain."

"Don't tell me she's left the windows open again."

"No, ma'am. She's taken her supper outside this evening."

Pretty wrinkles formed on Claudia's brow. "Outside? In November?" Panic took command of her voice. "What if she catches her death of cold? You know how susceptible she is to catching chills and fevers."

Mrs Bitton wrung her hands and shuffled on the spot. "They've built a shelter in the garden, ma'am. I'm sure it will keep the cold out."

"They?"

The housekeeper's bottom lip quivered. "Mr D-Dariell and Miss Emily are having a picnic."

"A picnic? In November? A picnic in a shelter?"

Lockhart suppressed a grin. He had to admit it sounded rather romantic. "Come, let us find this foolish pair and give them a piece of our minds."

Claudia raised her brows. "You said I could trust him to take care of her."

"And I'm sure he is doing a remarkable job." Lockhart fought the urge to mutter a curse. If Dariell had ruined any chance of Claudia returning to London, he would string his friend up by the ballocks. "Come. I presume they're in the garden."

"Yes, sir. They've made a tent inside the stone rotunda."

"A tent?" Claudia threw her hands in the air. After numerous huffs and puffs, she grabbed hold of Lockhart's arm as if he were a naughty boy about to receive his punishment. "You may return to your duties, Mrs Bitton, we will deal with this debacle."

And with that, Miss Darling marched him through the house, out through the terrace doors and along the narrow path lined with trimmed topiary. The light spilling from the house covered the garden in a faint golden glow to illuminate their way. It was a perfect setting if one were intent on seduction.

"I blame myself, of course," she muttered as she dragged him along. "Heaven knows, that scandalous nightgown should have been a clue. And he's friends with you, a man whose wicked tongue can render a woman helpless."

The compliment roused a sense of masculine pride. "My tongue renders you helpless, Miss Darling?"

She pulled him left as the path widened. "Helpless to the point I forget my own name. It's not healthy to be so consumed with passion that you lose the use of your faculties."

Lockhart cleared his throat. "There is nothing more healthy or invigorating than losing one's head to lust."

"Lust?" Claudia whispered through gritted teeth. "There you go again with—" She skidded to an abrupt halt and gaped open-mouthed at the Grecian-inspired rotunda at the end of the path. "Heaven above."

Lockhart drank in the sight of the magical scene. *Heaven* did describe the enchanting setting designed by Dariell to impress a woman who would never see its magnificent beauty.

Reams of white sheets hung in the spaces between the pillars, the material flapping and billowing in the breeze. Ivy trailed around each of the stone columns, ivy threaded with red November roses. Miss Emily lay stretched on a chaise in the middle of the rotunda, huddled beneath a mound of furs. Amber flames flickered in the copper brazier burning near the entrance. Supper was but an arm's reach away laid out on a trestle table. And Dariell sat on a rug piled with a rainbow of vibrant cushions reading to his transfixed companion.

The scene roused a feeling of inadequacy. Dariell certainly knew how to seduce a woman.

With her chin still touching her chest, Claudia stepped forward.

Like a deer sensing a distant sound, Emily looked up. Dariell glanced back over his shoulder and came to his feet upon noticing their approach. He said something to Emily, and the lady smiled in response.

"Oh, Hudson, I have never seen Emily look so happy," Claudia whispered as they neared the rotunda.

"No," Lockhart mused, noting the radiance in his friend's eyes, too. "I've never seen Dariell look so pleased with himself, either."

CHAPTER THIRTEEN

"I s everything all right?" Emily said as Dariell helped her to her feet and draped a fur stole around her shoulders. "We didn't expect you back so soon."

"Everything is fine." Well, except for the fact Claudia couldn't stop lusting after her new friend and employer. She took hold of Emily's hand and gave it a squeeze of reassurance. "We needed to take the country air to clear our minds. Isn't that right, Mr Lockhart?"

The sinful-looking gentleman at her side nodded. "Town can be stifling."

Dariell eyed them suspiciously before saying, "And your trip, it was successful? Everyone believes you are married?"

Hudson's arrogant grin stretched from ear to ear. "Our acting abilities would put any skilled thespian to shame." He glanced at Claudia. His brown eyes held the same look of restless longing she'd witnessed earlier in the carriage. "Except, of course, we hope our story will not meet a tragic end."

"No," Dariell mused. "I think it will be far from a tragedy."

"What do you think of our picnic?" Emily gestured to the

beautiful scene that looked like a home for Titania, queen of the fairies. "Isn't it splendid?"

Claudia considered casting Dariell a look of reproach but found she couldn't be angry with him, not when his ridiculous idea had brought Emily such joy. Perhaps it wasn't a ridiculous idea after all. Perhaps it was rather romantic. The Frenchman had clearly gone to an awful lot of trouble.

"Monsieur Dariell's efforts have produced excellent results," Claudia said by way of praise.

The Frenchman slapped his hand over his heart. "I'm afraid I cannot take all the credit, madame."

"No," Emily interjected, struggling to contain her excitement. "I'm responsible for decorating the pillars with ivy and roses."

"Then you've done a remarkable job." Guilt gnawed away at Claudia's insides. Was she just like their father when it came to doubting Emily's abilities?

Did nothing faze Monsieur Dariell? No doubt he'd have Emily climbing mountains, swimming in streams, dancing around the maypole and riding bareback across open country.

"There is food aplenty," Dariell said. "Join us."

Hudson cast Claudia a sidelong glance. "I am rather hungry after the journey. And we should make the most of being outdoors before the storm breaks."

Conflicting emotions made it difficult to make a decision. Things felt different at Falaura Glen. Emily had survived for two whole days without falling foul to her affliction. No, she hadn't just survived. Under Dariell's expert tutorage, she had thrived. And while Emily had found her inner spark, being home reminded Claudia that the warm feeling filling her chest was an illusion. Part of a complicated charade.

She was about to suggest they all return to the house when Hudson placed his hand on her back. "We must eat. We have a long drive to town tomorrow, and there's much to do."

Finding the strength to give him a half smile, she said, "Of course."

He led her past the brazier and into the rotunda tent. If not Titania's home it might be that of an exotic prince, a haven on his long trek through the desert. Taking a seat next to Emily on the chaise, Claudia watched Hudson Lockhart plate a selection of cured meats and plum chutney, a chunk of cheese and fresh bread.

He offered Claudia the plate after insisting on playing host, and then bent his head and whispered, "You seem different now you're home."

"Different?" *Fearful* would be the appropriate word. In such a short space of time, she had lost sight of her identity. Yes, she was the unmarried mistress of Falaura Glen, and yet somewhere deep inside she longed to be the wife of Hudson Lockhart. "Being home just makes me realise we're from different worlds."

Emily cleared her throat and came to her feet. "Excuse me while I assist Monsieur Dariell." Emily navigated her way around the chaise. Dariell reached out to her and Emily's hand slipped into his as easily as if she were blessed with sight. Without a word, Dariell drew her towards the brazier.

"We're not from different worlds," Hudson protested once Emily was out of earshot. "I despise pomp and ceremony and have always craved a simple existence."

Claudia glanced back at the house. "There is nothing simple about running a home when one is short of funds." Equally, she had come to realise there was something more than money missing from her life. Her fake marriage to Mr Lockhart had given her a glimpse of the intimacy a man and woman might share.

"Am I not helping you to rectify that problem?"

"Helping me? Am I not the one supporting you?" The sudden urge to argue came upon her like an errant devil. "Have I not embraced my role in order to help you settle your grievances?"

"You have gone over and above what is expected."

His compliment roused her ire for no reason at all. What was she hoping to prove by challenging him? That he cared? That he was struggling to separate fantasy from reality, too?

"This agreement is to our mutual benefit," he continued, confusion evident in his tone. "You said so yourself." Frown lines appeared on his brow. "What is this really about?"

A host of reasons flooded her mind. It was about the fact he could kiss her so rampantly, forget it so easily. It was about him telling her she could keep her wedding ring once he'd severed their connection. It was about the desperate yearning, the desperate ache for him that could not be tempered. Indeed, she was ready to pick up every damnable excuse to be angry and hurl them at him in the hope of seeing a flicker of pain.

But in a dusty corner of her mind reserved for logic, she knew this bout of anger was uncalled for and wholly undeserved.

"It's been an eventful few days," she said to excuse her erratic behaviour. "I think I might retire early."

"Without supper?" He glanced at the plate resting on her lap. "You've not eaten since this morning."

His concern touched her to the point she wanted to cry.

For all the saints! If she couldn't control these raging emotions, she'd be fit for Bedlam. Indeed, she might welcome being shackled in a dank cell if it brought an end to her torment.

"I shall take my supper upstairs." She forced a smile. "Will you be all right sleeping in the cottage tonight?"

Will you be all right sleeping alone, alone without me?

His grim mouth twitched, and she was relieved to see a flash of amusement in his bewitching brown eyes. "I've slept there for a month. One more night won't hurt."

He held her gaze for so long she might have kissed him had they been married.

"What time will we leave tomorrow?"

"I know you spoke about venturing to the village, but I need to return in the morning if I'm to hire the services of a doctor. Selina advised we visit at noon, but I'm reluctant to trust the motive behind her suggestion."

Talking about his problems in town was akin to downing a potent elixir, one that invigorated her spirits and chased away all painful thoughts. "I can take a trip into Flamstead the next time we return." Perhaps it might be then that they parted ways, parted ways for good. "Hiring a doctor must be a priority." And yet he had brought her home knowing that, too.

With a curt nod, he said, "Can you be ready to leave at seven?"

Claudia glanced at Emily. The sweet sound of laughter breezed from her sister's lips. She was warming her hands on the brazier while deep in conversation with Dariell. The urge to caution her sister not to venture too close lest she burn her fingers hung on the tip of her tongue.

"As long as Emily is comfortable with me leaving again, I shall be ready at seven."

An awkward silence ensued.

"We do have a bargain," he reminded her with some reluctance, "but I respect your need to ensure all is well at home." Hudson glanced briefly back over his shoulder. "Your sister seems most content."

"I'm sure she is." Claudia took hold of her plate and stood. Although it had been her suggestion to retire, she found it hard to leave him. "I'll send word to the cottage later this evening. And have no fear, Emily seems to relish her independence."

Mr Lockhart inclined his head. "Then I shall bid you a good evening, Miss Darling. Might I suggest you caution your maid to tuck in the blankets? Lest you wake in a state of dishabille."

Claudia laughed a little. "One cannot help being restless in bed."

"How fortunate I happen to know of a cure."

"You do?"

"I do." The words fell in a seductive whisper.

Once again, thoughts of kissing him filled her head as his mesmerising gaze held her rigid in its spell.

A sudden clap of thunder startled her out of the trance, but Hudson Lockhart would not be swayed from delivering one more tempting invitation. "Should you need me, my darling, you know where to find me."

"In the cottage?" The thought of paying him a midnight visit heated her blood. What if this was the only time in her life she would feel lust, lust with a sugar-coating of love? Because whether she wanted to believe it or not, she couldn't help but love him a little.

"No, you won't find me in the cottage." Hudson looked out at the black, billowing clouds swamping the moon. "You'll find me in the rain."

🐚

Rain hammered on the windows and pattered on the thatched roof of the small gatekeeper's cottage. The constant ping of droplets hitting the metal bucket kept Lockhart awake.

Not that he had any intention of sleeping.

As soon as he was assured Dariell had drifted into a peaceful slumber he would venture outdoors, hoping the mistress of the manor had taken to dawdling in the storm.

Perhaps it was wrong of him to throw temptation Miss Darling's way. Indeed, he was not in the habit of seducing virgins. But he could no more stop his desire to have her than he could stop the rain falling. Despite his desperate longing, he could not venture up to the house. If Miss Darling wanted him as much as he hoped, then he prayed she'd find the courage to seek him out.

Deciding he should linger beneath the cottage's front porch—holding a lamp to signal his intention should the lady stray from the house—Lockhart peeled back the blankets and slipped out of bed. He tiptoed to the chair in the far corner of the room, grabbed his shirt and dragged it over his head before throwing on his breeches.

Having left his boots near the front door so as not to wake Dariell, Lockhart was about to pad stealthily from the room when the Frenchman's voice penetrated the darkness.

"Is it not a little late for a stroll outdoors?"

Damnation. Could Dariell not mind his own business?

"It's never too late to take in the fresh air."

"Will you not catch a chill being out in the rain?" Dariell said, sounding highly amused.

"I'm used to the harsh elements." He'd brave a typhoon for a chance to kiss Claudia Darling again.

"And what of Miss Darling? The lady does not share your hardy constitution."

Bloody hell! Was it the man's mission to pry?

"Then I would have to say you don't know her as well as I do."

"No, my friend, that is quickly becoming apparent."

"The lady knows her own mind."

"And *you* must follow your heart."

Lockhart wasn't entirely sure what he was doing, but he'd heard enough words of wisdom from Dariell to know he should act on impulse. Particularly when that impulse had taken full command of his mind and body.

"Don't wait up," Lockhart said as he crept from the room to ready himself for his late-night rendezvous. Assuming Miss Darling came, of course.

After thrusting his feet into his boots and lighting the candle lamp, he yanked open the cottage door.

Rain pelted his face. The wind threatened to extinguish the flame. Thunder rumbled in the distance. Lightning could strike a foot away, and it would not deter him from his course. The earthy smell of the night called to his primitive needs. The darkness fed his lustful cravings. And yet it was his heart that pounded hard, his heart that throbbed with passion.

Waiting heightened his anticipation.

He wasn't sure how long he stood beneath the stone porch, his gaze fixed on the long gravel drive leading up to the house. Thirty minutes? Forty? Maybe more. He'd stared through the gloom, his face wet, water dripping from his hair as the rain battered his meagre shelter.

Disappointment flared.

He considered returning to the comfort of his bed when a flicker of light captured his attention. A yellow sphere hovered in the distance, swaying back and forth as it bobbed closer.

Stepping out onto the private road between the avenue of trees, Lockhart raised his lantern aloft—a sign he was also seeking something on this dismal night—and traipsed through the puddles to meet the advancing figure.

In a scene reminiscent of a gothic novel, the mistress of the manor approached, her cloak billowing and whipping about her legs, the lantern held high as if an evil presence had drawn her from the safety of the house to wreak havoc on her delicate sensibilities.

Miss Darling *was* in danger. In danger of being ravished by her husband. In danger of succumbing to the hunger flowing through her veins, too.

"There's nothing as refreshing as a walk in the rain," he said as they both came to an abrupt halt just a few feet apart. Rivulets ran down his face. His soaked shirt clung to his chest like a second skin. His sodden breeches were plastered to his thighs.

Claudia tugged down the hood of her cloak to reveal a flowing mane of golden tresses. She raised her face to the heavens, a broad smile of satisfaction sweeping over her pretty features.

"Someone once told me that they find the rain cleansing."

Water splashed off her cheeks and chin. The tip of her tongue traced the line of her luscious lips, lapping every drop of moisture.

Hell's fire. Had Lissette given her lessons in how to drive one's husband wild?

Lockhart brushed a dripping lock from his brow. "I fear I may have been mistaken."

"Mistaken?" She lowered her eyes and fixed her heated gaze upon him. Desire danced a teasing rhythm, holding him spellbound. "How so?"

Nothing could rid him of his wicked intentions. "No amount of rain can cleanse me of my sinful thoughts." His breathing grew fast and shallow. "No amount of rain can temper my raging blood."

He wanted her more than he'd wanted anything in his entire life.

"And yet the water seems to wash away my doubts." She blinked away the droplets clinging to her lashes.

"What doubts are those?" The husky tone of his voice should leave her in no doubt as to what he wanted. She'd found the courage to meet him. Would she find the courage to confess?

"Doubts about kissing you again." She swallowed. "Doubts about … about surrendering to these cravings that show no sign of waning."

The admission brought a shift in the air between them. The thunder groaned. A crack of lightning somewhere in the distance sparked a sudden sense of urgency.

Claudia gasped as her breath came quickly, too. "We should hurry indoors." Her gaze dropped to his shirt. "You need to get out of those wet clothes."

He had every intention of doing precisely that.

Lockhart placed his lantern on the ground and straightened. He held out his hand. The time for honesty was nigh, and yet he couldn't find the words to explain these foreign feelings swirling in his chest.

"Let me kiss you once, just once in the rain." Desire flamed his blood.

Claudia placed her lamp on the ground, a few feet from his. "What sort of kiss will it be, Hudson? A tender one to prove a point?" She stepped towards him and slipped her damp hand into his. "A wicked one to test my resolve?"

His heart hammered against his ribcage, harder than the rain battered the ground.

"Neither," he said, drawing her slowly into an embrace. "The only thing I can promise is that it won't be the kiss of actors on a stage."

She reached up on tiptoes, her eyes fluttering, her mouth achingly close. "Then kiss me, kiss me like you mean it. Kiss me for no other reason than because you want to."

Lockhart brushed away the wet tendrils of hair plastered to her cheeks and cupped her dainty face between his palms. He kept a tight rein on his desire, poured every honest thought and feeling for her into that first tender kiss.

One kiss was not enough to soothe the crippling ache within. One kiss soon became two, three. Each open-mouthed claiming spoke of his respect and admiration. With the first soft stroke of his tongue, he worshipped her strength and integrity. Claudia Darling touched him in a way no other woman had, ever could. He drank in her exotic taste—a unique blend of wanton innocence that proved highly addictive.

He kept a firm grip on his control, kept the rampant devil at bay, and made love to her mouth in the way he wanted to make love to her body. Slowly, and with long, deep thrusts of his tongue.

It wasn't the soft hum resonating in her throat that woke the devil. It was the two curious hands working their way up under his shirt, the two wandering hands creeping up to touch his bare skin.

A growl left his lips, the sound full of carnal longing.

He would take her here and now, against a tree, writhing on top of her on the muddy ground. Anywhere, as long as he drove home and buried himself to the hilt.

"Claudia, is this what you want?" A fleeting moment of logic forced him to drag his mouth from hers and ask. The flimsy thread of restraint would soon snap. "Do you want me? For I fear once we start we'll not stop."

She looked up at him through hazy eyes. "As an unmarried woman I should say no, but I cannot." Her hands drifted over his chest, grazing his nipples. "What if I never experience these feelings again?"

Hudson hissed a breath at her teasing touch. His swollen shaft throbbed in his breeches. "Then we need to get out of the rain."

"Where can we go?"

"Not the cottage," he said quickly before conversation dampened his ardour. "What about the house?"

"The house?" Her brief hesitation forced him to take matters into his own hands. Without warning, he scooped her up into his arms. She gasped, fidgeted a little but soon settled against his chest and twined her arms around his neck.

Leaving their lanterns on the ground, he strode up the drive and skirted left towards the stables.

"Where are we going?"

"We raised our glasses in salutation. A toast to our love of frolicking in forbidden places. There is nothing as daring as making love in a hay barn."

She pulled back slightly. "You've done it before?"

"No, but where you're concerned I am plagued with a vivid imagination."

The answer seemed to please her. Indeed, while one hand

cupped his neck, the other moved in caressing strokes over the muscles in his arms and shoulder.

"Making love sounds so much better than making lust."

He smiled as he marched across the courtyard, carrying his temptress. "Trust me there will be equal amounts of both."

CHAPTER FOURTEEN

"Perhaps we should wait until we return to London to further our acquaintance." Lockhart braced his hands on his hips and stared at the mound of hay in the stall at the far end of the small barn. His concern over their crude surroundings seemed to have quelled his desire.

Claudia felt quite the opposite.

The air smelt damp from the rain. The aroma of dust and wood and earth always appealed to her. Besides, in London how was she to know the difference between genuine feelings and those feigned purely for deception?

"If you've changed your mind," she began, but he did not let her finish her sentence.

"I have not changed my mind." Bewitching brown eyes travelled the length of her body. No, from the heat in his gaze that much was clear. "But I'll not treat you like a randy milk-maid in need of a quick tupping."

A chuckle burst from her lips. "Lust must play a part. You said so yourself."

"It's damp in here." A frown marred his brow as he surveyed the scene. "You'll likely catch your death in those wet clothes."

She should be flattered he cared. "If your reservations stem from concern for me—"

"Of course they stem from concern for you." He dragged his hand through his wet hair. "Love, is my need for you not perfectly evident?"

The comment drew her gaze to the thick rod of his manhood pressing against his soaked breeches.

Oh, my!

"Claudia, I'll die if I don't have you, but your comfort must be a priority."

An idea popped into her head.

She wasted no time in acting. "Then come with me." She grabbed hold of his hand and pulled him along behind. "Quickly."

The rain continued to pelt their faces as they hurried from the hay barn and around the back of the house in the direction of the rotunda.

The white sheets acting as walls were wet through. Clumps of damp ash filled the brazier. But the creeping ivy and red roses hinted it might be the perfect place for an amorous liaison. Inside, the chaise and furs were dry. The rug and the array of plush cushions made the hideaway seem like an exotic harem. After all, was she not about to become Hudson Lockhart's concubine, his mistress?

The thought should have roused her doubts. But such indelicate descriptions failed to convey the true depth of their intimate relationship. Dariell often boasted that the truth of all things lay in the heart, not the head. In her heart, nothing about this felt wrong. Everything felt right.

"Let's stay here instead of the hay barn." Claudia glanced out into the night, noted the house was shrouded in darkness. "No one will venture out into the garden at this hour."

Determined to appease Hudson's need to ensure her comfort, she moved the rug behind the chaise, and with his help made a bed out of the furs and cushions.

"You can be rather determined when you put your mind to something." Hudson grinned as he appraised their makeshift bed.

Nothing would prevent this union. She wanted to love him. Wanted to feel loved in return. And if her plans to thwart Mr Thorncroft went awry, she would always know what it was to be with a man she desired.

"We've spent so long focusing on the task, I wonder if you still feel as amorous as you did ten minutes ago." Perhaps the need for practicality had dampened his desire.

Hudson snorted as he clasped hold of her wrist and pulled her into an embrace. "With you, I can rise to the occasion in seconds." He brushed a soft kiss across her lips. "My blood simmers constantly, just waiting for that glazed look, that coy smile that tells me you want me."

Claudia blinked. Her blood simmered, too, though she wasn't aware she made any notable expressions when dreaming of caressing his naked body.

"Make love to me, Hudson." The words left her lips in a seductive whisper.

Make love to me as if I were your wife.

In all likelihood, she would never marry. Indeed, she could not envisage having any other man as her husband. Anxiety about what would happen once the week was out threatened to ruin the moment.

Refusing to surrender to her fears, Claudia came up on tiptoes and kissed him in the brazen, open-mouthed way that sent shock-waves to the intimate place between her thighs. Desire thrummed in her veins. Snaking her hand up to cup his neck, she deepened the kiss, slipping her tongue in his mouth to tease, to taste, to tempt him to respond.

A husky groan in his throat signalled the shift from slow and sensuous to desperate and depraved. He tugged on the ribbons of her cloak, pushed the garment off her shoulders to pool on the floor.

"You're wet," she gasped against his mouth as he crushed her to his chest.

"Isn't that my line?"

The comment threatened to remind her they were actors playing roles until he clasped her cheeks and kissed her again—the illicit kiss of a man keen to drain every drop of pleasure from the experience.

"Take off your shirt," she breathed.

He wasted no time in agreeing to her demand. He dragged the linen over his head, unbuttoned his breeches and pushed them low on his hips. It was then that he took a moment to notice her dress.

"I've missed that ugly thing," he said, trailing his fingers across the high neckline of her brown striped bodice, down over the swell of her breasts.

Claudia sucked in a sharp breath. "I've nothing on beneath it. No chemise. No stays or petticoat." She had dressed in a hurry. Intuition told her to do away with restrictions tonight.

Hudson's tongue swept over his bottom lip. "You certainly know how to tease your husband."

"A wife must find ways to titillate if she wishes to hold her husband's attention."

"You've had my attention since that first night in the cottage when you brought supper and tripped over the step."

The embarrassing image came flooding back. "How fortunate you were there to offer a strong arm of support." The memory of those large hands on her waist had kept her awake most of the night.

"By now, you must know I would use any excuse to touch you." He captured her hand and placed her palm on his chest. "I would give anything to feel your gentle caress."

The invitation to explore proved too tempting to resist. She ached for something. Touching him brought temporary relief.

Claudia splayed her hands over the solid muscles. His bronzed skin was damp, cool from the rain, as soft as silk though it sheathed a body as hard as marble. Rippling muscles in his abdomen drew her gaze down to the trail of dark hair that always teased a reaction. She caressed the solid planes, felt the thump of his heartbeat. Her fingers itched to delve lower, and she could not resist stroking the downy line leading to the waistband of his breeches.

Hudson's breath hissed between his teeth.

"You're beautiful," she whispered, pressing a kiss to the skin growing hotter with each graze of her fingers. He smelt of the rain, of the spicy incense and woody notes of his cologne. She inhaled his unique scent, too, the one that marked him as a hot, virile man.

Without warning, his hand slid round to cup her neck and he drew her to his mouth. The kiss was deep and long and passionate. It seared her soul, branded her body, marked her as his.

Despite the biting cold outside, inside she burned. The need to undress, to press her flesh to his flesh, proved overwhelming. But she would savour every second of this time with him.

"Wait," she breathed when his kisses grew more rampant. She stepped back. "Remove my dress." The tiny buttons were already undone, the consequence of rushing, of not wanting to call for a maid. "And don't worry about the cold."

"Oh, I'm not worried." The hypnotic timbre of his voice made her shiver. "I know of a few ways to warm your blood."

Without further comment, he gathered the hem of her skirt and slithered it up to her waist. His hands stroked the curve of her hips as he raised the garment up over her head. After draping it over the chaise, he took a moment to stare, to drink in the sight of her naked body as he had done the day she slipped into the bathtub.

"I'll try to be gentle," he said, the heat in his eyes scorching her skin, "but the hunger in my veins makes me want to thrust deep, makes me want to devour and claim and ride you hard until you cry my name."

Good Lord!

Nerves threatened to weaken her resolve. But she would not retreat now.

"Then be gentle until I'm used to you, and then you may satisfy your needs however you choose." She pulled back the furs covering their makeshift bed, settled down on top of the cushions, held out her hand and gestured for him to follow.

Hudson loomed over her, appraising her bare breasts, his gaze softening when he stared at her stomach. He grabbed one boot, yanked his foot free and tossed it aside, repeating the motion with the other foot. Then he grasped the waistband of his breeches and pushed them down past his hips to reveal the solid length of his arousal.

Thick and swollen, his manhood looked twice as large as it had before.

With a confident grin playing on his lips, he knelt beside her. "Touch me. Touch me if you dare."

Heavens above!

Claudia recalled a time when she struggled to look him in the eye. But that was because she was scared to like him, scared her dreams would lead to a life of disappointment. Now, she held his gaze as she wrapped her fingers around his throbbing erection. His large hand clamped over hers and moved back and forth in a slow, teasing rhythm. When he released her, she continued to stroke him, continued to bring him pleasure.

A moan left his lips as his head fell back.

There was something powerful about holding him, about having him at her mercy. Thoughts of closing her mouth over the glistening tip filled her head. Indeed, Lissette had been bursting with ideas when Claudia had asked how a wife might please her husband. Lissette seemed to know an awful lot about the desires of men.

But before Claudia could give the matter any further thought, her pretend husband—soon-to-be lover—clasped his hand over hers.

"As much as I'd like to make love to you all night," he said, moving to ease her knees apart and kneel between her legs, "the cold weather forces me to hurry."

"Then hurry," she said, desperately trying to ignore the fact she was so exposed, "but you must talk to me, prepare me for what I'm to expect."

The wolf in him flashed his teeth as he gripped her thighs. "Oh, I'll prepare you, have no fear of that."

When he lowered his head between her legs, she had no idea what he was about to do. Her only thoughts were of embarrassment until his tongue stroked and licked and teased her flesh in a slow, intoxicating rhythm. A gasp caught in her throat. Words of protest threatened to burst from her mouth. She dug her fingers into the soft cushions acting as a mattress as the waves of pleasure washed away any doubts. The muscles in her core tightened as she floated towards some unknown abyss.

"That's it, love," he said, offering words of encouragement as she rocked her hips in need of more. He moaned against her sex, probed her entrance with his tongue.

She should tell him to stop. But in the distant realms of her mind, her voice lacked conviction.

"Don't stop, Hudson," she panted, a traitor to morality. "I need … I need …" She didn't know what she needed. But she knew it was magical, knew she came closer with each suck of his hot mouth.

"I know exactly what you need," he said as his fingers slipped inside her.

She came apart instantly. The muscles in her core clamped around him. Months of worry and anxiety melted away as her legs trembled with the power of these bone-shattering pulses.

Before she could catch her breath, Hudson climbed on top of

her. The heat from his body penetrated her skin, warmed her to the depths of her soul.

"Are you sure you want this?" he said, his tone rough, husky. Not once did he glance at her bare breasts but kept his heated gaze fixed on hers.

Claudia cupped his cheek. He was asking her to choose between one wild, wicked moment of bliss or the aching agony of loneliness. Once would not be enough—she knew that—but the memory would sustain her on cold winter nights.

"It's not too late to change your mind," he continued, although the passion in his voice belied his calm words. "We can lie here for a while, sleep if that's what you want."

"Hudson, I don't know what is happening here—even Dariell might struggle to make sense of it—but I know I want to forget about the world for a moment. Regardless of all else, I need to be with you."

It wasn't lust that drew a soft hum from his mouth. It wasn't lust that drew him to brush his lips slowly over hers, to close his eyes and taste every inch of her mouth. She knew the feel and the look of it by now. It wasn't lust she saw playing across his handsome features when he took hold of his solid manhood and pushed gently into her body.

The feel of him inside her robbed her mind of rational thought. "Hudson." The word rang with invitation. "Hudson."

"I know, love, I need you, too." He kissed her mouth, her cheek, along her jaw and neck as he withdrew and then pushed inside a little deeper. "It will hurt, but only for a moment."

She held on to the bulging muscles in his arms, relished every small movement while fearing what was to follow.

"Tell me what you want, Claudia."

Surely he did not expect her to say the words. "What I want?" she panted.

"Do you want me? Do you want me inside you?"

Claudia gulped. "Yes, Hudson. I want you."

He lowered his head, his mouth closing around her erect nipple. The flick of his tongue dragged a moan from her lips. As she arched her back, relished the instant pleasure brought by his teasing, Hudson thrust hard, deep. "Christ!"

"Good Lord!" she cried through gritted teeth. Pleasure and pain whipped her insides. She didn't know whether to moan with ecstasy as he filled her full or to gasp at the intrusion.

"Trust me," he whispered, sliding in and out, in and out of her body. For a man who professed to trust no one, it was a surprising thing to say. But he was right. With every thrust of his thick shaft the pain subsided, and her desire grew.

"Why is it I feel the need to possess you?" he growled, his jaw just as hard and rigid as his impressive manhood.

Perhaps that was the way with lust. It grasped you in its powerful claws, teased, tormented, drove you to the point of insanity.

"Take what you want," she said, but it was the madness speaking, the addiction, the craving.

He needed no further inducement to take her in strong, deep strokes.

His breathless pants sent puffs of white mist into the air. "I want you, Claudia. I want you so damn much …" He broke off, withdrew from her body.

She wasn't sure what was happening, but she felt the hot liquid land on her stomach, heard the guttural groan of satisfaction that burst from her husband's mouth.

Her husband?

How strange that she was so entrenched in this deception that she almost believed the lies, too?

But as Hudson collapsed at her side, as he pulled her into his arms, dragged the furs across their sweat-soaked bodies and kissed her on the temple, one thought proved dominant.

She was in love with Hudson Lockhart.

So in love, she would never marry another man, not as long as she lived.

CHAPTER FIFTEEN

"I daresay you're right," Dr Hewlett said as he sat back in the worn leather chair behind his desk. He steepled his fingers and narrowed his gaze. "Your father's symptoms might indicate a number of ailments. Some severe, some less so. Without examining the patient, it's impossible to tell."

"Then will you come to Berwick Street this afternoon?" Lockhart infused a sense of urgency into his tone. He sat forward and stared across the desk. "I'm sure you will agree that time is crucial in such matters."

"Indeed." Dr Hewlett drew his appointment diary closer and scanned the open page. The doctor was younger than most, thirty by his estimation, though the man's thick unkempt side whiskers suggested he had little time for anything other than work. "My last appointment is in Newman Street. I could meet you in Berwick at three."

"We are grateful you can spare the time," Claudia said from her seat next to Lockhart.

Lockhart nodded in agreement. "Should you find anything untoward, I wonder if you might remain at the house for a day or two."

Dr Hewlett's brows twitched. "I have other patients. I'm not sure—"

"I will more than compensate you for your time and trouble."

The doctor hesitated. "Let us discuss the matter once I've examined your father."

"Very well." Lockhart stood. There was much to do. The early morning start for London, coupled with a lack of sleep, had left his energy flagging. "We'll reconvene in Berwick Street—number twenty—at three."

"At three," the doctor repeated.

Not wanting to detain the doctor lest he run late, they left the man to his work. Drake had assured him that Dr Hewlett was both thorough and reliable and so Lockhart trusted the fellow would meet at the appointed time.

"Where now?" Claudia asked, pushing her fingers firmly into her gloves as they waited on the pavement.

"We'll take the carriage to New Bond Street." Focusing on vengeance proved difficult when all he wanted to do was ferry his darling wife to Russell Square and make love to her more thoroughly than he had last night. "We'll inquire at the numerous apothecaries to find out which one supplies my father's medicine."

Intuition told him that if he delved deeper into his father's illness, he might find clues as to who had framed him for murder on that fateful night. Justin had everything to gain—money, position in the family. Terence did, too. As of yet, his enemy had not made any obvious move. That said, Lockhart's sudden trip to Falaura Glen might have stalled the fiend.

"We can but try," she said, "and we do have a few hours to spare until we meet the doctor."

"Dr Hewlett said there are at least five shops selling medicine on that street." He had not kissed her since this morning and could not resist the urge to touch her arm now. "Come. If we hurry, we might have time for a stroll in the park."

She eyed him suspiciously through half-closed lids. "How is it you make a walk sound positively sinful?"

Lockhart grinned. "It's not the walk that heats my blood, but the thought of dragging you into the bushes to steal a kiss."

Claudia shook her head. "What will you do when you no longer have a wife to tease?"

The question hit him like a hard punch in the gut. What would he do when she left? In whom would he confide his darkest secrets? Who would challenge his reckless decisions?

"You'll not get rid of me so easily," he said, sensing the truth in the playful words.

"Who said I want rid of you?" Claudia smiled and their gazes locked.

The sound of his carriage rattling to a halt beside them broke the spell. Lockhart spent the next fifteen minutes staring at her in the confines of his conveyance. His thoughts danced back to their illicit liaison inside the rotunda. Oh, the feel of her delicate hand pumping his cock had sent his head spinning. The feel of her tight body clamped around him had intensified his craving.

He would make love to her again.

Tonight, should she be willing.

Yes, tonight he would lavish her delightful breasts, would pleasure her aching flesh with his tongue until she begged him to fill her full. Last night, it had taken every ounce of willpower he possessed to withdraw from her needy body. Part of him didn't want to think what that meant. It had nothing to do with enhancing his pleasure and everything to do with making this fantasy real.

A sigh from the opposite side of the carriage dragged him from his lascivious musings. More than once, Claudia stifled a yawn before feigning interest in the passing scenery. That was until they rumbled to a halt outside the first apothecary shop on New Bond Street and she almost choked on a startled gasp.

It wasn't the rows of brown bottles in the shop's window that caused her mouth to drop open and her eyes to grow wide. It wasn't the small boy being dragged along the street by his irate mother that made her jerk her head back from the glass pane.

"What is it?" Panic gripped him when her bottom lip trembled.

A few seconds passed before she spoke. "That shop, the one two doors down from the apothecary, what can one buy there?"

Lockhart glanced at the swinging sign marked Higson and Son. From the various watercolours and assortment of quill pens displayed in the window, it was a stationery shop. "Many things. Art supplies, paintings, pencils. They print calling cards and invitations." He frowned, thought to make light of her odd reaction but found he could not. "Why do you ask?"

She shot back in the seat, her face ashen. "Oh, I thought I recognised the person who left the shop a moment ago, someone from Flamstead."

"So that's why you look as if you've seen the devil."

"Indeed."

Being seen in a carriage with an unmarried gentleman would undoubtedly stir the gossips in Flamstead. "We don't have to alight here. We can begin our enquiries at the top of the street."

Lockhart did not wait for a reply, but banged on the roof and relayed instructions to his coachman. Miss Darling struggled to sit still. She fiddled with her fingers, chewed her bottom lip.

"You don't have to come with me," he said. Guilt flared for having placed her in this awkward predicament. "Wait in the carriage if you're worried someone might notice you."

He expected her to laugh, to confess to being foolish, suffering from paranoia. He expected her to insist on standing by his side when he trailed from shop to shop badgering the proprietors for information.

"Would you mind? The last thing Emily needs is for someone to start vicious rumours."

Good God, she was lying.

He recognised the shifty look in her eye, the same one he'd seen when she sat opposite him in the cottage and professed to be a clumsy dancer.

Perhaps it wasn't a falsehood, the angel on his shoulder argued. She had no reason to lie. Numerous excuses filled his head. Perhaps the lady had a secret. No. Perhaps he was the one being foolish for jumping to conclusions.

"Very well," he said when the carriage stopped farther on the road. "Wait here. I'll be as quick as I can." Disappointment dripped from every word. Still, she remained resolute.

Lockhart found himself stomping along the pavement in a bid to banish these crippling suspicions. Mistrust was his constant companion. Why had she behaved as if she'd seen an evil spectre not a villager from Flamstead?

Trying to push his misgivings aside, he entered an apothecary shop. Despite offering a bribe for information, the proprietor could not recall a customer named Terence Lockhart. The same was true for the next two shops. Both men failed to recognise the name even after gentle persuasion.

Instinct told him he'd found the right place as soon as he crossed the threshold of Wilfred Wolfson's store. The name roused an image of a predatory beast. Indeed, the man behind the counter stared with bulging eyes as his tongue swept over cracked lips.

"Welcome." The fellow rubbed his red, blotchy hands. "How may I assist you today?" He had the slippery voice of a swindler. A man who lured the unsuspecting into believing they suffered from all sorts of terrible ailments.

"Are you Wolfson?"

"Indeed, I am, sir." The fellow scanned Lockhart's face. "You look like a man who struggles to sleep."

Well, that much was true, though it had nothing to do with an illness and everything to do with craving Claudia Darling's luscious body.

"I'm tormented by an addiction," Lockhart confessed as he prowled towards the counter. "Is there a cure for a man whose cravings keep him awake at night?"

Wolfson nodded. "There's a cure for most things, sir. If one is willing to pay the price."

"Is there a cure for lust?" And yet something more than lust flowed through his veins.

"There's a medicine that makes it difficult to perform if you take my meaning."

"Is there a cure for love?" Lockhart wasn't sure why he'd asked.

Wolfson chuckled. "That's called marriage. Three months of nagging and endless women's talk should see you right again."

Miss Darling didn't nag. And he could listen to her talk for hours.

Lockhart reached into his pocket and removed three sovereigns. He placed them on the counter. "Can you tell me if you supply a Mr Terence Lockhart with medicine?"

Wolfson glanced at the coins and then at Lockhart. "Can't say as I recall the name."

"Then permit me to prompt your memory." Lockhart removed another sovereign and added it to the pile. "He purchases laudanum in large quantities, cough suppressant and a range of other medicines without labels."

Wolfson frowned. "All the medicines sold here come with a full list of ingredients."

"I'm sure they do." Perhaps Terence removed the labels. Perhaps Justin and Selina had administered the wrong medication. Lockhart added two more sovereigns to the pile. "Terence Lockhart. I want to know what he purchased."

Wolfson licked his lips and stared at the coins as if admiring a huge chunk of meat pie. "Lockhart, you say."

"He looks like me but lacks my charm."

"He lacks your generous nature, too."

"Then you remember him?"

"A man doesn't forget the weird ones."

"Weird?"

"He orders laudanum, of course. The rest, well …" Wolfson flicked his gaze back to the coins.

"You drive a hard bargain," Lockhart said, adding another coin. "That's the last. So spill your guts unless you want me to spill them for you." He flashed the shopkeeper a look menacing enough to send the wolf scampering back to his underground den.

The man shuddered. "The cough suppressant, the invigorant, the fever tonic, they're labelled although there's nothing but castor oil, lavender or essence of peppermint in the bottles."

Lockhart slammed his hand on the counter. "You're charging for medicine when you know the contents will do nothing other than act as a relaxant?" And perhaps cause flatulence, which accounted for the sickly concoction of smells lingering in his father's room.

"At Mr Lockhart's insistence."

Why would Terence buy medicine knowing it would have little effect? Perhaps Terence didn't want their father to recover. Perhaps he didn't trust Justin to administer the required dose.

"Of course, the other fellow demanded something stronger."

Lockhart frowned. "The other fellow?"

Mr Wolfson flashed a greedy grin.

"You'll not get another damn penny," Lockhart hissed through gritted teeth. "What other fellow?"

Wolfson shrugged. "A right old dandy with an upturned nose and a fancy green coat. Came in here complaining about the quality of the laudanum. Demanded I use less alcohol in the tincture. He wouldn't leave until I'd prepared two bottles."

Justin Perigrew.

So his cousin was determined to keep Alfred Lockhart in a drug-induced state.

"Take the money," Lockhart said. He watched Wolfson slap

his hand over the coins and slide them off the counter. "You've been most helpful."

Lockhart left the apothecary shop feeling more confused than when he'd entered. He wished Claudia had accompanied him. Her insight proved invaluable, and she addressed matters from a logical viewpoint rather than one tainted with the need for vengeance.

As he strode towards his carriage, he hoped to find her spirits recovered. What he found upon yanking open the door was that the carriage was empty.

Claudia Darling had disappeared.

CHAPTER SIXTEEN

The shop's doorbell tinkled, drawing the curious gazes of two people examining the watercolours lining one wall. Another group was engrossed in surveying the row of pens until the woman slapped the child's hand when the boy insisted on tickling his sister with the feather of a quill.

Claudia scanned the items for sale, wondering what on earth had brought Mr Thorncroft to town and what had held his interest in the stationer's shop. The man liked writing letters—or contracts to be more precise. Perhaps it was the only place one might purchase an ink pot full of blood. Blood to represent the signing away of one's soul. Blood to represent a sinister deal with a devil.

Gathering her courage, Claudia approached the middle-aged woman behind the counter. "Forgive me, I am to meet my brother here, but I fear I've spent too long in the bookshop. Please tell me I haven't missed him." Heavens, Claudia's acting skills grew better by the day. "He's a rather dour looking fellow with sallow skin. But don't tell him I said that."

The woman scanned Claudia's clothes. The ones made purely

for the purposes of deception. "And you're to meet him in this shop?"

"Most definitely."

"Did he have business upstairs?"

Upstairs? That threw her somewhat.

From the woman's cautious tone and shifty eyes, whatever happened upstairs was neither legal nor moral. Perhaps she ran a bordello. A bordello masquerading as a stationery shop? Hardly.

But how was she to find out information without rousing suspicion or looking like a fool?

"My brother, Mr Thorncroft, has business of a delicate nature. He simply told me to meet him here." Perhaps he had come merely to buy sealing wax and a ream of paper. Then again, he looked to have left empty-handed. "Writing is his pastime if you take my meaning."

Claudia's arched brow and suggestive nod seemed to influence the woman.

"Then he'll have been to see Mr Higson."

"Mr Higson?"

"He's an expert when it comes to the written word."

The tinkle of the shop's doorbell forced Claudia to glance back over her shoulder.

The blood drained from her face as she locked gazes with Hudson Lockhart, whose broad shoulders blocked the doorway. He looked like he'd escaped a violent storm—flustered, breathless, scared. Fear quickly turned to barely contained rage. Indeed, he looked ready to throttle the first man foolish enough to raise a complaint.

Claudia turned back to the assistant. "Oh, it seems my brother has arrived."

Why on earth had she said that?

Hudson Lockhart had the bronzed skin of Adonis, and while he looked furious, there was nothing grim about his alluring countenance.

The woman eyed her suspiciously. She leant over the counter and whispered, "Then you've no need to come here again. No need to come prying."

Claudia swallowed past the lump in her throat.

Before the assistant skirted around the counter and chased her out of the door, Claudia turned on her heel and marched to meet the brooding devil waiting to rain fire and brimstone.

"I told you to wait in the carriage." Hudson stepped back for her to pass. "Can you imagine what went through my mind when I returned to find you missing?"

He strode over to the carriage door, yanked it open and more or less ordered her inside.

Now was not the time to argue, or demand he treat her as a loving wife and not the hired help.

Claudia settled into the seat, pursed her lips and waited until the carriage was rumbling along the road before saying, "Forgive me. I did not mean to cause you distress."

Dark, dangerous eyes stared back at her. "Perhaps you forgot that I'm a man who has been framed for murder. Perhaps you forgot that I promised to ensure your safety."

"No," she said, feeling the sudden urge to defend her position, "I did not forget."

"Then what prompted you to leave the carriage?" he growled. "What prompted you to enter that shop knowing someone from Flamstead had left a few minutes earlier?" He threw his hands in the air. "Hell, you insisted on remaining in the carriage because you were afraid to be seen."

What was she supposed to say? That she had been using Hudson so she didn't have to marry a wicked devil? That she suspected the wicked devil was guilty of some form of deception, too?

"I realised I was mistaken."

Hudson sat forward. "That's a lie."

The comment hurt even though it was the truth. Deflection

seemed the only way out of this mess. "You would know about lies, Hudson. Why didn't you tell me I was your second choice for a wife? Why didn't you tell me I was the inferior model, the one used because you grew desperate?"

A deathly silence descended.

For a moment, he merely gaped.

The tension in the air dissipated, the atmosphere growing sombre.

"You're far from the inferior model," he said so quietly she had to strain to listen. "After what happened between us in the rotunda, I thought you knew that."

Claudia swallowed down her guilt. "But I *was* the second choice?"

"Originally, I hired an actress to play the role, but Dariell insisted it was a sure road to failure."

"You hired an actress?" Perhaps he'd wanted a professional to help him solve his problem, a professional to please him in bed. "Why? To avoid emotional complications?"

He sighed. Sadness swam in his brown eyes. "Because I didn't know who else to ask, who to trust."

Having learnt more about the situation, she wondered if his only reason for wanting a wife was to prove a point to Selina. By his own admission, he'd been struck from his father's will. What need had he for pretending she was with child other than to annoy his brother? Other than to hurt the woman who'd left him alone on the docks. Where were the threats he warned her about, the attacks from his family?

Claudia's heart ached to ease his pain. But she could not rid herself of the crippling doubts inside. "I don't think you've come back for vengeance," she said. "I think you want the truth. And I am not speaking about the murder. You want to know what motivated Selina to marry your brother. You want to prove no one is worthy of your trust."

He flopped back in the seat. "I want to know who despises me to the extent they would ruin my life."

"Is it ruined?" If she focused on the negative aspects of her life, she might feel the same. "Are your friends not as close as brothers? Have you not amassed a great fortune that means you no longer need to crawl and beg to your parents? Have your experiences blackened your soul? No! You're a good man, Hudson, a good man who happens to be related to selfish people."

He remained silent.

"Promise me one thing," she urged.

"That depends what it is."

"Promise me, once we discover the truth you will lay the ghosts of the past to rest. Promise me, you will live your life without regret, without a heavy heart."

He studied her through narrowed eyes. "You still want to help me despite playing the understudy to an actress?"

"As you said, I am far from the understudy. I just wish you'd told me the truth in the beginning." It wouldn't have stopped her accepting his offer, but she might have had more realistic expectations. The word *hypocrite* rang loud and clear in her ears. Perhaps his expectations might have been different, too, had he known the real reason she'd accepted. "Based on my performance, every theatre owner in the country would scramble to hire me."

The last comment was said in jest to lighten the mood, but it seemed to have the opposite effect.

"Is everything part of the performance?" he said tersely.

Shocked that he could even ask the question, she said, "After what happened between us in the rotunda, I'm surprised you need to ask."

They continued the rest of their journey in silence.

When they arrived in Berwick Street, Claudia was somewhat glad they were meeting Dr Hewlett. The hours spent trying to solve this mystery would detract from the confounding thoughts filling her head.

Hudson dragged out his pocket watch and studied the time. "We'll wait here until the doctor arrives." His voice still sounded strained.

"You fear Simmonds will turn him away?" she said in an even tone for they could not continue like this.

"Mother will begrudge the expense."

"Even when the man might help save her husband?" Claudia would sell everything she owned to help Emily. She would sell everything she owned to help Hudson Lockhart, too.

"My father's illness gives her something to complain about."

"Some people thrive on drama," she agreed.

The atmosphere settled, and they sat in companionable silence while awaiting the doctor.

Dr Hewlett arrived fifteen minutes late. He scurried down the road clutching his leather case in one hand while holding on to his top hat with the other.

Hudson opened the carriage door and vaulted to the pavement. He held out his hand to her and Claudia slipped her palm into his. Touching him seemed to drain all previous stresses away. He inhaled deeply, evidently feeling the power of their connection, too.

"Forgive me," Dr Hewlett said as he came to a crashing halt and fought to catch his breath. "My last patient has a terrible addiction."

"To laudanum or gin?" Hudson asked.

"To talking," Dr Hewlett said with a chuckle.

"Well, you'll not have that problem here." Hudson glanced at an upper window. "For some reason, they're keeping my father sedated." He straightened. "Come, let's not talk of it here. You should examine the patient yourself."

Dr Hewlett gestured for Hudson to lead the way.

Simmonds opened the door and stepped back for them to enter the hall. No sooner had he closed the door than the dreadful din in the drawing room began.

"Who is it, Simmonds?" Hester Lockhart screeched the butler's name when he failed to reply. "Answer me, man. Simmonds? Simmonds? If it's the deserter, book him passage on the next boat sailing to India."

The butler inclined his head. "Excuse me, sir. I must attend to the mistress." Simmonds plodded to the drawing room and squared his slumped shoulders before entering.

Dr Hewlett's anxious eyes flitted back and forth in their sockets.

"Have no fear, doctor," Hudson said without a hint of embarrassment. "My mother is a heartless harpy, but it is a truth to which I am reconciled." He gestured to the stairs. "Permit me to lead the way."

As they mounted the stairs amid the abusive complaints and infernal noise echoing from the drawing room, Claudia wondered which family member was attending Alfred Lockhart. While Selina had implied that Hudson might find her alone if he called at noon, it proved somewhat of a surprise to find both Selina and Mr Perigrew huddled together, deep in conversation.

Selina practically jumped out of her skin when they entered. Claudia stared, convinced the couple had been holding hands. Selina took one look at the doctor and her face blanched.

"It must be my father's lucky day," Hudson said, ushering Claudia and the doctor into the room and closing the door. "What a pleasure to have both of his devoted relatives at his bedside."

"I arrived ten minutes ago." Justin tugged at the sleeves of his maroon coat and gave a mocking snort. "I must admit, I'm surprised to see you here, surprised my aunt permitted another visit."

"Your aunt is a foolish woman with no power over me," Hudson retorted. He glanced at his father's sunken cheeks as he lay asleep in the bed. "Dr Hewlett has come to examine the patient."

"Then I'm afraid I must object," Justin snapped, though his

tone lacked conviction. "How do we know this fellow is a doctor? How do we know you're not going to drag the poor man from his bed and commit him to an asylum?"

Dr Hewlett placed his leather case carefully on the bed. "I was apprenticed to Mr Bartholomew Hunt at Guy's Hospital for five years. I am a Licentiate of the Society of Apothecaries and as such am qualified to attend this patient."

Justin's jaw quivered, and he snapped his mouth shut.

Selina moved closer to the bed. "As you can see from the assortment of bottles on the side table, doctor, my husband has tried many things to cure his father's ailments." The raven-haired beauty locked eyes with Hudson and moistened her lips.

Jealousy roiled in Claudia's stomach.

Dr Hewlett moved to examine the bottles. His nose twitched, and his brows wiggled as he sniffed and tried to determine the ingredients. "Remind me of the gentleman's symptoms."

Selina repeated the list of ailments.

"And he's often delirious," Justin added, gesticulating his frustration with a dandified wave. "Says ridiculous things during bouts of paranoia."

Dr Hewlett turned to Hudson. "That could be attributed to the excessive use of laudanum."

"It's not," Justin protested, shaking his head so vigorously a lock of golden hair flopped over his brow. "He's been like that for years. Muttering and mumbling to himself like an imbecile. All poppycock, of course." He approached Selina and placed a comforting hand on her back. "I honestly don't know how we've coped."

The lady shuffled uncomfortably, and a blush stained her cheeks. When Justin failed to move his hand, she edged left, forcing his arm to flop to his side as limp as a fish.

"It has been a terrible strain that has impacted our lives to an immeasurable degree," Selina said, somewhat desperate to incite pity. It did not stop her eyes widening as she feasted on the breadth of Hudson's chest.

Justin nodded. "We're at the theatre tonight for the first time in months."

Selina squirmed. "Only because it's the last time Mr Maverick is to play Solinus in *The Comedy of Errors*."

With tales of wild mishaps, mistaken identities, madness and infidelity, perhaps the Lockhart family found similarities to their own lives while watching the play.

"But I intend to return after supper," Selina added.

"There is no need," Hudson said. "Dr Hewlett will remain here tonight."

Thankfully, the doctor made no objection.

"That's outrageous." Justin's cheeks ballooned. "You cannot come home, storm in here and expect to take over."

"As the eldest son, I can do as I damn well please. What's wrong, Justin? Afraid my father might change his will?"

Saliva bubbled between the fop's lips as he attempted to control his temper. "Tell him, Selina. Tell him we'll not allow him to ride roughshod over us, to undermine our authority."

Selina batted her lashes and fixed a hungry gaze on Hudson. "There's no need for hostility. We can all work together to serve your father's needs." Her sibilant voice slipped across the room like teasing fingers eager to stroke Hudson Lockhart into submission.

"Drugging him is hardly serving his needs," Hudson countered, seemingly unaffected by her womanly wiles.

Numerous times, Dr Hewlett tried to ignore the hullabaloo and focus on the patient, but the argument proved distracting.

"Perhaps we should leave the doctor to his work," Claudia suggested. "Complaining is helping no one."

Justin screwed up his nose as if he'd suddenly caught a whiff of a foul stench. "This has nothing to do with you, so I suggest you remain silent."

A growl resonated in Hudson's throat. He marched around the bed, ready to throttle his cousin. Justin stumbled back, his hands outstretched in protest, but Hudson grabbed him by his fancy collar and dragged him to the door.

"Speak to my wife like that again, and you'll be chewing on broken teeth." Hudson opened the door and threw his cousin out. He ignored the man's prattling and turned to Selina. "*We* will attend my father. Good day, Selina."

Selina flung sharp daggers Claudia's way. She snatched her pelisse from the chair and swept from the room.

Hudson closed the door and muttered a curse before turning to Dr Hewlett. "My wife is right. No man can work under such stressful conditions. Please, Dr Hewlett, I would be grateful if you would examine my father."

Dr Hewlett nodded.

While the doctor retrieved various instruments from his leather case, Hudson drew Claudia to the opposite end of the room.

"What if this is all my fault?" he whispered, guilt evident as he brushed his hand through his mop of dark hair. "My father's condition worsened a month ago. Perhaps Greystone's return brought painful memories flooding back, caused some mysterious malaise." A weary sigh breezed from his lips. "I should have remained in India. Heaven knows I wanted to."

"Then why come home?" She touched his forearm, found that it wasn't enough to ease her craving and so touched his upper arm in a soothing caress.

"It was always Greystone's plan to seek retribution. The same was true for Drake. Sometimes the need for vengeance is too powerful to resist." His brown eyes grew distant. "And the thought of being alone had little appeal."

"What is it you seek, Hudson, vengeance or the truth?"

Hudson shrugged. "Maybe both. Maybe neither." His weary sigh tore at her heart. "I want peace, peace to live my life without feeling the sharp stab of betrayal. I want the peace that comes with knowing who I can trust."

She slid her hand up over his shoulder to cup his cheek. "Trust yourself. Love yourself. Forgive yourself. Don't let your happiness be dependent on what others say or do."

That was a sure road to misery and failure.

Moisture formed in his eyes as he stared at her. He captured her hand and kissed her tenderly on the palm. "Dariell was right."

"Right about what?"

"You're perfect—"

"Perfect?" she interjected, scared of what he might say. "Perfect to play the wife of a rogue? Perfect when it comes to challenging your opinion?"

He shook his head. "Just perfect."

The air between them thrummed with energy. It was all Claudia could do not to kiss him.

A groan from the bed sent all amorous thoughts scattering.

"The effects of the laudanum are wearing off," Dr Hewlett said. His comment drew Claudia and Hudson back to the bed. "I advise we wait before administering any medicine, and certainly anything contained in these bottles." He gestured to the assortment on the side table.

"I spoke to the apothecary who dispensed them." Hudson related the extent of his conversation with a man named Mr Wolfson.

"Do you think that's the reason your father isn't getting better?" Claudia said. What other reason could Terence have for requesting essence of peppermint instead of cough suppressant?

"We'll know more once we wean the gentleman off laudanum."

"Wean him off?" Hudson frowned. "But that can take days. And I've heard enough horror stories to enquire as to your meaning."

Dr Hewlett arched a brow. "I'm not talking scalding baths and mustard plasters if that is your fear. I shall monitor him tonight and make a more definitive decision then."

"So you will stay?"

The doctor nodded. "For the next eight hours at least."

"Eight hours is all we may have," Hudson said gravely. "You must do what you can before my cousin returns tomorrow."

Claudia glanced at the frail figure in the bed. What if there was nothing wrong with the man other than a lack of food and fresh air?

While contemplating that thought, she was drawn to a black mark on the coverlet. She stepped closer to examine the stain.

"Is something wrong?" Hudson asked.

"This mark on the coverlet, what does it look like to you?" She dabbed the strange blotch with the tip of her finger.

Hudson studied the mark for a moment. "It looks like ink."

"It wasn't there the last time we called, and the maid hasn't changed the bedding."

"It's dry." Hudson looked up and met her gaze. "You think it's relevant?"

"I don't know. But it is odd."

"Indeed." After scouring the room and finding nothing to account for the stain, Hudson turned to the doctor. "We shall return later tonight on our way home. I'll inform Simmonds to expect us around midnight."

Claudia frowned. "On our way home?"

Surely he wasn't planning another trip to Falaura Glen. Lord knows what wonders Dariell had created in their absence. The image of the rotunda flashed into her mind, swiftly followed by the image of a bare chest and the wickedly handsome face of Hudson Lockhart.

"Are we going somewhere?" Claudia asked, desire pulsing in her veins.

"We're going out." Hudson smiled. "Did I not promise you a trip to the theatre?"

CHAPTER SEVENTEEN

"You might have given us more notice," Drake complained as he tugged the sleeves of his black evening coat and settled into the padded velvet chair in Greystone's box. "I hate plays almost as much as I hate masquerades."

"Oh, but this is the first time you've brought me to the theatre." Juliet touched his arm, and the giant softened.

"Then I shall sit quietly," Drake conceded, "for you must concentrate if you intend to follow this one. It's a farce made to muddle a man's mind."

"That doesn't mean it will muddle a woman's mind," Juliet countered.

Valentine chuckled. "Then you should come to the theatre more often, Drake. Perhaps there's a play about a man who converses with dogs."

Drake smirked. "I'd be more interested in one where a wild monkey attacks the patrons."

Greystone laughed.

"I know how you hate large crowds, Drake. I had but a few hours' notice myself," Lockhart explained by way of an apology. He drew out the chair for Claudia and waited for her to sit before dropping into the seat next to her. She wore a sumptuous burgundy gown, another splendid creation that drew his gaze to the soft swell of her breasts.

He had deliberately chosen seats at the rear of the box, behind Devlin Drake. With such a large crowd, it afforded him the privacy to observe the horde unnoticed. The gossips were just as interested in his friends, and so he hoped he might shrink into the shadows.

"I presume you're going to tell us why we're here," Greystone enquired, though he kept his gaze fixed centre stage.

"I need you to locate Terence and inform me when he leaves the auditorium." Lockhart had more than a few questions for his brother. He refused to call on Terence while Selina was at home. And having not seen him since the masquerade, he couldn't help but think his brother was avoiding a second meeting.

Aveline gripped the ivory handle of her opera glasses and studied those in the private boxes opposite. "Oh, Lucius, I see Honora with Mrs Madeley."

"Damnation," Valentine muttered. "Now my mother will want to know why we didn't tell her we were coming."

Greystone borrowed Lydia's glasses and observed the crowd. "What makes you think Terence is here tonight?"

"Selina said they were coming. Apparently, it is Mr Maverick's final performance." Then again, she had made no mention of Terence attending. "Justin should be here."

During the first act, Greystone continued to scan the sea of heads. Lockhart sat silently with his thoughts. Whenever he felt a spark of anger at both his and his father's mistreatment, he took hold of Claudia's hand and stroked her palm. She wasn't particularly interested in the play, either, and they spent more time looking at each other than the fools on stage.

"I've found your cousin," Greystone said, looking to the middle tier and to the left of the plush boxes. "He's sitting with Selina, but Terence isn't with them." Without warning, a muttered curse burst from Greystone's lips, and he almost dropped the glasses. "Damnation."

"What is it?" Panic rose in Lockhart's chest.

"I locked gazes with Selina. She's watching me through her glasses."

"Let me see." Lydia took the glasses and stared into the crowd. "Yes, she is most definitely watching this box."

What was Selina's problem? Was it dissatisfaction with her husband? Was it guilt for abandoning Lockhart on the docks? Was it fear? Perhaps when it came to caring for his father, she was the villain, not the nurse.

Lockhart pondered those thoughts during the second act until a comment made by the character Dromio disturbed his reverie.

Every why hath a wherefore.

The words tormented him. There was a reason someone had framed him for murder. He just couldn't see it. There was a reason Terence had married Selina. He just needed to ask his brother to learn the answer.

"Wait," Greystone whispered. "I see him. I see Terence."

It seems the Divine had heard Lockhart's musings and extended a helping hand.

"He's in Mrs Fanshaw's box and looks remarkably relaxed. The woman can't take her eyes off him."

"Mrs Fanshaw?" Lockhart grimaced. "The woman is old enough to be his mother."

"Some men are happy to overlook the age difference when weighted against her yearly income," Aveline said. "She's had endless suitors these last few years. Most of them riddled with debt." When Valentine stared at his wife and arched a brow, she said, "What? Lady Cartwright told me. The matron prefers gossip to examining literary texts."

Lockhart contemplated the information.

Was Terence in financial trouble? His brother had a fondness for the card tables. Was he simply hoping their father would die so he could get his hands on his inheritance? Lockhart suppressed a gasp when another thought struck him. Had the fiend at the inn mistaken Lockhart for Terence? The rogue had come looking for money. Had Terence set the trap?

Anger burned in Lockhart's veins.

Every why hath a wherefore.

And he'd damn well learn the truth before the week was out.

"Excuse me for a moment." Lockhart pushed to his feet. He bent down and kissed Claudia on the forehead. "Wait here. I'll be back soon."

"Where are you going?"

He brushed her cheek with the backs of his fingers. "To speak to Terence."

She grabbed his arm. "Please be careful." Fear danced in her eyes. "Promise me you won't do anything foolish."

Valentine glanced in their direction. His knowing smirk mirrored Drake's wide grin.

"My friends will keep you company until I return." Lockhart looked into her eyes. Despite it not being written in the stage directions, he placed a chaste kiss on her lips and exited the box.

Something told him he was getting closer to the truth. The thought drew him along the corridor, towards the grand staircase. He would knock on Mrs Fanshaw's box and demand answers.

As he moved past the impressive chandelier hanging from the domed roof, a figure stepped out of the shadows.

"Hudson. Wait. I must talk to you."

He would know Selina Lockhart's voice anywhere. Not because it stirred fond memories but because it grated.

"What do you want, Selina?" He moved to walk past, but she grabbed his arm.

"Just a few minutes of your time. If you ever cared for me at all, surely you can spare me that. It's about Terence."

Perhaps he *had* cared for her once. Not in the way he cared for

Claudia. And he considered the possibility that she might have useful information.

"Five minutes," he said reluctantly, before offering a weary sigh. "Five minutes. That is all."

A smile formed on her lips. It was the first time he'd seen a glimmer of happiness since his return. "Come," she said. "We might have some privacy in the saloon."

Selina hovered at his side. If she expected him to offer his arm, she was mistaken. He strode off in front, past two Grecian statues standing guard in the alcoves. Their coy expressions made him doubt his decision.

They slipped into the room occupied by men lighting candles and polishing glasses, men waiting to serve those who came to gorge on food and drink when they'd grown bored with the play. A few stragglers were already sitting around a table at the end of the long room.

"Perhaps you might start by telling me why Terence is enjoying the play from the luxury of Mrs Fanshaw's box." Lockhart drew Selina towards the window. The saloon's intimate setting, with its red flock wallpaper and gleaming gilt sconces, added an illicit air to this secret conversation that did not sit well with him.

"Why do you think?" Selina replied evasively.

Lockhart shrugged. "He's your husband. I imagine you might have something to say regarding the fact Mrs Fanshaw is hanging on his every word."

"Terence has never been a faithful husband."

So why the hell had he married her? For propriety's sake? Perhaps Terence despised him and marrying Selina brought an element of satisfaction.

"Do you love him?" How she answered would prove telling.

Her eyes brightened. "I love you. I have always loved you."

Ballocks!

Claudia Darling would have slipped her hand into his at the docks, would have walked the gangplank and never looked back.

"Then what a shame you lacked the courage of your convictions. That said, your loss proved to be my gain."

"Your gain?" She jerked her chin in the air. "Oh, you're referring to your obedient little wife."

"You don't know what love is, Selina." Claudia's sweet face flashed into Lockhart's mind. "Thankfully, your selfish actions provided an opportunity for me to experience what trust and devotion truly mean."

"My selfish actions?" Selina snorted. "I wasn't the one who ruined everything because I couldn't control my temper." She gritted her teeth and muttered, "I wasn't the one who drove a blade into a man's heart and was forced to flee."

A fury to surpass all others, a raging tempest set to clear the room in one fell swoop whirled in his chest. Despite everything Selina knew of him, she still believed he was guilty of committing such a vile atrocity. Bile bubbled in his stomach.

Lockhart snarled. "You cold, heartless—"

"Cold? Perhaps you're mistaking me for your wife." Spite dripped from every word. "She doesn't love you. Any fool can see that. And you certainly don't love her."

The comments threw him. For a second he wondered if they had let their guard slip. Had Selina witnessed a wooden performance, the work of amateurs?

No!

He desired his wife, lusted after her, craved her company. It had nothing to do with stepping into roles and everything to do with the magnificence of the woman in question.

"Make no mistake," he said, his words dripping with conviction. "I am in love with my wife."

For all the saints!

He felt the truth of it as soon as the words left his lips.

"I adore her," he continued. Now he had started he couldn't stop. "I would lay down my life for her, sail the stormy seas, venture to lands unknown, just for the opportunity to gaze at her face, to hold her hand. So don't dare presume to know what I think or feel."

Selina gulped. The veil of arrogance fell, leaving naught but a quivering wreck in its wake. Tears filled her eyes.

"I married Terence for you," she blurted, shaking visibly. "So you would be free to pursue a new life. And now you're happy, and my husband is a philanderer, a gambler, a liar and a cheat who would see his father dead to get hold of his inheritance."

Two men stumbled through the saloon door, laughing and joking. One caught sight of Lockhart and Selina huddled in the corner and gave a knowing wink.

Bloody hell!

He'd not have the gossips spread rumours of infidelity. The story of two brothers fighting over the same woman always proved popular.

"Then it's time I spoke to Terence and dragged the truth from his lying lips." Lockhart straightened. He'd wrap his hands around his brother's throat and squeeze out a confession.

"Wait." Selina grabbed and tugged at Lockhart's arm. "He's not worth the time or the trouble. Oh, Hudson, can't we begin again? Can't we go back to that night on the docks?" Selina touched his chest, clawed at his shirt, gripped his cravat. "Can't you make love to me like you used to?"

Hell's teeth, the woman knew how to make a scene.

Lockhart captured her hand as her other hand snaked up to tangle in his hair.

"You loved me once," she whispered. "You can learn to love me again."

"Selina," he began. He was about to tell her that he'd never loved her, that marrying her would have ruined both their lives. He was about to tell her to get her damn hands off him when the saloon door opened and closed again.

The feminine gasp reached his ears before the gentleman's discreet cough.

Still clutching Selina's hand, Lockhart glanced over his shoulder to find Claudia and Valentine staring back. Water welled in Claudia's eyes, eyes that spoke of disappointment, heartbreak and pain.

Valentine arched a brow. "Terence left the theatre a few moments ago." His tone carried more than a hint of disapproval. "Your wife feared something had happened to you."

Lockhart released Selina's hand as if it burned his skin. One could not deny how it all looked. But he was innocent of any wrongdoing. Hell, he wasn't even married and yet guilt crept through his veins like deadly poison. Excuses formed in his mind, hung on his lips, all tainted and toxic, all dripping with deceit.

"Didn't I say she'd grown suspicious?" Selina said, offering a smug grin. As he suspected, this woman would use any means necessary to advance her position.

Goddamn!

He considered yelling in protest, dropping to his knees and begging for Claudia's forgiveness. No doubt people were staring.

"Claudia," he managed to say.

She held her hand up to silence him. For a second she looked ready to turn on her heels and race from the room, back to Falaura Glen. But something changed as she stepped into the light, stepped into a new role as easily as she donned a new dress.

Claudia prowled towards him, her gaze dark, predatory. She glared at Selina and whispered in a calm yet sinister voice, "Remove your hand from my husband else I shall do it for you."

Selina grinned, the arrogant smirk fading when Claudia took another step closer.

"We share a history," Selina said, drawing her hand around Lockhart's neck and letting her fingers trail down his chest, "a rich, vivid history. One developed long before he met you."

Claudia offered a mocking snort. "And we share a future,

though I am not the sort of woman who grovels and begs for a man's attention. But let us solve this problem by putting my husband's loyalty to the test."

Lockhart wasn't sure what Claudia would do. A simple explanation would solve the problem and yet how would he convince her it was him speaking and not the damn actor?

His wife moved closer. "It's time to choose, Hudson." She came up on her tiptoes and kissed him open-mouthed on the lips. Her tongue slipped into his mouth to tease a reaction, succeeded in setting his body aflame. Regardless of the fact they were in company, he wrapped his arm around her waist and drank as if he were dying.

But he wasn't kissing the kind, loving soul who brought him supper in the cottage. He wasn't kissing the temptress who stripped naked to prove a point before sinking into the bathtub. He was kissing an actress, a highly skilled performer who had learned how to use lust against him.

Lockhart broke contact, knowing he had to do something real, something honest, something true. He stared into her eyes, drew on the warm feeling that flooded his chest whenever he thought of her. Cupping her cheeks, he kissed her forehead, kissed the salty taste of tears off her cheeks, kissed her mouth in the tender, affectionate way that resonated deep in the depths of his soul.

"Let me take you home," he said with a level of devotion reserved only for her. He didn't mean Falaura Glen or Russell Square. Home was anywhere he could take her in his arms and drift off into a peaceful slumber. "Let me show you how much I adore you, why I will always choose you."

Claudia nodded.

He ignored Selina when he took hold of Claudia's hand and made for the door.

He grabbed Valentine's shoulder as he passed. "Forgive me. Please express my sincere apologies for dragging you all here this evening."

"You do not have to apologise to your friends." Valentine clutched Lockhart's arm, a gesture of brotherly affection. "We're more than familiar with the situation. If you need anything at all, advice, assistance, anything, you know where to find me. I'm sure I speak for Drake and Greystone, too."

Lockhart smiled. "Anything?"

"Anything."

"What if I asked you to look after Claudia's pet monkey?" he said, unable to resist an opportunity to tease the viscount.

Valentine's lips twitched in amusement. "For you, my friend, I would of course oblige. But don't be surprised if you return to find the creature locked in a crate on a ship bound for India."

CHAPTER EIGHTEEN

L *et me take you home.*

Hudson's words replayed over in Claudia's mind as she sat huddled next to him in the carriage. Inside, her heart still ached from the shock of seeing Selina's hand curled around his neck, from seeing the look of desperation swimming in her eyes. The woman was a spiteful wildcat, and yet Claudia couldn't help but pity her a little.

Let me take you home.

Home was Falaura Glen, a place of love and comfort, a place she had always cherished, and yet her heart no longer resided there. The time spent with Hudson these last few days—days that felt like months—had changed her in some inexplicable way. Falaura Glen would always be missing something—missing the enigmatic man who made her body ache and her soul soar.

The sudden realisation that she must make every second with him count forced her to wrap her arm around his waist and shuffle closer.

Hudson kissed her hair as he held her in an embrace. "I feel nothing for Selina," he reminded her for the fifth time in as many minutes. "You do know that?"

"I do," Claudia said with confidence as she inhaled the notes of exotic incense clinging to his clothes. What really worried her was what would happen when this was all over. But worrying wasn't living. And had she not just decided to treasure every moment? "You haven't forgotten we're to visit Dr Hewlett before returning home?"

"No, I've not forgotten. It's almost eight hours since we left him, so he should have some news to impart."

Claudia prayed the doctor had something positive to say. Selfishly, she couldn't wait to get Hudson home to Russell Square, to take him by the hand and slip into bed. Of course, she would demand he strip naked, demand he press his hard body on top of her, demand he claim her in the possessive way that brought immense pleasure.

The fire between her legs flamed with each illicit thought. Heat flooded her entire body. It took every effort not to beg him to touch her, to massage her sex, to bring relief to this addiction. She was addicted to the woody tones of his cologne, the taste of his mouth, the warmth of his skin. The rhythmical rocking of the carriage only heightened her desire.

With her mind lost in a sensual haze, she wasn't sure what happened next.

One minute she was cupping his cheek, making him kiss her in the wicked way that drove her wild. The next, she was gathering her gown to her waist and straddling his muscular thighs.

"I need you inside me, Hudson." Uncontrollable passion and mindless lust dragged the words from her mouth. She yanked down the blinds. "If only until we reach Berwick Street."

Looking somewhat bewildered, yet equally excited at the prospect of joining with her, Hudson fiddled with the fall of his evening breeches and positioned himself at her entrance.

"There's no time to pleasure you as I did in the rotunda," he growled. "Are you sure you're ready for me?"

"Oh, I'm more than ready." Tonight, she was a milk-maid in need of a quick tupping.

The first thrust into her body tore a moan from her lips. He was so large, so hard and hot.

"Christ, Claudia." He grabbed hold of her hips and showed her how to move. "Ride me, love. Ride the hell out of me. Hold nothing back."

Driven by an intense hunger unlike anything she had experienced before, she sank down and sheathed his solid erection. It took a few seconds to find a rhythm, but once she did, she slid up and down his delicious length, taking him deep, deep into her body.

Hudson's head fell back against the squab as his breathing grew ragged.

She ran her hands over his chest, grabbed his waistcoat in her fists like reins and rode hard.

"Goddamn, you're so wet, so tight." He raised his head. "Wait. Come up on your knees."

She sucked in a breath and did as he asked.

Hudson took hold of his manhood and blindly rubbed the slick head back and forth over her sex. Claudia ground against him as the ache inside grew. Soon she was close to the glittering finale, the moment when her chaotic world shattered into one of sheer bliss.

"I need to be inside you when you come," he groaned.

"Then do it now."

He slid into her body, and she could not help but cry out with pleasure. "Hudson."

His expert fingers continued to rub her as she came down on him harder, so hard her buttocks slapped against his thighs. She came apart panting his name, shuddering in his lap.

He tried to pull out of her body, but she couldn't stop loving him, couldn't stop grinding against him in a frantic rhythm.

"Claudia, stop." Panic infused his tone. "I need to withdraw else there *will* be a child."

For one foolish second, she wanted him to pump his seed inside her, wanted her stomach to swell and grow. Quickly dismissing the thought as folly, she came up on her knees again and tumbled into the seat beside him.

She watched him take hold of his glistening erection, watched him hiss a sharp breath as he pumped hard, slowing just as he spurted into his hand.

Hudson's head fell back, and he closed his eyes. Their rapid pants filled the air in the confined space. The scent of their love-making teased her nostrils. It took a minute for her to drag her head out of the clouds.

"My handkerchief," he gasped. "It's in my pocket."

Claudia fumbled in his pocket and removed the silk square. "Allow me," she said, fascinated by the sheer size and strength of his manhood. She refused to give him the handkerchief and set about wiping up the evidence of their passionate encounter.

Hudson watched her intently before suddenly saying, "I don't want this to end."

The comment caught her unawares. "I don't want it to end, either." Love filled her heart. She considered telling him but what if it was sated desire talking? What if he meant nothing more than to continue their illicit affair?

Silence ensued while they set about righting their clothes. The carriage jerked to a halt as he fastened the buttons on his breeches.

"Let's see what Dr Hewlett has to say." Hudson folded his handkerchief and pushed it into the inside pocket of his coat. "We can talk later, once we're alone."

Claudia nodded, though fear crawled through her body like strangling ivy.

What if they wanted different things?

What if they felt different things?

They had no need to knock on the front door of number twenty Berwick Street. Simmonds was waiting ready to prise it gently from the jamb.

"So your mistress hasn't thrown the doctor out?" Hudson whispered to the weary-looking butler.

"No, sir. The doctor is still upstairs."

Hester Lockhart was one of those women who liked to voice her opinion but lacked the courage of her convictions.

"Then we won't be long," Hudson said, tapping the butler on the arm. "I'm sure you're keen to retire."

They crept upstairs, found the doctor sitting in a chair next to the bed. Light from a single candle penetrated the darkness. The room smelt of herbs yet the stench of sickness still hung in the air. Alfred Lockhart looked just as weak and pale. The bottles had disappeared from the side table, replaced with a pot of tea.

Dr Hewlett stood. "There's not much to tell, I'm afraid. It seems the last few doses of laudanum were particularly potent. When he grew restless, thrashed and mumbled, I fed his dependency with a less concentrated dose."

Hudson stepped closer to the bed. "Do you think we might wean him off it completely?"

"Yes, but it will take time and a concerted effort." Dr Hewlett's expression turned grave. "I do not wish to speak out of turn, but I suspect the gentleman might have an ulterior motive for keeping your father sedated."

"You speak of the dandified fop I threw out earlier?"

"Indeed." The doctor pursed his lips. "I do have other patients to consider but fear what will happen should I leave your father unattended."

"I cannot see Justin staying away," Claudia said, trying to concentrate on the conversation but she had caught Hudson's unique scent lingering on her clothes. "The man is desperate to control what happens here."

"Too desperate," Hudson added. "What I cannot understand is why Terence permits it."

Perhaps Terence was simply hoping their father would die. Perhaps he was too interested in fleecing Mrs Fanshaw, too concerned with paying his debts.

Hudson rubbed his chin and stared in thoughtful contemplation.

"I can stay for another twelve hours, until noon tomorrow," Dr Hewlett said. "The only other option is to move your father somewhere else."

Claudia had a sudden epiphany. "Could we not move him to Russell Square?"

"And have my family accuse me of wanting him dead? Should anything untoward happen to him, they will lay the blame at my door."

Claudia considered the fact that Terence or Selina might threaten Hudson, might resort to blackmail. But how could they? In disposing of the body and ferrying Hudson to Portsmouth, both were guilty of aiding and abetting a supposed criminal.

"You have powerful friends," Claudia said. Two of which had seats in the House of Lords. "I think we should move your father tonight. Dr Hewlett can attend him in Russell Square."

Hudson arched a brow. "My mother will raise an objection."

"Is she not asleep in bed? I doubt she'll learn of it until morning." Claudia shrugged. "Besides, what can she do? Dr Hewlett will testify that he considers the patient at risk if he remains here."

"If asked, that would be my expert opinion," the doctor agreed.

Hudson paced back and forth for a moment before saying with some determination, "You're right. We will move him to Russell Square. Should my mother dismiss Simmonds for assisting a heathen, I shall offer him employment." He turned to the doctor. "But I must question if my father is well enough to be moved."

"In the interests of the patient's safety, I fear there is no other option."

Hudson nodded. "Then I'll fetch Simmonds to assist us."

They didn't need Simmonds' help or that of the doctor. Alfred Lockhart was so frail and thin, Hudson was able to carry him in his arms and place him in the carriage. Simmonds brought blankets and packed a small valise.

As they crammed into Hudson's conveyance, Simmonds loitered at the carriage window. "Your offer, sir, to come and work in your household should the mistress turf me out without references. I wonder if I might join your staff regardless."

The poor man shuffled nervously while awaiting an answer. How he had the strength and patience to serve Hester Lockhart, one would never know.

"Climb in, Simmonds," Hudson said, sporting a huge grin. "I'm sure we can make room for one more."

CHAPTER NINETEEN

With his father settled into a bedchamber, and an extra bed moved into the room for Dr Hewlett, Lockhart advised his staff of the current arrangements and then went in search of Claudia. He was both disappointed and relieved not to have found her in the master bedchamber.

Despite a desperate need to sleep, his hunger for her could not be abated. Never had he known such an all-consuming desire. Never had he met a woman capable of hugging his heart while she hugged his cock. But his admiration for her ran deeper than these lustful urges.

I don't want this to end.

He'd meant every word he'd said in the carriage. This love affair meant more to him than clearing his name. If she would agree to board the next ship to India, he would leave with her in a heartbeat. But she had problems at Falaura Glen, a sister to consider. He'd come home to find a murdering blackguard, and with suspicions regarding his father's illness, he had no option but to sort out this damnable mess.

"I expected to find you asleep," he said, stumbling upon her sitting in a chair in the drawing room.

A smile touched her lips. "I'm so tired I could sleep for a week, but I cannot stop thinking." She snatched the glass from the side table, swallowed the amber liquid and placed the vessel back on the table.

"Thinking about what?" Was it their current predicament or her feelings for him that kept her awake?

She shrugged. "About everything. Your father's illness, Emily, those scoundrels who call themselves your family—" She stopped abruptly, yet he suspected the list was endless. "Do you think Justin and Selina will come banging on your door?"

"Undoubtedly."

"Will you let them in?"

"Definitely not. Not until I've spoken to Terence and discovered what the hell is going on."

Claudia pushed out of the chair. "Then we should get some rest. Lord knows what dilemmas we'll face tomorrow."

She looked tired, weary. Then again, an hour before she had ravaged him senseless in a moving carriage.

A smile touched his lips.

He loved her—was in love with her.

It wasn't that he'd become so rooted in his role that he'd lost sight of reality. The need to be her lover and husband lived and breathed inside him.

"Do you think you might sleep in the carriage?" he said, capturing her hand as she came towards him. "If Justin and Selina come, it will be sometime after midday. There's no telling when I'll find the time to take you back to Falaura Glen."

She pursed her lips and seemed to mull over his suggestion. "It's important you're here when your family arrive to cause mayhem. If I check on Emily tonight, I won't need to go back for a couple of days."

"That's what I thought, and it means I can collect the private papers I left with Dariell. I want to examine the letter from my father stating he'd struck me from his will." With his parents' erratic behaviour he had never thought to question its legitimacy. Pride had stopped him asking for proof. "The letter did not come from his solicitor, which leaves me questioning its authenticity."

"Under the circumstances, I understand why you're suspicious." A frown marred her brow. She stared into nothingness for a few seconds before saying, "How easy is it to forge someone's signature, do you think?"

"For fraudulent purposes?" He shrugged. "For the average person, I imagine it would take many hours of practice. But for a few pounds, one might hire someone to do the deed."

"Someone skilled in penmanship?"

"Indeed, and someone without a conscience."

She stared at him for a moment and then her eyes widened. "Then let us hurry to Falaura Glen and retrieve the items you need."

Lockhart brought her hand to his lips and pressed a kiss to her knuckles. "I shall inform Simmonds and Dr Hewlett. Call Lissette to help you out of that gown and be ready to leave in twenty minutes. It's cold out. I'll have extra bricks warmed but wear a thick cloak."

Claudia came up on her tiptoes and kissed him on the lips. "I like it when you worry about me."

Lockhart smiled. "This may sound perverse, but I like worrying."

Darkness permeated every corner of the conveyance. While it served to aid Claudia's need for sleep, a deep sense of foreboding forced Lockhart to remain awake and alert. Unease settled in his chest for no apparent reason—an omen some might say. It had nothing to do with the wind rattling the windows or the coachman's cautious pace.

To distract his thoughts, he leant forward and tugged the tartan blanket around Claudia's knees. She had fallen asleep within minutes of leaving the chaos of London behind. And while he missed her conversation, just looking at her proved comforting.

By Lockhart's estimation, they'd been navigating the bumpy road for forty minutes when the coachman's sudden shouts and wild cries held him rigid.

Saints and devils!

The carriage picked up speed, rocking and swaying on the road as the coachman pushed the team to their limits. Panic forced Lockhart to lower the window, to thrust his head out and enquire what the bloody hell was going on.

"Stay inside, sir," Fleet cried. Dariell had hired the coachman two weeks ago and assured Lockhart the man was highly respected in his field. "I'll not outrun the blighter, but I'll ride the last breath outta that 'orse."

The blighter?

Lockhart yanked his head back inside the carriage and shuffled around on the seat. He removed the loose padding to reveal the small viewing window at the rear.

In the dark, it was impossible to make out the identity of the rider chasing their heels. A black neckcloth covered the lower half of their pursuer's face. The peak of a black tricorne—a fashion that had fallen out of style twenty years earlier—hid his eyes.

Lockhart had no reason to fear the rogue. Dariell had taught him how to knock the largest oaf on his arse. But a glint of metal caught his eye, the barrel of the devil's pistol.

Pushing panic aside, for one did not shoot well when one's hands shook, Lockhart removed the oak box from the cupboard beneath his seat and attempted to load the flintlock pistol.

"Bloody hell."

The carriage careened to the right as Fleet swerved around a bend. The swift movement caused Lockhart to drop the damn tamping rod. After brushing powder from his breeches, he tried again, but the carriage bumped down a rut in the road sending him sliding off the seat.

Claudia shrieked. Her eyes flew open as she jerked forward.

"Damnation." He scrambled up, thumped the roof and shouted out of the window, "Stop the blasted carriage before one of us suffers an injury."

"What's happening?" Looking more than alarmed, Claudia blinked rapidly and gripped the seat. "Hudson, why are you waving that pistol?"

"Because we're about to be held up on the King's Highway."

Claudia didn't clutch her throat as ladies wearing fine jewels were wont to do. She wrapped her arms around her stomach as if her first instinct were to protect their imagined child.

"Heaven help us. Are you sure?"

"Quite sure."

Fleet slowed the horses and brought the carriage to a grinding halt next to a coppice.

Frantic, Hudson closed the box but kept hold of the pistol. "During highway robberies, ladies make the mistake of hiding in the carriage, waiting like sitting ducks. You won't. You'll climb out with me. You'll stand slightly behind my right shoulder, and if I tell you to run, you will run. Don't say anything. Don't look back no matter what you hear." He broke for breath. "Don't run in a straight line. Use the trees to your advantage."

Claudia stared at him, her eyes wide. "You're scaring me."

He shuffled to the edge of the seat, cupped her cheek and poured every ounce of love he felt for her into one tender kiss. "I'll protect you with my life."

She pressed her forehead to his, kissed him with the same abiding devotion. "If I loved you, I would tell you now," she said, stroking his cheek. "I'm in love with you, Hudson."

His heart soared and ached at the same time. He saw a bright future ahead. A bright future brought to an abrupt end by the firing of a single lead ball.

"And I am deeply in love with you." It felt so damn good to say the words. If he died tonight, he'd not have that regret.

"Stand and deliver!" The cold, masculine command pierced the air.

"Don't go out there. Please," she begged. Water welled in her eyes.

"I must. We must." He tucked the pistol into the waistband of his breeches before offering his hand. "Remember, when I tell you to run, run and don't look back."

"I know what you said, but I am not Selina. If there's a remote chance I might save you I will."

Pride and love filled his chest. Terror found a way in, too.

"Get out of the damn carriage!" the rogue cried.

Without another word, Lockhart opened the door and vaulted to the ground. He studied the assailant, looking for clues to his identity should he need to hunt the reprobate down and seek retribution.

Claudia climbed out of the carriage. Her knees buckled, and she crumpled to the ground. "It's all right. I'm fine."

The rogue's ugly laugh ignited a burning fury in Lockhart's chest. He helped her to her feet, noticed she clutched something in her hand.

"Give me your jewels and your purse." The blackguard spoke in an affected voice, as deep a timbre as any Lockhart had heard.

Lockhart snorted. "I don't have a purse, and my coachman only carries coin enough to pay the toll."

"Hand me your purse else I'll shoot." Agitated, he aimed the pistol at Lockhart. "And every lady of quality has a ring."

"No," Claudia muttered beneath her breath, "not my ring."

"She has no jewellery. Ours is a short journey." Lockhart spoke in a clipped tone. "We have no luggage, nothing of any value."

"Didn't anyone tell you these roads are unsafe?" The blackguard snorted. He seemed to find the notion of highway robbery somewhat amusing. "A man might take a ball between the brows should he fail to comply."

Should he fail to comply?

Lockhart had been away from England for five years, but to his knowledge, murderous thieves rarely spoke with the phrasing of a gentleman. Was this a ruse? The timing proved perfect. Was it Justin or Terence sitting astride the horse? Even with the light of the carriage lamp, it was impossible to tell. But one thing was certain. Both men had a reason to pull the trigger, which made this rogue more dangerous than any highwayman.

The blackguard teased the hammer. "Perhaps if I put the ball between your wife's brows it might force you to reconsider."

The chance that this man was either Terence or Justin grew more likely by the minute. Still, Lockhart couldn't risk pulling out an unloaded pistol. "How do you know she's my wife? I made no mention of the fact."

An awkward silence ensued.

"It was an educated guess," the fool replied in a higher pitch. Lockhart could teach him a lot about acting. In his panic, the devil forgot to speak in a deep voice.

"Then I shall repeat my earlier statement. We have nothing of any value."

The villain aimed his pistol at Claudia. "Perhaps I'll shoot your wife, anyway."

Lockhart's blood froze in his veins. What if his father hadn't amended his will? What if killing them was a sure way to gain Lockhart's share of the inheritance? Then again, it would be better to kill him first and deal with Claudia later.

Thankfully, Claudia stood slightly behind him which made her a more difficult target. And so Lockhart decided to take a chance.

"You'll not hit her from that range." Lockhart stepped to the right to shield Claudia. "I know of only one man capable. So, unless you're Lucius Valentine, I suggest you lower your pistol and be on your way."

"I could always shoot you."

Lockhart opened his arms. "Then take your best shot."

Behind him, Claudia gasped. "No, Hudson. Don't be a fool." She tugged on the back of his coat.

The blackguard aimed at Lockhart's heart.

And then chaos erupted.

Claudia jumped out from behind Lockhart's back and hurled a stone at the masked man sitting astride his mount. It whisked through the air and smacked the rogue hard on the hand.

"Bloody hell!" Yelping in pain from the accurate shot, the fool loosened his grip and his weapon tumbled to the ground.

Then Fleet made his move.

A loud crack of the coachman's whip sent the rogue's horse skittish. It reared, threw the rider back onto the ground before darting off into the coppice.

Lockhart broke into a run. He dived on the man lying squirming on the ground. A scuffle ensued, but Dariell had taught him how to use his opponent's strength to his advantage. Two deflects, and a hard punch to the rogue's gut rendered the fool helpless.

"Don't kill me," the coward choked when Lockhart straddled him on the ground. He wrapped his fingers around the black-guard's throat and pressed the pad of his thumb into the man's Adam's apple. "The ... the pistol isn't loaded. I s-swear."

In the fall, the tricorn hat had slipped to the left to reveal a wave of blonde hair. Lockhart tugged down the black neckcloth, unsurprised to find it was Justin Perigrew playing the part of an arrogant thief, though no theatre manager in the land would hire him after such a shoddy performance.

Lockhart supposed he should ask a few questions, but the urge to punch his cousin proved too great. The smack sent Justin's head whipping to the left. A stream of blood and spittle shot from his mouth. The dandy coughed and spluttered.

Satisfaction thrummed through Lockhart's veins.

"That's for threatening my wife." Lockhart flicked Justin's tricorn, and the hat went skittering across the ground. He grabbed a fistful of his cousin's hair, raised the fool's head and punched him again. The crack, quickly followed by Justin's pained groan, rent the air. "And that's for taking advantage of a helpless man."

Claudia came to stand at Lockhart's side. "What did you hope to gain by threatening us with a pistol?" She kicked Justin in the thigh. "That's for threatening to shoot my husband." She kicked him again for good measure. "Well, what were you hoping to gain?"

Silence ensued.

"You've insulted my wife on more than one occasion." Lockhart raised his fist. "Don't insult her now by refusing to answer."

"All right. All right." Justin closed his eyes briefly. "I just want rid of you."

"Rid of me?" Lockhart narrowed his gaze. "You said the pistol wasn't loaded."

"I was attempting to frighten your wife." He dabbed his tongue to the corner of his mouth. "I thought if she felt unsafe here she might beg you to take her back to India."

Lockhart couldn't help but glance at the woman standing at his side. The woman who hadn't run at the first sign of danger, but who had risked her life to save him. When it came to loving her, he didn't have to pretend.

"What, and leave you to drain my father dry?" While watching Claudia sleep in the carriage, Lockhart had contemplated the dark stain on his father's bedsheets. Only one plausible reason sprang to mind. "I know why you sit there, day after day. A visit to the bank will prove my theory."

"What theory?"

"That you wait until my father rouses from his drug-induced state. That you thrust a quill into his hand and persuade him to sign his name to numerous banknotes." Why else would there be an ink splatter on the bed?

Claudia placed a comforting hand on Lockhart's shoulder before continuing the verbal attack. "It is why you object to the doctor's presence, why you object to ours. One might wonder if Selina isn't aware of your trick. Perhaps you share your ill-gotten gains."

"That's preposterous." Justin's eyes widened in disbelief. "I would never do such a thing. And Selina is a paragon of virtue. Look, I admit to pestering my uncle, admit to playing the doting nephew in the hope he leaves me a large portion in his will."

"Then why drug him when there's nothing wrong with him?" Lockhart countered. The doctor was yet to confirm the diagnosis, but something told him his father suffered from nothing other than the effects of an excessive use of laudanum.

Justin groaned. "Can I stand? My stomach aches like the devil."

"Not until you answer my question."

"At least give me my handkerchief so I can clean the damn blood off my lips."

Claudia kicked Justin in the thigh. "Answer my husband's question."

"Goddamn," Justin groaned. "All right. As far as I know, he *is* ill. He's been suffering from some odd malaise ever since you left. Had it not been for Selina then your mother might have sent him to an institution."

"What were his symptoms?" Claudia asked.

"Disquiet, a general weakness of the body, disinterest in food and conversation. Every time someone mentioned your name he'd clutch his chest and take to his bed."

The answer tugged at Lockhart's heart.

During his time in India, he had concocted a very different story. In his chronicle, Alfred Lockhart ranted and raved. He destroyed his son's belongings and cursed him to the devil. He stomped down to his solicitor and demanded to have the name

Hudson Lockhart wiped from his will, scratched from their family's history.

"Your father pleaded with Terence to set sail and bring you home. He begged until he became too weak to utter the words."

A lump formed in Lockhart's throat, so large he had to swallow numerous times to breathe.

"Of course, your brother cares for no one but himself," Justin continued. "If you knew what he'd put his wife through, you would understand why she spends so much time with your parents."

Perhaps Terence lacked integrity. Perhaps he did have a gaming addiction that left him no option but to pander to the likes of Mrs Fanshaw. Lockhart imagined Selina was not an easy woman to love. And the absence of any children only added to the strain.

And yet something about the ink stain on the bed bothered him.

He was busy phrasing another question in his mind when Claudia said, "So Terence rarely visits Alfred?"

"Rarely?" Justin scoffed. "He's been once this last month."

"To bring the medicine," Claudia clarified.

"Yes."

"And both you and Selina attend to Alfred around the clock."

Justin frowned. "From ten in the morning until ten at night, yes."

That left twelve hours unaccounted. So Terence might have visited during the night without their knowledge. Lockhart would check with Simmonds upon his return.

"And my father's symptoms worsened when Lord Greystone returned from India," Lockhart confirmed.

Justin winced as he nodded. He pressed his fingers to his cheek. "By Selina's reckoning, Greystone had been home for a few days when Alfred started vomiting and lost his appetite."

Was it a natural sickness of the heart or was foul play afoot?

"And you're in love with Selina," Claudia blurted.

The statement came as a shock. Justin was too much of a fop to satisfy a woman with Selina's voracious appetite. Then again, he was easy to control, easy to manipulate. Many times in the past, Selina had tried to use her body to get what she wanted. Nothing of any great importance—attention, new dresses, jewels to show how much he cared.

"Selina needs a man who loves her to distraction, not one who abuses and humiliates her publicly," Justin replied. "Terence didn't even have the funds to pay her modiste. The poor woman was beside herself with worry."

And no doubt Justin came to her rescue.

The fool should be pitied, not beaten.

Lockhart climbed off his cousin and dragged the fop to his feet.

Panic flashed in Justin's eyes. "What are you going to do? Kill me?"

For a second, Lockhart wondered if the comment was said in reference to what had happened on that fateful night at the inn. But if Justin had known the truth, he would have used the information as a weapon to attack, a shield to defend. Unless of course, he was the one hiding behind the oak tree, the one guilty of murder.

No. Justin didn't have the strength of mind or body to drive a blade into a man's heart.

"Answer one last question, and I shall release you," Lockhart said. He would ask Greystone to monitor Justin's movements for the next two days. "Why would Lord Greystone's return affect my father so deeply when he believed I was dead?"

"I can only think it was something Captain Connor said on his return from Meerut."

"Captain Connor? Of the 8th dragoons?"

During his time in India, Lockhart and his friends had spent many drunken nights with the captain. Captain Connor had inherited an estate in Harrogate and returned two months before Lockhart's ship landed in England. What the bloody hell was he doing in London?

Justin brushed dirt off his coat and breeches. "I've never met him. Selina told me Terence spoke to the captain at his club, that the man was happy to inform him you'd not died from a tropical fever but was very much alive and well."

Damnation!

Lockhart had spent a month in a ramshackle cottage for naught. A month eating pheasant and stew. A blasted month sleeping next to Dariell. He glanced at Claudia's heart-shaped face, at her sparkling blue eyes, eyes that held the power to caress him with one sweep of her lashes. How could he be angry? He'd spent a month with a wonderful woman who had changed his life.

"So you were all awaiting my return?" Lockhart couldn't help but feel foolish.

"The captain mentioned that you and Greystone were inseparable. Once Greystone returned, Terence knew it was only a matter of time before you ventured into town."

And yet both Terence and Selina had appeared shocked to see him at the Comte de Lancey's masquerade. Was it shock or were they just as skilled when it came to acting?

Feeling a renewed flow of vengeance rushing through his veins, he captured Justin by his blood-stained cravat and yanked him forward. "Make any attempt to hurt my wife again, that includes making snide remarks, and I will put a lead ball between your neatly trimmed brows. Is that understood?"

Justin gulped and nodded vigorously.

"The wild dogs at the Westminster Pit are desperate to tear a man's flesh from his bones," Lockhart added. "There are numerous ways I might dispose of your body."

Lockhart released him, and the fop stumbled back before landing on his arse. Taking hold of Claudia's arm, Lockhart drew her towards the carriage. "We'll continue to Falaura Glen as planned, spend an hour there and return to London posthaste."

Claudia touched his upper arm. "Your cousin is no more than a besotted fool. I believe he would do anything for Selina, anything to secure a portion of your father's estate. And yet I doubt he is capable of committing a violent crime."

"I agree." A heavy sadness weighed in Lockhart's chest. It was time to track down his elusive brother and wring the truth from him if necessary. "Had Justin betrayed me I might have learnt to live with that, but not Terence."

"I know." She pursed her lips as her gaze softened. "The truth can be painful yet enlightening at the same time. But you cannot assume your brother's guilt until it is proven."

Frustration surfaced. "What other explanation is there?"

She gave a half shrug. "Soon, we will know."

For some reason, her words acted as a balm for his wounds. "Then let's be on our way."

Lockhart climbed into the carriage behind Claudia and slammed the door shut.

"Wait!" Justin raced over and knocked on the glass pane. "What about me?"

Lockhart lowered the window. "I suggest you start searching for your horse. Failing that, you can always walk back to town."

CHAPTER TWENTY

Everything was as it should be at Falaura Glen. Emily lay sound asleep in bed, the corners of her mouth curled in a satisfied smile. Mrs Bitton confirmed all was well and so Claudia spent ten minutes ferreting around in her father's study.

It was something Hudson had said earlier, that his father might not have written the letter he received while in India, that fanned the flame of doubt. Claudia found the document she wanted, locked in the bottom drawer of the desk. It was a legally binding contract—the sale of two acres of land—made between her father and Mr Thorncroft some three years earlier. Then she hunted out the receipts for household expenses.

Richard Darling made a point of signing and dating all receipts and marking them as paid. If one compared the signature on the bills from three years ago to the one on the contract, they were identical. However, examining the signature on the bills dated during the time of the supposed loan, revealed a discrepancy. Yes, they were almost similar to the naked eye. But as her father's illness progressed, he lacked dexterity, and the pen strokes were not as smooth or fluid.

It wasn't enough to approach the magistrate and declare something was amiss, but it was a start.

After securing the evidence and locking the desk drawer, Claudia made her way to the cottage to find Hudson. He, too, had gathered the leather satchel full of papers.

"Are you ready to leave?" he said, sliding his arm around her waist and pressing a kiss to her lips. "Dariell assures me your sister is happy. Last night, she beat him at cards."

"Cards?" Claudia whispered so as not to disturb the Frenchman resting in the next room.

"Apparently, he cut numbers into each card and a symbol for each suit. He taught her to trace the symbols in order to identify which card she wished to play."

Hudson spoke with admiration. Admiration and a deep abiding gratitude filled Claudia's chest, too. No wonder Emily slept with a smile on her face.

Claudia was about to say that her sister would miss the Frenchman when he left, but that would only raise questions as to what would happen once the week was out, and there were other matters to attend to first.

The drive back to London passed without incident.

Claudia would have stared out of the window, hoping to see Justin Perigrew trudging back to town, had she not spent the entire journey sleeping.

The hustle and bustle of the city roused her from a blissful dream about the man seated opposite. Having taken full advantage of the few hours of peace to rest, too, he stretched his limbs and yawned.

"Will you check on my father while I speak to Simmonds?" Hudson said, rubbing his hand over the bristles on his chin. "I must know if Terence called during those hours my father was left unattended."

Claudia studied the dark circles beneath his eyes, the frown between his brows that was swiftly becoming a permanent feature. These troubling events had taken their toll. Only when his mouth melded with hers, when he drove hard into her willing body, did his troubles melt away.

Thoughts of seduction filled her head.

She might lead him upstairs and take advantage of such a large bed. She might delve into the hat box and snatch the red and black mask, have their own illicit masquerade.

By the time the carriage rattled to a stop in Russell Square, her pulse was racing.

Before the footman opened the front door and came to offer assistance, a loud rap on the window made them both jump back in shock.

Terence Lockhart pressed his face to the glass. "Where the hell have you been?" he mouthed.

Hudson hesitated, and his wary gaze flicked in Claudia's direction. Mistrust lingered in his eyes. "No doubt he thinks I've kidnapped Father. Or perhaps he's seen Justin's bruises and wants to know why I've taken to beating my own cousin."

"Well, you can sit here inventing stories, or you can open the door and find out."

Terence knocked on the window, his gaze darting left and right. He tried to open the door from the outside, but Hudson grabbed the handle and gripped it in his strong fist.

Lockhart gritted his teeth. "As God is my witness, if he lays a hand on you they'll still be looking for his body five years from now."

Claudia leant forward and touched his knee. "Open the door, Hudson."

Exhaling a weary sigh, Hudson released the handle. He opened the door and said, "What do you want, Terence?"

His brother climbed into the carriage without invitation, slammed the door shut and dropped into the seat next to Claudia. "Tell your coachman to drive, drive anywhere."

"Tell me what the hell this is about."

"What it's about?" Terence asked incredulously. "It's about the fact you're alive and didn't bother to tell me. It's about the fact you turn up here, ignorant to the scheming villain at work and presume to ride roughshod over all of us."

Hudson sat forward, his eyes as dark and dangerous as any devilish fiend. "Do not dare lecture me when you've left Father to rot in his room. The man has spent the last damn month in a laudanum-induced sleep."

Unable to contain his anxiety, Terence thumped his fist on the roof and shouted, "Drive!"

The carriage jerked forward. The brothers' voices carried a similar cadence—though Claudia didn't melt a little inside when Terence spoke—and with the order given from within the confines of the carriage, it must have confused the coachman.

Hudson did not protest when the vehicle picked up pace. "Is there a reason you cannot take tea in the drawing room and converse like any other civilised person?"

Claudia shuffled closer to the window. The tense atmosphere proved suffocating. A volatile energy vibrated in the air, so volatile she wouldn't be surprised if either brother lashed out.

"I'll not have the servants listening to our conversation," Terence snapped. "I'd rather avoid being the topic of gossip in the saloons tomorrow."

"No, we wouldn't want that," Hudson mocked. "Better to avoid scandal than to fight for the truth."

A brief silence ensued.

"We seem to be singing from different hymn sheets," Terence said. "I don't know why you have an issue with me."

Hudson glanced at Claudia, his brows raised in amazement at his brother's ignorance. "Perhaps it might have something to do with the fact you're avoiding me," he said to the brother whose jaw was less defined, lips too thin. "Or could it be that you'd rather spend your evenings pandering to Mrs Fanshaw when your father is ill in bed?"

Terence flopped back in the seat. A mirthless laugh escaped him. "That goes to prove my earlier statement. You're charging around, completely ignorant of the facts."

Hudson's cheeks turned crimson. Fire flashed in his eyes. "Then tell me what the hell this is about."

"It's about five miserable years spent with a woman who still loves you. It's about the fact our cousin is determined to steal our inheritance, and my wife will do everything possible to ensure she bleeds us all dry."

❦

The sudden revelation defused the tension in the air.

Lockhart remained silent. No part of Terence's dramatic monologue came as a shock. Indeed, Selina had professed her love at the theatre and yet they were empty words. Unlike Claudia's declaration, they lacked real sentiment. He had not felt the truth deep in his bones.

"Justin held us up on the road, dressed in the garb of a highwayman." Lockhart couldn't help but grin when the image of the dandy in a tricorn flashed into his mind. "It was his intention merely to frighten and intimidate. He hoped we would pack our trunks and book passage on the first boat back to India."

Terence arched a brow. "Then our cousin is a fool. You're not a man who frightens easily."

Except when threatened with the gallows after being bludgeoned by an unknown assailant.

"We both know that's untrue. I fled the inn in terror, crossed vast oceans, and I haven't stopped running since."

Claudia's sigh drew his gaze. Compassion filled her pretty blue eyes.

"I gave you no other option," Terence admitted. "To this day I cannot make sense of what happened that night. I've returned to the inn many times, hoping to discover something new, but to no avail."

Suspicion flared. In this game of deception whose word could he trust?

Devils wore disguises. They masqueraded as kind, considerate citizens—lovers, brothers, cousins and neighbours. Was this just an alternative retelling of the biblical tale? Did Terence have Cain's jealous streak? Or was this a gentleman's curse—the curse of the eldest son?

"What did Selina tell you on the night she came to you for help?" Lockhart's abrupt tone held the depth of his disdain.

Terence settled into the seat. "She said you were fighting with a man in the woods, that you told her to run, and that she feared you'd killed him."

The same lines she had repeated on the journey to Portsmouth. "And rather conveniently, you happened to be at home."

"Conveniently for you, yes," Terence argued. "Selina sent the coachman to the door and summoned me to the carriage." His brother shook his head. "But you know all of this."

"No, I don't. I remember very little after the incident." Hudson rubbed the back of his head recalling the painful lump that had throbbed for weeks, the place that still ached when the temperature plummeted. "Did she speak to you on the journey back to the inn?"

Terence gave a nonchalant shrug. "She cried most of the way. Complained about her life being ruined."

Claudia cleared her throat. "May I ask what Selina was wearing that night?"

Lockhart knew why Claudia had asked. Indeed, he had added Selina to his list of suspects. But she lacked the strength to thrust a blade into a man's heart—she did that with words— and there had not been so much as a speck of blood on her dress.

"I don't recall. She'd wrapped a lap blanket around her shoulders."

Thankfully for Terence, he didn't stare down his nose at Claudia as Justin had done. That saved Lockhart having to punch his brother, at least.

"And when you arrived at the inn she brought you straight to the woods?"

Terence shook his head. "She remained in the carriage for a few minutes. She was scared of what we might find. The coachman directed me to the spot where you lay next to a blood-soaked body. Selina only came when the servant returned to confirm you were alive."

Lockhart remembered hearing Selina's sobs. They'd sounded heartfelt at the time, not so now. "And you thought I had murdered that man."

It was perhaps the one thing he would struggle to forgive. Not once during the long carriage ride to the coast had Terence accepted Lockhart's pleas of innocence.

Terence dragged his hand down his face and rubbed his jaw. "Not intentionally, but I believed you killed him in self-defence. You were always a little wild and unpredictable."

Lockhart almost reeled from the pain of the imagined punch. "I did not kill him," he reiterated, grabbing hold of the overhead strap lest he throttle his brother. "Not in anger. Not in self-defence."

Noting his mounting frustration, Claudia crossed the carriage to sit at his side. She found his hand and gripped it tight. It was a show of solidarity, of support, a testament to her loyalty.

"Do not let what others think or believe feed your anger," she said softly.

Her words were like an elixir, a soothing tonic to douse the flames.

Lockhart took a deep breath before asking, "What happened to the body?"

The question had haunted his nightmares for years. Lord knows how many times he'd looked at a mound of earth and imagined a hand bursting up through the soil.

Terence glanced at their clasped hands and sighed. "I have no idea."

A host of questions flooded Lockhart's addled brain. "What do you mean?" Panic choked his throat. "You said you'd dealt with things."

"Selina's coachman dealt with the matter while I scoured the woods looking for his accomplice."

"So what the hell did he do with the body?"

Claudia placed her other hand on his arm. "Terence said he doesn't know."

Lockhart narrowed his gaze. Was this all part of the plot to overthrow him?

"Selina gave the instruction," Terence informed. "She said it was best we remain ignorant. Should the incident ever come to light, we wouldn't be forced to lie."

So despite her distress, Selina had considered how the event might impact her in the future. How courageous. Then again, maybe Lockhart had inherited his mother's cynical view.

Either way, the declaration presented a far more serious problem.

"The coachman's devotion to his duties surpassed that of any servant I've ever known," Lockhart said.

The man's loyalty to Selina went above and beyond the call of duty. Particularly when one considered he was employed by her father, Mr Garthwaite. But her father had died two years ago. So where in hell's name was the coachman?

"The impression I got was that Selina could have asked him to do anything and he would have obliged."

"And where is he now?" Lockhart tried to keep the desperation from his voice.

"Dead."

"Dead?" Why was he not surprised?

"All I know is he left Mr Garthwaite's employ and boarded a boat to Boston. Somehow during the journey, he fell overboard."

People did not fall overboard—invariably they jumped or were hurled into the water by someone with a grudge. "And you don't think that's odd?"

"What's odd is the series of events that have occurred since Lord Greystone's return to London," Terence countered. "And yet through the confusion, there appears to be a common thread."

"Money," Claudia said with confidence. "Money is the impetus. It is certainly not love, for I do not believe you love Selina."

A month ago, Lockhart would have scoffed at the mere mention of the word *love*. Now, he could not deny that one could develop a profound and passionate connection. Trust had been a problem for him, too. And while he still doubted the integrity of most people, he would place his life in the hands of the woman sitting at his side.

"About Selina ..." Terence's chin dropped. He glanced at the buttons on his waistcoat. When he sighed, his shoulders slumped forward. After taking a few deep breaths, he raised his head. "There was a profound attraction, an attraction I could not deny."

"Is that why you grew distant those last few months?" Lockhart recalled his brother making excuses to avoid his company.

"I assumed it was just a passing phase." His cheeks flushed crimson. "On the journey back from Portsmouth, she was inconsolable. One embrace led to a kiss ... a kiss led to something of which I am deeply ashamed."

Lockhart waited to feel another sharp stab—the pain of betrayal—but it didn't come.

"So you're saying you loved her once," Claudia attempted to clarify. "A man who cavorts with another lady in her box in full view of the audience cannot possibly love his wife."

Claudia was right. When Lockhart thought of touching any

other woman other than the delightful Miss Darling, his stomach roiled.

With tense shoulders and pinched lips, Terence looked like a man who'd been stabbed in the heart, not the back. For a moment it sounded as if he'd stopped breathing.

"It took a few years to realise the truth," Terence eventually said. "Selina is an extremely good actress." He gathered himself. "You're right, Mrs Lockhart. Money is the impetus for all Selina's decisions."

"With your predilection for gambling," Lockhart scoffed, "I imagine you fought often."

Terence frowned. "Is that what Selina told you? I'm not the one who loses money at the tables. Every matron in the *ton* knows not to invite her to their card games. Ask around if you distrust my word. Since I restricted Selina's funds, she's taken an extreme dislike to me."

Hence the reason the lady was keen to spend more time with Justin. Had the fop really paid her modiste bill or just another gambling debt?

"Is your interest in Mrs Fanshaw merely a means to make her jealous?" Claudia asked.

Terence shook his head. "I was attempting to use charm to extract information. Mrs Fanshaw was Mr Garthwaite's mistress at the time of the incident five years ago."

Lockhart relaxed back in the seat. Perhaps he needed to erase the story he had created in his mind and begin again. He'd come home believing he had no family. Now it appeared his father cared. From the snippets of information he was piecing together, it seemed his brother might care a little, too.

"And you think that has some relevance?" Claudia asked.

"It does if you consider the fact Garthwaite had borrowed money to the sum of ten thousand pounds. A debt he could not repay. Mrs Fanshaw had stopped funding his habit. The image he projected to society does not reflect the true nature of the man."

Perhaps spending so much time with Claudia Darling had awakened Lockhart's senses. Instinct told him his brother spoke the truth. Everything he'd said sounded logical, plausible.

But there were still unanswered questions.

"So why not approach me sooner?" Lockhart said. It would have saved time and trouble. Then again, he would have missed the opportunity to spend time in Claudia Darling's company. "Why insist we leave town?"

"Because I believe my wife is dangerous." Terence's grave expression proved unnerving. "She is cold and calculating, and I feared what she would do to your wife should you remain here. I needed more time to gather evidence and your presence has made her panic."

"Good God! You think she is dangerous and yet you permit her to spend hours alone with our father?"

"Oh, she won't hurt him, not when I'm convinced he is funding her habit. I'm in the process of bribing a clerk at the bank for information."

Claudia gasped. "There's an ink stain on the bed. What if she structures her visits around the time your father regains use of his faculties?" A delightful hum left her lips. "But why go to such lengths now?"

"Because now Hudson is home, he might discover our father has been giving her money for years. She's played the doting daughter card extremely well. Keeping him sedated buys her a little time. I've been monitoring the situation daily without her knowledge."

"You attend him at night," Lockhart stated. "You realise Justin visited the apothecary and insisted on a stronger tincture of laudanum."

Terence nodded. "I decanted a lesser dose into the bottle though I fear Selina is bringing her own tincture with her now."

Claudia muttered something under her breath. "If Selina suspects you know the truth, she may harm your father. He is the only person who can attest to the fact she is drugging him against his will, to the fact he is giving her money."

Lockhart considered the last point. Based on his father's supposed illness no one would believe his ramblings. The only proof lay with the bank.

"It's of no consequence now as I've moved Father into my home. Simmonds is under strict instructions not to let her cross the threshold."

Terence snorted. "I received word from Mother this morning that the heathen had gone on the rampage, although she seems more concerned that you've abducted Simmonds."

Lockhart snorted. "The butler begged me to take him."

"As would I if I had to suffer Mother's infernal complaining." After a brief silence, Terence sighed. "Well, I have an appointment with the clerk at the bank. I trust you will watch Father while he's in your care."

"Of course." Lockhart inclined his head. "Dr Hewlett is tending to him as we speak." No doubt the doctor was eager to attend to his other patients, too.

Terence glanced out of the window. They were approaching Russell Square for the third time, and so Lockhart rapped on the roof. As the carriage drew to a stop, Terence shuffled forward and gripped the door handle.

"I'll let you know my findings. In the meantime, be on your guard." Terence turned to Claudia and smiled. "Allow me to congratulate you on your marriage and the upcoming birth of your first child."

Claudia smiled, too. "Thank you."

It was the forced smile of an actress. Beneath it, Lockhart wondered if she'd experienced the same rush of regret that currently plagued him. How was it possible to feel the loss of a child who had never existed?

Terence exited the carriage, and they followed closely behind.

When Terence climbed into his own carriage, Lockhart took hold of Claudia's hand, and they entered the house.

"I suppose I should relieve Dr Hewlett," he said, snatching the note from the salver on the console table. "And then we should retire to the privacy of our bedchamber." Making love to his soon-to-be wife would banish the ghosts of the past.

"Perhaps I should have Lissette draw a bath." From her seductive lilt, she wanted him, too.

Lockhart broke the seal and read the few scrawled lines. "Damnation."

"What is it? Is something wrong?"

He scanned the missive again, the prickle at his nape racing down his spine. "It's from Selina." The damn woman would say anything to gain attention. "She wants to meet us tonight on Richmond Bridge. Reading between the lines, it sounds as though she's threatening to jump."

CHAPTER TWENTY-ONE

A grim silence filled the space inside Lockhart's carriage. The creak of rolling wheels and the pounding of horses' hooves on the hard ground permeated the uncomfortable stillness. The road's uneven surface proved problematic amidst the heavy fog. Twice they'd almost bumped down a ditch. But it wasn't Devlin Drake's driving or the choking mass outside that roused a deep sense of foreboding.

Wickedness hung in the air.

Evil lurked in the shadows.

Selina Lockhart had devious intentions, else why had she not begged him to come alone? What possible motive prompted her to insist on Claudia's attendance, too?

Lockhart withdrew his pocket watch. He angled the face but struggled to read the time. Damnation. Arriving late would only rouse the woman's ire. In the distance, the bells of St Mary Magdalene tolled eight, but the sound echoed like an ominous warning.

"Do you think Selina will realise it is Mr Drake and not Fleet sitting atop the box?" Claudia's strained expression revealed her apprehension, too.

"They're of a similar size and build. With the collar of his greatcoat raised, Drake could pass for my coachman."

Valentine would have been Lockhart's first choice. The viscount could shoot an apple off a tree from two hundred yards. But the lord's trim, athletic physique would have drawn Selina's attention. Drake could beat five men to a pulp, but he would never assault a woman. Still, having his friend close at hand brought comfort.

"Do you think she means to jump?" Claudia asked. "Or is it all just a ruse to dim the light of suspicion?"

With Richmond being an hour's ride from town, Lockhart had considered the possibility that, in their absence, Justin might attempt to steal Alfred away from Russell Square. Hence the reason he'd paid Dr Hewlett a handsome fee to keep a bedside vigil.

"A woman as selfish as Selina would never take her own life."

"A woman as cunning as Selina would not call us both to Richmond Bridge unless she had a plan."

Panic threatened to choke him. His fears were not for himself but for the woman seated opposite. Seventeen hundred pounds was a pittance when he considered what he'd put her through— treachery, deceit, highway robbery and now this. Not once had she raised a complaint. Not once had she demanded they renegotiate their terms, demanded more money. If he could do anything for her, he would ensure she had every penny she needed to fix the problems at Falaura Glen. She never need worry about a leaking roof or an empty store cupboard again.

"We will follow the same procedure as we did the night Justin chased our carriage and pulled a pistol," he said, shaking his head as he recalled the pathetic attempt to scare him. That said, he had been scared, scared of losing the love of his life.

"You want me to pretend to trip so I can grab a stone?" she said with mild amusement.

"Do not underestimate her. She'll sob in your arms whilst

driving a blade into your back." Suspicious thoughts invaded his mind. Had Selina been more than a spectator on that fateful night at the inn?

Every why hath a wherefore.

Every new piece of information brought answers. Tonight, he hoped to bring an end to his midsummer's nightmare.

The carriage rumbled to a halt.

Lockhart glanced out of the window, noted the light of a lantern swaying from the hook outside the toll house. "Drake is paying the toll."

With the transaction completed, Drake led the carriage across the bridge, bringing it to a stop on the brow. He climbed down from his perch and knocked on the pane.

Lockhart lowered the window. "Can you see her?"

"The fog is so dense a man would struggle to see his feet." Drake glanced left and right. A white puff of mist left his mouth as he sighed. "The tollman said a carriage crossed twenty minutes ago, but he hasn't seen a soul since."

"We'll wait here. The note said to meet on the bridge."

"What if she has jumped and we're too late?" Claudia said. "It's so cold her muscles would seize as soon as she hit the water."

"She hasn't the courage to jump." In his gut, Lockhart knew that's what Selina wanted them to think. "No, we'll wait."

Drake nodded. The carriage rocked as he climbed back up on the box.

Minutes passed before Drake rapped twice on the roof—a signal to say someone approached.

"Are you ready?" Lockhart shuffled to the edge of the seat. "Drake is under instructions to save you regardless of all else. By now, Terence will have received my note and will join us soon." He was about to lean forward and claim her mouth in a kiss filled with lust and love and hope for the future, but Drake rapped on the roof again.

"I saw a figure in the mist," Drake said as Lockhart climbed out of the conveyance. "The person wore a long cloak, but I can't tell if it's a man or woman."

"Where?" Lockhart peered through the grey cloud swamping everything in its path.

"Just beyond the next gas lamp." Drake pointed to the faint yellow glow in the distance.

"I'll go on foot. Roll slowly alongside." He would not leave Claudia alone and vulnerable in the carriage.

Drake flicked the reins but did not shout instructions to the team.

The clip of Lockhart's boots on the stone path rang like a death-knell. The eerie noises of the dark echoed from the depths of the ghostly mist. Boats moved like phantoms in the water beneath them, the creak of oars the only sign of their presence. The sterile smell of cold air might have cleared his mind, had the wind not whipped up the foul stench of death and decay from the river below.

At first, Lockhart feared his eyes deceived him. The black figure measured ten-foot tall. But as he drew nearer, he realised his mistake. Selina Lockhart had climbed the parapet. She stood on top of the capstones as if on stage, gripping the post of the gas lamp to steady her balance.

"Selina?" Lockhart spoke softly so as not to startle the woman, but she knew he was there.

Shrouded beneath the folds of her hood, he could see nothing but her dark, wild eyes staring back. "The invitation was for two," she said. "I want your wife to hear what I have to say."

"This is just between us," he said, wishing he'd left Claudia at home. "We share a history no one else understands."

"A history?" she spat. "What happened on that terrible night ruined everything."

"And it is in the past, Selina." Had she dragged him all the way to Richmond to incite his pity? "You're married to Terence now. What good will any of this serve?"

She shook her head, clutched the post with both hands. "But I want to be married to you."

Lockhart firmed his jaw. He could not lie. He could never lie about his feelings for Claudia. "It's too late. I love my wife. I am so deeply in love with her there will never be anyone else for me."

A heart-wrenching sob burst from Selina's lips. "No! That's not how it was meant to be. I was too weak then, too weak to fight for us, too foolish to understand how conniving he could be, but I'm stronger now."

Lockhart tried to make sense of her ramblings. "To whom are you referring?" Hell's teeth surely she didn't mean Terence.

"I want to speak to your wife," she suddenly said.

"I don't see what good it will do." Lockhart glanced left and right, scoured the haze to ensure no one else lingered, waiting to pounce.

"You said I don't know what love is, but you're wrong," Selina continued. "At the theatre, your wife made her claim, and I didn't get to make mine."

"Have I not already explained my position?" He exhaled a white puff of frustration into the cold night air.

To make matters worse, the carriage door opened and Claudia stepped out.

Drake muttered a curse. He climbed down from his perch and set about checking the horses.

"You're right," Claudia said, the rattle of fear evident in her voice. "I stated my case but did not give you the opportunity to state yours."

Gripping the post with one hand, Selina tugged down the hood of her cloak. "When you see us together, there is no comparison," she said, brushing her loose ebony locks over her shoulder.

"I have an elegance, a natural charm that comes with good breeding. There is something of the country bumpkin about you."

Selina had clearly spent too much time with his mother.

Lockhart opened his mouth ready to jump to Claudia's defence, but his soon-to-be wife placed a reassuring hand on his arm.

"Your argument is weak." Claudia raised her chin. "In assuming my husband is a man lured by the superficial, you do him a disservice."

Selina snorted. "It was the superficial that enabled me to tempt him into bed."

"You're right," Claudia said with confidence. "Lust is a powerful emotion. But I am talking about love."

"In bed, there is no difference."

Lockhart coughed into his fist. "I beg to disagree." When he entered Claudia's body, the pleasure gleaned from each vigorous thrust satisfied on a level deeper than that of casual bed sport. "Making love to my wife satisfies on an emotional and physical level rather than just relieving an ache in my ..."

Drake hummed in agreement.

Selina shook her head, unable to accept his explanation. "It would have been the same with us if only you'd stayed in the room, if only I'd not had my hand forced."

Her hand forced?

"You didn't love him," Claudia protested, ignoring the vital clue. "If you did, you would have run into the inn to fetch help. You would have trusted in his innocence. You would have boarded the boat and never looked back."

"You know nothing about the circumstances of that night," Selina countered, growing more agitated by the second. "You don't know what I've endured, what I've sacrificed."

Lockhart shook his head. "What you've endured? I was bundled on to a ship and sent halfway across the world." Anger flared. "My wife is right. You've never loved me. You think I'm guilty of committing vile atrocities."

"No!" Selina cried. "That's not true. I know you're innocent. You did nothing that night. I was there."

The comment confused him. "But you said you heard a scream and didn't know what happened. On your return, you remained in the carriage because you didn't know if I was alive or dead."

A sudden gust of wind caught her off guard. Her cloak whipped about her legs, and she gripped the post with both hands.

"Get down, Selina," Lockhart demanded. The woman thrived on drama. "Get down before you fall."

She shook her head. "Listen to me! I can't risk you walking away when I need you to know that I did love you. You didn't hurt that man, my father did. My father arranged it all. He lied to me, made me believe he was acting in my interests."

It took a few seconds for the words to penetrate.

Every drop of blood in Lockhart's body turned cold. His heart skipped a beat. Bright lights danced in his eyes. It took every effort to focus on the image of Selina balancing on the capstones.

He wanted to speak but couldn't.

"How was murdering that man supposed to serve you?" Claudia asked on his behalf.

"I was supposed to follow you outside," Selina said, ignoring Claudia to address him. "When the thug threatened me, my father said you would realise how much you loved me, would save me and offer marriage."

Every why hath a wherefore.

Lockhart tried to piece together the snippets he'd learnt from Terence. It had been about money. The rogue had come expecting payment and received a knife to the heart.

"But instead, your father killed the man because he couldn't afford to pay his debt." Bile bubbled in Lockhart's throat. "Garthwaite blamed me for the crime, and his loyal coachman concealed the evidence." Judging by the brusque nature of the coachman, perhaps he was the one who delivered the fatal blow.

"That is what I am trying to tell you," Selina said. "I wanted to come with you, but my father knew of our secret liaisons. When you didn't offer to marry me, he realised Terence was the better option. My father had mortgaged the house. I would have lost everything had he gone to debtors' prison."

Parts of the puzzle slotted into place. Terence was the easier target, the man with more integrity, the greater conscience. No doubt Terence offered to marry her on the journey back from Portsmouth. And she'd spent years funding her father's gambling habit, not her own.

"You used my brother to pay your father's debts," he said. Guilt surfaced. In his mind, he had made his brother his enemy when in truth they had both been betrayed.

"If only you had married me." Selina reached out her hand to him as if expecting he might grasp it, might save her. "We could have paid the debts, freed my father from his obligations and then lived happily."

Deluded did not even begin to explain her thought process.

"Happily?" he mocked. "Knowing that you value your position in society over all else. You watched me board that ship a broken man when one word from you could have saved me. For five damn years, you let me wallow in confusion, let the bitterness of vengeance consume me, blacken my soul."

"That is not love." Claudia's sweet voice breezed over him.

No. It was cruel.

The abominable act of a heartless harpy.

"What did you hope to achieve by telling me this?" Daresay, whatever her reason there was no logic involved. "If it was to prove that you loved me, you have done the opposite."

The echo of footsteps racing along the stone bridge captured their attention.

Lockhart grasped Claudia's hand. He considered bundling her

into the carriage so Drake could spirit her away. For a few seconds, he stared at the thick, rolling fog, as blind as he had been for the last five years, watching, waiting.

Relief, tinged with a sliver of apprehension, took hold when Terence and Justin burst through the bank of grey cloud. His brother took one look at Selina balanced on the bridge and came to a crashing halt.

Justin, his face a rainbow of blues and purples, gasped in shock. "What the devil?"

Silence descended, as suffocating as the swirling mist clawing at their throats.

Selina looked dazed. She reached out to Terence, her shaky hand mimicking the tremble of her bottom lip. "Save me. Your brother is beside himself with rage and won't rest until I'm lying dead at the bottom of the Thames. He blames me for what happened that night."

"Blames you for what?" Justin sounded confused.

She ignored Justin and focused on Terence. "But I had to send Hudson away," she said, gripping the post as another gust of wind whipped at her hair and cloak. "It was the only way we could be together."

"Will someone tell me what is going on?" Justin persisted. "Come down from there, Selina, before you do yourself an injury."

"Oh, Justin." Selina feigned a sob. "Can you not see what's happening here? Hudson wants rid of us. He's kidnapped Alfred and won't rest until he's stolen every damn penny. Twice, he's tried to push me off this bridge."

Drake growled. He threw off his hat and lowered the collar of his greatcoat. "The woman is lying. She lured us here under some misguided notion of love. Every word from her lips is riddled with deceit."

"Your aunt is right. They're all heathens." Selina choked on her fake tears. "Call the watchman, Justin. Tell him these men are trying to kill me." She turned to Terence, bared her teeth and glared. "I should have known you'd stand there looking gormless."

While Terence retaliated with numerous accusations, Lockhart glanced at Drake.

His friend sidled next to him and whispered, "Perhaps we should call the watchman. He patrols the bridge nightly. Anyone caught causing malicious damage risks transportation to one of His Majesty's colonies."

"You think we should shout *vandal*?" The thought of Selina serving a sentence abroad had vast appeal.

"Are you going to stand there and let him insult me?" Selina had turned her beady stare on Justin. "You said you loved me. You said once you inherited you would keep me in the luxury I deserve." She stamped her foot. "You said all of those things. Deny it."

Justin shuffled uncomfortably. "That was before Terence told me you've been stealing money from my uncle. Goddamn, at this rate, there'll be nothing left once he passes."

"So that's it," Selina complained. "You're all so consumed with money you're willing to turn on those you love."

Drake bent his head and whispered, "The woman has lost all grasp of reality. I'm beginning to think an asylum might be better than the colonies. Either way, we need to get her down from that bridge."

"Agreed."

"Let me try," Claudia said, having been a party to their hushed conversation. Lockhart had reservations, but before he could air them, Claudia said, "Selina, why don't you come down. We'll find a quiet inn and take supper, talk about this in a calm, rational manner. I'm sure we can resolve our differences."

Despite Claudia's charitable protestations, Lockhart would never forgive Selina. He would never speak to her again.

The prolonged and pained silence should have told him something was amiss. They were all waiting for Selina's reply when the crazed woman drew a small pistol from the pocket of her cloak.

"Oh, we can resolve this," she said, waving the pistol back and forth between Claudia and Terence. "The only way I can marry Hudson is if I shoot both of you."

"You've only got one shot," Claudia countered. "Who will you choose?"

As Selina considered her dilemma—and Lockhart debated how the hell he would grab the pistol out of Selina's hand without knocking her into the Thames—the echo of booted footsteps rendered them all frozen to the spot.

"Help!" Selina blurted. "They're trying to kill me!"

The approaching figure broke into a sprint.

Curse the devil!

The watchman appeared through the mist, puffing and panting. He scanned the scene, noted Selina waving the pistol and gasped.

"They're trying to kill me," Selina repeated.

Claudia turned to the watchman. "She lured us here and then threatened to shoot us. I fear she is unstable. My husband has the letter she sent, and any one of these gentlemen can testify to her insanity."

Lockhart wasn't entirely sure what happened next, but he would replay the event over and over in his mind for some time to come.

The gust of wind struck at precisely the same moment Selina fired the pistol. Claudia crumpled to the ground, and yet it was Selina's scream that pierced the air.

Good God!

"Claudia!" Lockhart dropped to his knees. "Are you hurt?"

"No," Claudia panted, her face deathly pale. "At least I don't think so."

Lockhart glanced behind him at the sudden flurry of activity.

The shock of firing, coupled with the sudden wind, forced Selina to release her grip on the post. Arms flailing, she fell back, back over the bridge. Her fearful cries died as soon as she hit the water.

While Terence, Justin and the watchman raced from the bridge to the water's edge, Drake calmed the horses, and Lockhart checked every inch of Claudia's body searching for signs of blood.

"I think she hit the lamp," Drake said, pointing towards the opposite side of the bridge. "I heard the glass shatter."

"Christ, I don't think I've ever been so scared." Lockhart took Claudia's hand and helped her to stand. He captured her cheeks and kissed her on the mouth. "For a second, I thought I'd lost you."

She smiled. "There's no chance of that." Her expression turned sombre. "We should go down to the waterside and see if we can help."

Keeping a firm grip of Claudia's hand, they crossed the bridge and descended the flight of stone steps leading down to the riverbank. It took a few minutes to find Terence in the fog. Indeed, the weather had prevented them from locating the place where Selina had plunged into the water. The watchman roused the help of two men in a boat. After an hour spent searching, one shivering and soaked fellow dragged Selina's body onto the shore.

They spent the next few hours giving statements to the magistrate. No one mentioned the incident at the inn five years ago. With the information Terence had discovered from the bank clerk, and the watchman bearing witness to the madness, the magistrate concluded that guilt had robbed Selina of her mental faculties.

Drake drove them back to Russell Square.

"Fleet will take you home, Drake." Lockhart stood with his friend on the pavement as they watched Claudia enter the house. "I'm sure Juliet will be keen to know you're safe and well."

Drake gripped Lockhart's shoulder. "It must be a relief to

know the truth. Now you know what happened that night at the inn you can put the past behind you."

Indeed, he had to stop thinking about the injustice of it all. Despite Selina's treachery, he would not have wished for her death.

"The truth is always enlightening." Lockhart clutched his friend's arm. "I cannot thank you enough for your help tonight. Now that my return is no longer a secret, you should all come to dinner."

Drake's smile reached his eyes. "It will be good to eat a meal together without talk of retribution and vengeance."

Lockhart laughed. "What the devil will we talk about?"

"We could talk about our love for our wives. I think we all have that in common."

The comment brought a rush of euphoria when he thought about Claudia. It brought a pang of anxiety, too, for there was still the matter of the fake marriage to address.

"Except for Dariell," Drake added.

"I'm not so sure. The last time I saw Dariell, he looked besotted. But I'm sure he'll tell you himself when he returns to town."

Drake arched a brow. "What will you do now?"

"Do?"

"About the fact Claudia is your wife in everything but name."

"There is only one thing to do. I shall make Miss Darling an offer."

One he prayed she would not refuse.

CHAPTER TWENTY-TWO

Perhaps it was the traumatic events of the last few days that forced them to slide into bed as soon as the doctor waved goodbye at the door. Perhaps it was lust that caused them to strip naked amid frantic pants and groans, lust that made Claudia take Hudson's impressive erection into her mouth.

The urge to control and dominate proved to be a powerful thing.

But it was love that brought tears to her eyes when Hudson entered her body. Love that made her wrap her legs tightly around him, not wanting to let go. Love that split her heart in two when she realised the grave error she had made by not being completely honest with him in the beginning.

Everything had come to a climax quickly. She was speaking of betrayal and deceit, for the man lying sated between her damp thighs had a stallion's stamina.

Fear over what would happen now Hudson had satisfied his need for retribution played havoc with her mind.

"You're quiet," he said, lifting his head to look at her. He could not mean during the act of lovemaking for she had writhed and moaned from the dizzying heights of pleasure. "Are you thinking about the problems at Falaura Glen, about Emily?"

Claudia gave a weak chuckle. "I have my lover's sweat-soaked body between my legs, and you imagine I'm thinking about the repairs to the cottage roof?"

"I don't like it when you use that term." Disapproval rang heavy.

"What? Lover?" Oh, she'd give anything to say "husband."

"There's more to our relationship than that, and you know it." He sighed. "You were thinking about something. You had that hazy look in your eyes."

She could say it was the look of desire but decided on the truth.

"I cannot help but feel sad that things are coming to an end."

"Coming to an end?" Hudson came up on his knees, a frown marring his brow. "Love, it is only the beginning."

"You know what I mean," she said, drinking in the sight of his bare chest and the flaccid manhood she could tease to attention in seconds. "We learnt the lines, played the part. Now, it's as though we're reading from a blank script."

"Then we make our own scenes. We decide on a structure, what form our lives will take. And then we live, and we love, and we make a life together."

How could she make a commitment when bound by Mr Thorncroft's ridiculous contract?

Foolishly, Claudia had put the problem to the back of her mind. She had not felt the need to tell Hudson, believing that the fantasy of becoming his wife would come to naught, and so she would pay Mr Thorncroft and go back to her quaint existence.

"It sounds like a wonderful dream," she said, her heart heavy, aching. "But I cannot consider my own needs when there are problems at home."

"Of course you must consider the upkeep of your home, the welfare of your sister." Tension radiated from the hard muscles in his shoulders. It clung to every word, every syllable. "I'm not asking you to abandon your responsibilities."

What was he asking?

She was frightened he might tell her, might make a beautiful declaration for her to trample over, spoil and ruin. How could she tell him she had made a commitment to marry another man? How could she tell him she had accepted this role because she cared only for the money?

Heaven help her!

Did she not sound as cold and conniving as Selina?

Honesty is a rare trait. You have it in abundance.

The truth would alter his opinion.

And yet her heart was honest and true. Perhaps he would understand her intentions were good. Perhaps doubt and mistrust would surface, and he would forever wonder if she truly loved him or if she had married him simply to escape her debts, escape marriage to a devilish fiend.

Water welled in her eyes.

Tears rolled down her cheeks, but they failed to wash away her fears.

"Don't cry," he said, his voice softening. He moved to settle on the pillow beside her, used the pad of his thumb to wipe away the evidence of her pain. "Our lives have been whipped up by a whirlwind. It will take some time to adjust."

Oh, why was he so wonderful, so understanding?

Love burst from her heart like the sun's powerful rays.

"The problems at Falaura Glen relate to money," she said, knowing she had to find some middle ground between lies and truth.

"I know. I spent a month in the cottage." Hudson snorted. "When the raindrops hit the metal bucket, it's like a weird form of torture."

"The money you're to pay me for playing your wife is to

cover a debt not fix the roof. Mr Thorncroft is rather anxious to see the matter settled."

"Then if you need more money, you only need ask." He raised his hand when she was about to protest. "What you've done for me, what you've had to endure, it's worth more than a king's ransom."

Endure? Every single moment had been sheer bliss. Perfect beyond belief.

She placed her palm on his chest. "Oh, it's not been such a hardship."

Hudson captured her hand and pressed a kiss to her palm. "No, together we make a remarkable team. Still, let me settle your debts."

A painful lump formed in her throat. "This is something I must do on my own."

"You don't want my help?"

Claudia cupped his cheek. "I must solve the problem that I created. It took courage to accept your offer, a little foolishness, too. We've been so engrossed in playing fictional roles, a few days apart will give us both an opportunity to consider where we go from here."

He came up on his elbow, his brows drawn together in confusion. "You doubt the depth of my feelings?"

"No, not at all." Claudia would have knots in her hair the number of times she shook her head whilst lying on the pillow. "You've never lied to me."

Suspicion flashed in his eyes.

Claudia shuffled closer. "I love you. I am in love with you. I want to be with you in any capacity—friend, lover—" She daren't be so presumptuous as to say "husband." "But you must let me deal with the issues at Falaura Glen."

Besides, she could not make any decisions without speaking to Emily. The problem with Mr Thorncroft affected her sister, too.

"You tell me you love me and yet I feel a great weight

crushing my chest." He dragged his hand down his face and sighed. "Love should be easy. So why is it proving so damn difficult?"

It was because she loved him that she could not be completely honest. If she told the truth about Mr Thorncroft, Hudson would ride to Flamstead and throttle the man. And yet, lies weakened the foundation of any relationship.

"You must trust me," she said. "Have faith that I will deal with this dilemma and then return to you."

He flopped back on the pillow. A weary sigh burst from his lips as he stared at the ceiling. "The signed banknotes are in the leather satchel in the armoire. I am in debt to you for seventeen hundred pounds but take what you need."

His phrasing reminded her that this had started as a business arrangement. Money sealed the deal. Payment reflected a job well done. But nothing about her time with him felt like a transaction.

Good Lord!

The sudden realisation that she could not take his money stole her breath. Money devalued everything that had occurred between them. Money tainted their love.

Claudia glanced at the diamond and amethyst ring on her finger. She could never part with something so precious.

So where in the devil's name would she get the money to pay Mr Thorncroft?

"Return to Falaura Glen and deal with your problems," Hudson said, the richness of his voice pulling her from her reverie. "Know that I will be waiting here for you should you wish to return."

"There is nothing I want more than to come home to you." Claudia tried to fight the tears. "Will you do something for me?" she said, choking back a sob.

"I would do anything."

"Hold me. Let me sleep in your arms tonight."

She did not need to ask twice.

Hudson gathered her to his chest, stroked her hair, kissed her brow. "Our paths are entwined, our fate shared. We must have faith that life will give us what we need."

"You sound like Dariell."

"He's an intelligent man." Hudson drew the coverlet up around their shoulders. "I am attempting to use wisdom as a crutch."

Claudia closed her eyes as she listened to his heartbeat.

She had to trust that this was not goodbye or farewell. She would put her faith in the only thing she believed in—she would put her faith in love.

The second Lockhart opened his eyes he knew she was gone.

The house was quiet, the bed cold.

A huge hole filled his chest.

Despite fighting against it, the urge to turn his head and glance at her pillow proved overwhelming. The empty space confirmed his worst fears. For a few minutes he strained to listen, hoping to hear the pad of footsteps, hear the giggle that left her lips whenever she whispered secretly with Lissette.

Silence.

This was not how he envisioned things would end.

Then again, nothing about his time with Miss Darling—his darling—had gone according to plan.

He supposed he should dress, check on his father, wait for the doctor. He supposed he should visit Terence, offer his condolences, meet with his mother and revel in the prospect of informing her she'd been duped by a devil. He supposed he should bring some semblance of normality to his disordered life, and yet he could not find the strength to drag his body out of bed.

An hour passed, maybe two or three.

He missed the rhythmical sound of her breathing, missed the soft breeze of her breath on his neck.

Everything about his world felt different, felt wrong.

Anger surfaced.

Goddamn, she hadn't even bothered to say goodbye. A rush of rage enlivened his spirits. He imagined her creeping into the armoire, emptying his satchel, sneaking off into the night like a thief who had stolen his heart.

The painful organ beating in his chest told him that was untrue.

She'd abandoned him, then. In effect, she was as good as standing on the dock in Portsmouth, telling him she couldn't come with him, forcing him to board the boat alone.

The need to prove a point forced him from the bed. He marched into the dressing room, yanked open the armoire and snatched the leather satchel.

He returned to his chamber, stood at the end of the bed and with a violent shake emptied the contents onto the coverlet. Banknotes, letters, bills and receipts tumbled out. He sorted through the pile, paused when he counted the notes.

Three thousand pounds' worth of signed notes stared back at him.

Miss Darling had not taken a penny.

Rejection replaced anger. Was his money not good enough?

He continued this odd form of self-flagellation until fear crept up on him unawares. It wrapped its bony fingers around his heart and squeezed so hard he wanted to cast up his accounts.

How would she pay her debts?

Who the hell was Mr Thorncroft? And why in the devil's name did she owe him money?

What if the blighter took advantage of her when she couldn't pay?

He stared at the ceiling and yelled in frustration before dropping onto the bed to grieve, to wallow in morbid thoughts for another three hours.

The loud rap on the door—the fourth since he'd woken —no doubt brought another concerned member of staff, wondering when he wanted to break his fast. The soft, masculine burr of a French accent calling to him from the other side of the door forced him to sit up and pay attention.

"Enter."

Dariell walked into the room. "Is it not a little late to lounge in bed?"

"Bugger off!" he imagined saying, but the love in his heart drew one important question from his lips. "Have you seen Miss Darling? She returned to Falaura Glen this morning. I trust she is safe and well."

"Yes, she arrived safely. Fleet brought me back to town." Dariell's curious gaze fell to the papers and banknotes sprawled on the bed. "Ah, I see Miss Darling forgot to take her fee."

"Her fee?" Lockhart almost spat the words. It undermined the true value of their connection.

"The money you were to pay her for pretending to be your wife." Dariell sauntered over to the chair flanking the fire and dropped into the padded seat. "She tells me she did a remarkable job convincing your family that she loves you."

"She is an exceptional actress."

Dariell smiled. "And you lack her skill, my friend. If you're going to use arrogance to hide your pain, you must learn to convey it in the eyes."

"Of course, you're as easy to read as an open book."

Dariell shrugged. "Why complicate matters?"

"As a man who rarely speaks about his own feelings, I imagine that's an easy feat."

"I like to keep life simple."

Lockhart snorted. Dariell might think differently if persecuted by murderous scoundrels. "So in simple terms, can you explain your interest in Emily Darling?"

"Of course," Dariell said with an exaggerated wave of the hand. "I am in love with her and intend to marry her."

Damnation. He did make it sound simple. But then Lockhart had been of a similar mind until Claudia Darling disrupted his plans. "And I trust the lady feels the same and welcomes your attentions." Maybe she might find an excuse to whip his world from under his feet.

Dariell inclined his head. "She has accepted my proposal, professed that it is a sentiment shared. Simple."

Blast.

"Well," Dariell continued. "I have an urgent call to make in New Bond Street. You're welcome to come if you can drag your weary body out of bed."

"New Bond Street?" The mere mention of the name roused thoughts of Claudia, of the time spent together in his carriage. It felt like a lifetime ago. "I have no need of new gloves."

"And stationery? Might you have need of a new quill?" Dariell came to his feet. "I'm told Mr Higson has a remarkable skill in chirography."

Mr Higson? It could not be a coincidence.

Lockhart narrowed his gaze. "Clearly you are party to a secret and intend to tease me to the point I might lose my mind." Snippets of conversation came flooding back. Claudia's desperate interest in the stationery shop, her questions relating to forged signatures. "If this is about Claudia, then I deserve to know."

"Because you love her?" Dariell probed.

"Yes, because I love her."

"And yet she did not tell you about the deceitful devil she has promised to marry." Dariell snorted. "Well, that is what the contract says. I have seen it for myself. Though how she expects to marry this fellow when she loves you is rather perplexing."

A black cloud descended to obscure Lockhart's vision. His

heartbeat thumped so loud in his ears he convinced himself he'd misheard.

"I beg your pardon?"

"Miss Darling is being blackmailed over her father's debt. The lady accepted your proposal to avoid marrying Mr Thorncroft. Fifteen hundred pounds or her hand in marriage, that is how I read it."

Lockhart swallowed past the lump in his throat. "And you know this how?"

"Emily sought my advice. She believes this fellow will find any means necessary to marry her sister." Dariell strode towards the door. "Of course, Miss Darling faces a dilemma considering the fact she did not take her fee."

"It's not a damn fee. It's the money I agreed to pay her for her assistance."

"Yes, the money she was going to use to pay the debt. Strange that she did not take it."

Numerous questions bombarded his mind.

A plague of emotions sought to torment and harass.

Why had Claudia not trusted him with the truth?

Why in God's name had she not taken the money?

"You obviously know more and intend to dangle the bait and wait for me to snap."

"One cannot put a price on love." Dariell smiled. "Love is simple. People make it complicated. And while I would prefer to leave you to come to the same logical conclusion, time is a constraint. But I will give you a moment."

Silence descended.

Dariell folded his arms across his chest and stared while Lockhart sat on the bed, lost in thought.

The simple truth was that he loved Claudia Darling to the depths of his soul. He didn't care about the money. Taking *the fee* would have made their time together seem like just another contract, a business deal for their mutual benefit, and it was so much more than that.

He did care that she had not told him about this bastard Mr Thorncroft. Men could be devious. They knew how to take advantage of unmarried women living alone. Then again, Selina had almost destroyed his life. Deceit lived in the hearts of the wicked, regardless of gender. But there was not one deceitful bone in Claudia's body, and so he had to do what she'd asked.

He had to trust her.

Lockhart cleared his throat. "Put simply I love Miss Darling. I intend to marry her and will bring the devil's wrath on anyone who seeks to prevent our union."

"Excellent." Dariell clapped his hands. "Hurry. Get dressed. Our friends will meet us in New Bond Street. I called on Greystone en route, and he will rally Drake and Valentine."

"Is that necessary?" Did it take five men to descend on Mr Higson?

"*Oui*, we will need an army when we launch our attack."

CHAPTER TWENTY-THREE

Claudia sat behind her father's mahogany desk, picking at the worn corners of the green leather surface. A distant clock struck ten. Another rang the hour a few minutes later. The damnable things had never kept good time. Indeed, a heavy heart and crippling trepidation forced her to glance at the mantel clock, just as that infernal timepiece donged, too.

Had she been waiting for Hudson, she would relish every tick, welcome every chime. Knowing that it was Mr Thorncroft coming to call made her want to steal all the pendulums in the house and lock them away in a dusty drawer.

To add to the assault on her nerves and her eardrums, the knocker on the front door fell with a loud bang. Not once. Three times. Mr Thorncroft liked to make a grand entrance.

A long minute passed before Emily entered the study, her mouth drawn into a grim line. "Mr Thorncroft is here. I've told Mrs Bitton to keep him waiting in the hall, just in case you needed a moment to gather your thoughts. Mr Hollingsworth is with him, too, as you requested."

Heavens! Claudia felt sick to her stomach.

She resisted the urge to press her forehead to the desk, to curse and weep and lament her reckless decision.

"Before I speak to them, Emily, I must ask you the same question I have asked five times already." Claudia gathered herself and straightened her shoulders. "Are you certain you wish to marry Monsieur Dariell?"

Emily's face brightened, and she clasped her hands to her chest. "I cannot think of anything I want more."

"And your decision has nothing to do with the fact we might have to sell Falaura Glen?" If not the house, then they would have to part with the contents. "You're not worried about my growing attraction to Mr Lockhart?"

Growing attraction was somewhat of an understatement.

"I love Monsieur Dariell." Emily edged closer to the desk. "When I am with him I feel alive, so alive I could conquer the world. He doesn't treat me like an invalid, like my lack of sight must mean I'm a simpleton, too. Oh, we talk about the most amazing things."

Claudia certainly knew what it was like to feel the power of love flowing through one's veins. And yet this was not a sudden revelation. Every day for the last month, she had watched the beginnings of their love blossom.

"And during my absence, he behaved like a gentleman?" The image of Hudson's naked body flashed into Claudia's mind. *Hypocrite* some might say, but she hated the thought of anyone taking advantage of Emily.

"Of course," Emily said, like it was the most ridiculous question in the world. "But I have kissed him. I just couldn't help myself. One minute we were waltzing about the room, the next …"

The declaration brought a smile to Claudia's lips. Passion was potent, powerful. "Monsieur Dariell will make a fine husband, I'm sure."

Indeed, the Frenchman had a charm that went beyond gentlemanly manners. He listened with his penetrating gaze as if he could read every thought in her mind. Ten minutes spent in his company this morning and Claudia had told him she'd not taken Hudson's money and, more surprisingly, the reason why. The man had a mystical power, one capable of dragging a confession from the Cato Street conspirators.

"So, I have your permission to treat Mr Thorncroft with the disdain he deserves?" Claudia asked.

"Most definitely." Emily's smile faded. "Do what you must, but you cannot marry him."

No, she could most certainly not do that.

The dilemma regarding the contract had kept her awake for most of the night, amid daydreams about Hudson Lockhart, and crying into her pillow. It would be unwise to come out and directly accuse Mr Thorncroft of fraud, not in front of the magistrate, but she might lead the conversation in that direction. The penalty for breach of contract would most probably involve financial compensation. It would take months for Mr Thorncroft to bring a private prosecution, giving her time to investigate further.

Months!

One night away from Hudson felt like forever.

"Call Mr Thorncroft and Mr Hollingsworth into the study." Claudia straightened the papers on the desk and attempted to look composed.

Emily nodded. "I might hit Mr Thorncroft with my stick when he's not looking," she said, gripping the walking cane Dariell had given her to help navigate the furniture and doorways.

"What a splendid idea." Claudia feigned an amused tone yet inside her heart thumped hard, and her stomach roiled.

Emily left the room and returned a few moments later with both gentlemen in tow.

Claudia did not stand to welcome them or offer a curtsy, mainly because she feared her legs might buckle under the strain.

Mr Thorncroft looked smug as he clutched his cane and

dropped into the seat opposite. Mr Hollingsworth—a stout gentleman with ruddy cheeks and a shock of white hair—looked mildly irritated. No doubt it was all a dreadful inconvenience.

"I trust you've had an eventful week, Miss Darling." Mr Thorncroft's beady stare sent a shiver from her neck to her navel.

"Eventful?" Oh, yes, she had attended a masquerade, the theatre, bathed naked in an unmarried gentleman's bedchamber. She had been shot at, kissed, ravished, devoured by her hot-blooded lover.

"I imagine regular trips to the pawnbroker might be your only hope of paying the debt," the devil said.

"Then the answer is no, sir. Pawnbrokers pay a pittance."

Mr Thorncroft scanned the cluttered room as if it were a hovel for the poor and needy. "Yes, and I highly doubt there's anything here worth selling."

The magistrate's weary sigh and numerous glances at the clock conveyed his thoughts about being dragged from Meadow-brook to listen to Mr Thorncroft's irritating snobbery.

"Precisely why I did not waste my time." Claudia drew the papers towards her in a bid to look efficient. "Indeed, having some reservations regarding the contract, I took a trip to town to consult a solicitor."

"A solicitor?" Mr Thorncroft frowned. His hawk eyes flicked back and forth in their sockets. "We signed the document in front of the magistrate." He gestured to the gentleman at his side, who had suddenly sat up and taken notice. "Your sister acted as a witness, too."

Claudia shook her head. "I am not referring to the contract made a week ago, but of the agreement made by you and my father when he supposedly asked for a loan."

"Look, my dear," Mr Hollingsworth began, leaning forward in order to appear intimidating, "we are here to discuss payment of a debt not what occurred more than a year ago. Are you able to settle? That is the only question of any consequence."

"It is not the only question, sir. During my visit to London, I happened to see Mr Thorncroft exiting Higson's stationery shop in New Bond Street." Dariell had extracted that piece of information from her, too.

"The gentleman's shopping habits have no relevance," Mr Hollingsworth snapped.

Mr Thorncroft remained silent, his intense gaze boring into her.

"Imagine my surprise when I discovered the proprietor's skill with a quill extended to forgery," Claudia said with the confidence of an actress used to playing demanding roles, for it was pure supposition after all.

Perhaps it was foolish to make such a sweeping statement. Perhaps she risked being charged with slander for challenging the authenticity of the signature. But having begun her case for the prosecution, Claudia wouldn't rest until she had proven Mr Thorncroft was guilty.

Mr Thorncroft snorted. "Buying paper and ink is hardly a crime. And my only dealings with the proprietor extended to paying the bill." He cleared his throat. "Let us stop this nonsense. Do you have the funds to pay or not, Miss Darling?"

Undeterred by their menacing glares, Claudia sorted through the papers on the desk. She offered the magistrate examples of her father's signature, documents signed three years ago.

"As you can see from the evidence shown, the signatures on both documents are identical. Please note the dates."

The magistrate looked down his nose and gave the items his brief consideration.

"Here, you see that the signature on the loan is identical to those already shown," Claudia said, pushing the other examples across the desk.

"What does this prove, Miss Darling?" The magistrate's words carried a veiled challenge, a sinister threat that she should think carefully before making accusations.

"I shall tell you if given a chance." Claudia's patience was wearing thin.

"It proves that the lady is stalling," Mr Thorncroft replied. "It proves she is trying to undermine the legitimacy of the contract. The only notable question worth an answer relates to the debt of fifteen hundred pounds."

Mr Hollingsworth huffed. He shook his head as he glanced at the clock. "Just answer the question, Miss Darling, so we can bring this matter to a swift conclusion. Do you have the funds to settle the debt?"

"No." Claudia raised her chin. "I do not."

Mr Thorncroft's eyes brightened. "Excellent. Then as per our agreement, we shall arrange for the vicar to read the banns on Sunday."

Claudia would rather spend a year in Newgate than a day married to this buffoon.

"I cannot marry you, Mr Thorncroft," she found the courage to say. The bang of the brass knocker hitting the front door plate made her jump, but she would not veer from her course. "You may prosecute me. The magistrate may conduct an inquest and haul me before the assizes. Do what you must. Either way, nothing would induce me to accept a proposal."

The devil shot forward, his eyes sharp and black, his teeth bared. "Oh, you will marry me if I have to drag you to the damn church myself." Without warning, he lunged and grabbed hold of her wrist. "You'll marry me else you'll rue the day you made me your enemy."

She heard Emily's frantic mutterings in the hall. Never had her poor sister sounded so afraid.

Anger flamed hot in her chest. "Release me at once," she commanded.

Mr Thorncroft's sharp talons dug into her skin. "Not until you agree to abide by our contract." He firmed his grip and twisted her wrist.

The magistrate's eyes widened. He opened his mouth, made an odd popping sound, but no words came out.

"You're hurting me. Release my hand at once."

"For twelve long months I've pandered to you, Miss Darling." Mr Thorncroft's wild stare froze the blood in her veins. "I always get what I want, so make no—"

"Then you're about to be sorely disappointed." An eloquent, determined voice cut through the chaos. Lord Valentine stepped into the room, accompanied by Lord Greystone, Mr Drake and Hudson Lockhart. "In this instance, you'll get what you deserve."

Mr Thorncroft relaxed his grip as he glanced back over his shoulder and considered the four men.

Claudia's eyes met Hudson's furious glare. Mr Drake gripped Hudson's forearm as one might hold the leash of a savage dog.

Claudia used the distraction to her advantage. She grabbed the heavy glass inkwell and brought it crashing down on Mr Thorncroft's arm.

"Blast!" The devil howled as he snatched his hand away and cradled his injured limb.

It took the magistrate a moment to haul his rotund figure out of the seat. "What is the meaning of this intrusion?"

Hudson turned to Mr Drake and cursed. "Goddamn, I will rip their heads off their shoulders."

"All in good time," Mr Drake replied, looking pleased at the prospect of brawling in the study.

"Let us dispense with formal introductions," Lord Valentine said in the arrogant tone one might expect from a member of the aristocracy. "We know who you are. But in case you should have any doubts regarding our authority to burst into this lady's home, permit Miss Darling to correct any misconception."

The magistrate's anxious eyes fixed on Claudia. "Am I to understand you know these gentlemen?"

Claudia nodded. "Lord Valentine, Lord Greystone and Mr

Drake are dear friends of Mr Lockhart." Excitement, gratitude and relief filled her chest. "Mr Lockhart is … Mr Lockhart is …"

"Miss Darling's betrothed," Hudson said in a murderous tone.

The magistrate's eyes bulged. "My lords." Looking somewhat flustered, he could not decide which gentleman to bow to first. "I fear there has been a terrible misunderstanding."

"There is no misunderstanding." Hudson snatched his arm free of Drake's grasp and stepped forward. "Miss Darling is betrothed to me, and my illustrious friends bore witness to the fact."

Just hearing his rich voice, seeing his handsome face, sent her stomach flipping.

"That's impossible," Mr Thorncroft protested. "Miss Darling signed a contract agreeing to marry me."

Lord Valentine cleared his throat. "A contract based on black-mail and forgery. Richard Darling did not borrow a damn penny, and yet you have persecuted his daughter to your own devilish ends."

Mr Thorncroft's face turned ashen.

Claudia gasped. It was as she had always suspected. "Is that true?"

"Whether Mr Thorncroft deceived you out of love or greed is the only matter up for question," Lord Valentine said.

"Preposterous lies. All lies." Mr Thorncroft was about to make further protestations when Monsieur Dariell entered the study, clasping the arm of a terrified-looking fellow.

"Mr Higson, he has come to confess." Dariell pushed the man forward.

After a prod in the back, the scrawny, red-haired man explained his business dealings with Mr Thorncroft, which extended to forgery and copying her father's signature.

"We have Mr Higson's sworn statement," Lord Greystone said, "and intend to advise his punishment is commuted to trans-portation in light of a full confession."

Silence descended.

A volatile tension hung in the air.

Mr Thorncroft turned to the magistrate who had edged away from the devil and moved to stand near Lord Greystone. "You'd better send these men on their way, else I shall explain you're a man who can be persuaded to turn a blind eye to the truth."

"Now listen here," the magistrate said, but Lord Valentine raised his hand to silence the men.

"Mr Hollingsworth," Lord Valentine began, "together we will take the prisoner into custody on the charges of fraud, intent to extort money and blackmail. Am I correct that the court will hear the case in Hertford?"

The magistrate nodded. From his sallow complexion and trembling lips, anyone would think he was the one being committed. "After the formal inquest and indictment, the judge will hear the case at the Shire Hall, although not until Lent."

"This is ludicrous!" Mr Thorncroft protested. He swung around to face Claudia, his movements so erratic that Hudson darted forward and grabbed the rogue by the collar. "Let me go. Get your hands off me. You've got no proof, nothing more than the word of a shopkeeper."

"And the discrepancy in the signatures," Claudia added.

"One thing I cannot abide," Lord Valentine said, "is a man who takes advantage of a lady living alone. As a viscount and peer, I shall do everything in my power to see you charged. Indeed, we will retire to your residence, Mr Hollingsworth, and have your clerk record the details."

In the presence of two peers, the magistrate could do nothing but agree.

A scuffle broke out when they tried to drag Mr Thorncroft from the room. The devil wielded his walking stick like a sword, swinging it high and low until Lord Greystone caught hold of the cane and Hudson smashed his fist into Thorncroft's face.

The next twenty minutes passed by in a blur as the gentlemen bundled Mr Thorncroft into Lord Greystone's carriage. Mr Drake accompanied the magistrate, and the men left for Meadowbrook, except for Hudson Lockhart.

Claudia stood beneath the portico, her arms wrapped across her chest while Hudson stood a few feet away and watched the carriages rattle down the drive. Nerves held her rigid. She would have to explain her reasons for not telling him the truth, for not trusting him with the facts.

Hudson turned to face her.

Claudia tried to read his mood, though his face remained expressionless. Relief brought water to her eyes when he opened his arms, smiled and beckoned her forward. In a rush of excitement, she almost tripped on the bottom step but Hudson was there with a steady arm and a warm embrace.

Determined to offer an explanation, she opened her mouth to speak, but he captured her lips in a searing kiss hot enough to make her toes curl.

"Don't ever do that again," he panted as he dragged his mouth from hers. "Don't ever feel as if you have to battle your problems alone."

"But after what happened with Selina, I thought—"

Hudson placed his finger on her lips. "You're not Selina. You were right not to take the money. I was wrong to assume you would. For the last week, you've done everything to support me and help solve my problems, and not once did I enquire as to the nature of yours. I am the one at fault, not you."

Claudia swallowed hard. "I would have told you about Mr Thorncroft, but I wanted you to know that my problems had no bearing on my feelings for you."

He stroked her hair off her brow, kissed her so deeply the muscles in her core clenched, begging for him to enter her body.

"None of that is important now," he said in the husky voice that suggested he wanted her, too. "Only two questions matter. Two simple questions that require two simple answers."

"Oh." Her heart thumped against her ribcage.

"Do you love me, Claudia? For I love you more than life itself."

Her throat grew so tight she could hardly speak. "To the depths of my soul."

A wicked smile touched his lips. "Will you marry me?"

"In a heartbeat."

CHAPTER TWENTY-FOUR

FALAURA GLEN - TWO WEEKS LATER

"So your father did send the letter threatening to strike you from his will," Claudia said as they waited for their friends to join them at the rotunda.

Dariell and Emily had spent the previous day decorating the structure with roses and ivy, used fresh white sheets to give the place the same magical air. Instead of a chaise, a harpsichord took centre stage. Two braziers blazed with enough heat to keep the winter chill from settling into their bones.

"It was a desperate attempt to force me to come home," Lockhart said, unable to resist the urge to stroke her cheek and press a chaste kiss to her cool lips. "Of course, he had no notion why I'd left in the beginning."

Claudia touched his upper arm. "The main thing is that your father is on the road to recovery. Dr Hewlett seems happy with his progress."

"Yes, but Father insists it's too soon to send him back to Berwick Street." Indeed, he'd pleaded to stay for another month to recuperate.

"And who can blame him?" Claudia chuckled. "How is your mother coping?"

"Apparently, she suspected something was amiss." Lockhart had spent the last week in London, preparing for their honeymoon in Scotland, before heading back to Falaura Glen. "She complained about being a victim of deception, about having no option but to accept Selina's help because I was away living like a heathen." Someone had to take the blame for the matron's lack of judgement.

"Has your mother found a replacement for Simmonds?"

Simmonds had begged to remain in Russell Square, too, after Hester's numerous attempts to coax him back to Berwick Street.

"The new butler lasted three days before packing his bag and disappearing into the night. And I'm afraid to tell you that as of ten o'clock today she's your mother, too."

Claudia grinned. "Oh, so now I'm your wife I have to share in your burden?"

"Absolutely."

She stared into his eyes for a moment. "You didn't mind the fact your family weren't at the church today? You could have confessed. You could have told them the truth about hiring me to play a role."

Lockhart shook his head. He refused to give the gossips a reason to shame his wife. "As far as my family are concerned we were married last year in Meerut on the second day in November."

"You remembered."

"How could I forget?"

Claudia's smile faded, and she sighed. "Soon they will learn that there isn't a child."

"Then we will have to do something to rectifying the problem." Lockhart slid his arm around her waist and drew her to his chest. The need to make love to her thrummed in his veins. "Perhaps we should leave our guests to fend for themselves. It's been a week since I've dragged a pretty moan from your lips."

"You certainly know how to tempt a lady, Mr Lockhart."

"Can I help it if I have a charm you find irresistible?" Lord, as much as he loved the company of his friends, he couldn't help but wish they were alone. "Kiss me, then, in the way that makes me know you want me. Kiss me as you did that night in the rotunda."

Claudia's blue eyes sparkled. She moistened her lips and came up on her tiptoes just as Drake's loud laugh reached their ears.

"Damnation." Lockhart released his bride as their friends approached. "Anticipation is said to heighten one's desire."

"Then by this evening, I imagine we'll be clawing at each other's clothes."

"What is so funny, Drake?" Lockhart said in an effort to dampen his ardour.

Juliet smiled as she gripped her husband's arm. "Dariell has taught Emily to deflect a punch by using instincts alone. Devlin did his best to prove it was an impossible feat."

Claudia gasped. "Good Lord, you attempted to strike my sister?"

"No," Emily said as she stepped up to the rotunda. "He didn't use his fist. He used my walking cane."

"Sometimes the eyes are deceiving," Dariell said as he sauntered behind Emily. "It is always better to use one's intuition. My wife has just proved the point, no?"

The comment drew Lockhart's thoughts to the blood-stained body at the inn. Anyone stumbling upon the scene would have assumed his guilt, and yet he had known in his heart that he had not committed the heinous crime.

Greystone and Lydia, and Valentine and Aveline, joined them outside for Dariell's surprise. Lockhart glanced at his friends as they embraced their wives. Happiness radiated. It filled the cold air with a vibrant energy that brought hope for new beginnings.

"Well, Drake?" Dariell said, wearing a wide grin for it was his wedding day, too. "Are you ready to take your seat?"

Drake inclined his head and sat down on the bench at the harpsichord. "The keys are slimmer than I'm used to, but I shall do my best." He flexed his fingers and adjusted his posture.

Dariell and Emily stepped into the rotunda. The Frenchman took his wife in his arms and muttered words of reassurance. When the music started, the couple moved slowly at first, following the steps of the waltz.

Drake performed with great mastery and skill. While Lockhart knew his friend played, he had no idea how well. It was a piece of music he had never heard before, more dramatic than any waltz heard in the ballrooms in London. It had a Hungarian flavour filled with passion and energy.

"Devlin composed the music himself," Juliet said, looking extremely proud.

It was then that Dariell and Emily took to twirling about the floor in the rotunda, circling Drake as he tinkled the keys, sweeping about with poise and grace.

Claudia gripped Lockhart's arm. "Heavens, I don't think I have ever witnessed anything so beautiful." Love for her sister clung to every word.

"I have," he whispered as he studied his wife's delicate profile.

Overwhelmed with the need to feel Claudia's body pressed to his, Lockhart took her in his arms and swayed in time with the music. He held her far too close for the dance to be considered respectable. After all, had she not accepted a proposal from a scandalous rogue?

Using a strategy of carefully planned steps, he steered her away from prying eyes, to a secluded spot behind the flowing white sheets. "Now that we have a little privacy, perhaps we should share a passionate kiss, one that conveys the depth of our love."

When he stared deeply into her eyes and his hands skimmed

the curve of her hips, Claudia arched a brow. "While that is the look of love, Mr Lockhart, your wandering hands speak of lust."

Lust and love burned hot in his veins. "Won't you permit your husband this one indulgence?"

Claudia looked into his eyes and gave a dreamy sigh. "For you, my love, anything."

Made in the USA
Columbia, SC
14 August 2020